A Dangerous Place

A Dangerous Place

Robin Herne

MOON BOOKS

Winchester, UK
Washington, USA

First published by Moon Books, 2013
Moon Books is an imprint of John Hunt Publishing Ltd., Laurel House, Station Approach,
Alresford, Hants, SO24 9JH, UK
office1@jhpbooks.net
www.johnhuntpublishing.com
www.moon-books.net

For distributor details and how to order please visit the 'Ordering' section on our website.

ISBN: 978 1 78279 211 6

A CIP catalogue record for this book is available from the British Library.

Design: Stuart Davies

Printed in the USA by Edwards Brothers Malloy

CONTENTS

The author would like to express thanks to…

Young Tom Chadwick, who first gave the idea of this book a positive reception, and who I hope remembers me when I am a degenerate wreck and he has won his Nobel Prize for medicine!

Mark Salmon, formerly of the Ghost Club, for advice on the world of psychical research;

The immensely learned Nick Ford for the suggestion of the central character in one of the stories;

Finally to the members of the Gippeswyk Storytelling Circle, who have endured my tales over the decades.

"Some places speak distinctly. Certain dank gardens cry loud for a murder; certain old houses demand to be haunted; certain coasts are set apart for shipwrecks."
Robert Louis Stevenson

"The world is a dangerous place to live; not because of the people who are evil, but because of the people who don't do anything about it."
Albert Einstein

Introduction

The animist and polytheist religions of the ancient world embraced, and continue in their modern expressions to embrace, the notion of the spirit of place. The Romans called it the *genius loci*, and virtually all cultures have their own counterparts – *landvaettir, wights, kami, bocain* etc. The interactions between the *genius* and the humans (and other creatures) that dwell within its remit are a subject for considerable reflection for polytheists and animists.

A comparatively new branch of psychology, ecopsychology, is beginning to take a non-religious look at the impact a place can have on the minds of the humans living, working, or otherwise spending prolonged periods there. A polytheist myself, I believe in the existence of these spirits of place as real beings rather than just as poetic abstractions. The relationship flows in both directions – not only does the *genius* influence people but we, in turn, impact upon it. However, as the *genius* undoubtedly lasts much longer than a human lifespan, it is probable that the spirit has a greater influence on the human than vice versa.

As the old saying goes, like attracts like – and this is as true of places as it is of people. Some places are fundamentally joyful, whilst others radiate an atmosphere of anger and corruption, and each attracts people suitable to its own nature. Those who do not feel comfortable in such a place soon leave, if they have the freedom to do so. For those that lack an escape route, perhaps their natures are eventually moulded in tune with the place. Spending a prolonged period in a depressing place will wear down even the most ebullient of souls – and perhaps it is to be wished that the reverse is true, and a person deep in the doldrums may be lifted by associating with a vivacious *genius*.

So often we think in terms of owning houses, farms, woodland and other places or property. We have become used to thinking of the places we inhabit as passive possessions to impose our own decorative tastes upon – but perhaps they also view us as possessions, as things which they encompass or contain, and either enjoy having us within them or resent every minute of it.

Whilst ecopsychology, operating in an essentially atheist paradigm, speaks in terms of the unthinking impact an environment has upon a thinking human, from a pagan viewpoint I suggest that the world around us is very much aware and capable of a form of sapience (albeit not in a human manner), or perhaps rather that the many different parts of the world around us have their own multiple sapiences.

What determines if a *genius* is happy or hostile in the first place? In honesty, I have no idea (though I'd love to learn, and have helped form a group in Suffolk whose intent is to get on better terms with the local spirits of place and find out more about them). My suspicion is that their character is in part the consequence of experience (much as it is with humans) but also of function. Some places have a function in the grander scheme of things, and the *genius* regulates this. Some places heal, and doubtless feel wonderful as a result, others act rather like psychic rubbish dumps, breaking down patterns and recycling the forces directed there – a process that may not be pleasant to be around, and so we tend to feel uncomfortable near such unseen activities. That doesn't make such *genii* evil, merely unwelcoming – though humans are prone to cast others in a moral context based largely upon how friendly they are towards us rather than a grasp of the bigger picture.

When talking of the purpose of place I am not only referring to the function imparted by humans, but of a pre-existing raison d'etre. Having said that, experience suggests that even short-term human activity can have a major impact, and especially where the focus of people is to a common goal.

Each of these short stories is set in a different century, but all have their central action taking place in the same location, namely Castle Hill in Ipswich. This is a real place, though it bears little resemblance to the fictional version presented in these pages. Interestingly there is an area of the Massachusetts Ipswich which is also called Castle Hill, the location for a number of films. These days the area of the British Castle Hill is a housing estate, as unremarkable as a thousand others like it. Its past is rather more intriguing than its present, having been the location of an extensive Roman villa, then later a wooden castle (hence the name) which was finally demolished on the orders of Henry II in 1176. The succession of buildings which replace the castle in these stories are fictional – but inspired by real sites elsewhere in Ipswich and its surrounding villages.

As well as exploring the nature of the spirit of place, these stories are also united by themes of religion, mysticism and superstition. This latter word is interesting, one of those opprobrious words that are normally applied only to the beliefs of other people for whom we have a low regard.

The stories use a number of different literary styles (first-person narratives, epistolary accounts etc.) largely because I enjoy experimenting, and short stories are a great avenue for doing just that.

A couple of these stories, such as *A Contention of Druids,* have appeared in shorter versions in magazines and newsletters. *Angel Blood* was broadcast on Ipswich Community Radio many years ago, having won a competition for people writing stories with a local flavour.

Whatever dwells in the fictional Castle Hill is angry and vindictive, and its poison spreads like a canker amongst all those who come to live upon the hill over the two and a half millennia that separates the first story from the last.

Chapter One

A Contention of Druids

Senorix ran the string of amber beads through his fingers, a gesture that his handsome bodyguard Luccus recognised as signifying deep thought. The old Druid's eyes took in the desecrated grove where flies gathered on the carcass of the frail old man whose blood splattered the wooden altar. They had delicately searched the diminutive body, the investigator looking at the three small items found in a leather pouch – a knucklebone, a Greek coin, and a wooden talisman.

Riomandus had been his tutor, many decades earlier, and they had remained close after Senorix had attained the Druid's mantle and been sent out into the world to serve the Iceni. That such a noble life should end in such violence sickened him, inured as he was to the sight of sudden death.

"I don't like this place," commented the tactless young warrior as he shooed away a crow that hovered hungrily nearby. "He must have been hated with a passion. The first blow must have killed him, but to go on and on hacking at the body in that manner—"

"Suggests a mind unhinged by rage or fear. See those three wounds to Riomandus' throat? They have nearly severed his head. I wonder if the murderer was especially incensed by something that my old teacher said?"

"According to the Uerdruis, old Riomandus only arrived here a week ago. What on earth could somebody say in the space of a week to produce such a reaction? Did he have an especially poisonous tongue?" Luccus ran a hand through his long hair.

"Never in all the years I knew him; Riomandus was a man of peace. Even when dealing with idiots he was uncommonly kind and gentle. I had so looked forward to hearing him speak again.

His insights into the ways of the Gods were profound, and I have never met anyone who knew more about medicine than he. Come, Luccus, let us consult with the revered Uerdruis."

"We cannot go ahead with the convocation until the spirit of my dear friend has been satisfied." The senior Druid's voice trembled with emotion.

Senorix already understood the importance of the gathering, and the necessity of resolving the vexed issue of rightful sacrifice that threatened to pull the Druid world apart. "Tell me, honoured Dubnos, how did this terrible waste of life come to be discovered?" the sun-browned sage asked, as they stood on one of the few dry patches along the marshy banks of the river and watched the passage of the birds across the grey waters.

"Trenus, guardian of this sacred grove, and his assistant Catus came to prepare the area for the morning prayers – and were nearly knocked down by Riomandus' own nephew, the warrior Atto, fleeing the scene. That was about an hour after dawn, as Trenus was late waking. I had kept the poor man talking nearly all night, discussing his somewhat eccentric religious views. I was summoned immediately. Riomandus was quite cold and I will swear that he had been dead since no later than midnight, maybe a couple of hours earlier. The last anyone admits to seeing him alive was at the evening meditation."

The tall, cadaverous Trenus made a comical contrast to the short, rotund Catus as they led the procession carrying the bier with a pale woollen shroud covering the corpse. They wound their way awkwardly down the path that spiralled from the grove atop the hill. Senorix and Luccus waited patiently at the base of the hill until the tubby man sonorously finished chanting the prayers for the dead. The two investigators approached, making the gestures of greeting, and Senorix noticed the thick cataracts that must have rendered Trenus all but blind. The sombre Druid gestured for them to follow him back up to the sacred glade, where his assistant began gathering some articles left upon the wooden altar slab.

"I commend you on the beauty of the holy nemeton that you guard, honoured Trenus. I see that you have recently installed an intriguingly carved pillar behind the altar."

A smile twitched the sombre features of the guardian, as he indicated his assistant and introduced him as not only the tribe's gutuator but also an accomplished wood carver.

The short man positively bloomed under the dry praise, gazing puppy-eyed at his superior. "Not only a great singer but an artisan too? I wonder that you are not a devotee of Lugus of the Many Skills, yet I do not recall seeing any of the symbols of the blessed God in the nemeton. Though I am sure I had heard that this glade was dedicated to Belinos – is there not a healing spring near here? But I have not seen the Radiant One's signs here…nor do I recognise the curious swirling symbols on the new pillar."

"No," Trenus cut across Catus's flustering, "our tribe did once pay homage to Lugus and Belinos amongst others, but we have been blessed with many visions of recent years which have led us to dedicate ourselves almost exclusively to Croucacrumbas. We have always been an impoverished community, this land being little suited to farming. Yet since the Great One called to me, we have had excellent harvests."

It was something of a running joke that the tiny clan that dwelt in the small village on the banks of the River Ura never knew if they were Iceni or Trinovantes, until the royal messengers passed through. The interminable petty disputes between the two kingdoms meant that the marshy hinterland was often traded back and forth.

"Then I must learn more of this God, for I confess his name is unknown to me. Tell me, had you spoken much to poor Riomandus since his arrival at your community?" Senorix asked, running a hand over his hairless sun-browned pate.

"Very little," the lips pressed tightly together in disapproval, "our humble nemeton is honoured to have been chosen by the noble Uerdruis for this gathering of the learned. Yet I could wish that some would confine their minds to the needs of their own tribes and not dictate what others should do."

Catus's chins wobbled in vigorous agreement, and he suddenly burst into a voluble description of the murderous mannerisms of the warrior Atto who had that very dawn fled the scene of his unspeakable crime of kin slaying. Senorix and his assistant had considerable difficulty tearing themselves away from the singer's repeated demands for advice on how best to purify a holy place violated by such a deed.

The wretched nephew stared up at his interrogators with grief-swollen eyes. Alcohol had robbed much of his memory of the previous twenty-four hours, and he repeatedly cursed himself for having over-imbibed with his fellow swordsmen. Luccus, who had been one of his drinking companions showed little sympathy and demanded to know the nature of his last meeting with the revered Riomandus.

"It is true that I was unkind to him, may Brigantia forgive me for such churlishness. I was keen to get to the feasting hall for the drinking and…other distractions, and Uncle kept asking me silly questions. I became impatient and snapped at him, but that is all. There was no bad blood between us."

"What questions did he ask?" Senorix leaned forward, his piercing blue eyes fixing the young man.

"He kept asking me if I'd heard tell of battle captives held for ransom by the local tribe, and then started on about the paw bones I gave him. He always wore a bracelet of dog bones, being especially devoted to the god Noudens, but it broke on the journey and most of the bones were lost in a river crossing. I found a couple of new ones for him, auspicious ones too because they must have been left over from a sacrifice made in the nemeton."

"And did you know of any captives?"

"No, the Ura clan are peaceful to the point of monotony. They never go to war. I went to the nemeton to tell him as much, but he was dead when I got there."

They sat on a fallen tree gazing out over the slowly undulating river, Luccus describing a strange dream that had come to him in a grove of Noudens many years earlier and Senorix admiring the passing swans. A tall woman approached them from the direction of the temporary druids' encampment, and Venerable Senorix recognised her bleached ash staff before he recognised her lined face. He stood and greeted Illica in the traditional manner.

"Why have I not been questioned in the matter of Riomandus' death?" she thrust her jaw out pugnaciously and glared at him, ignoring Luccus, "I am a natural suspect given the many arguments I had with the dead man."

"I was not aware that any of these arguments were other than philosophical disputes, Illica, or did you take them as some personal insult?"

"Of course not!" she sounded genuinely shocked, running her hand so vigorously through her iron-grey hair that the tight knot came loose. "I am not some silly maid given to tears and tantrums when her ideas are challenged."

Luccus looked away, even he was aware of Illica's reputation for temperamental mood swings since leaving her fertile years behind. He had noted that she was also quite a powerfully built woman, and looked as if she might be easily capable of delivering the fatal wounds.

"I last saw him," she continued as if Senorix had actually asked the question, "just before dawn. I awoke early, unable to sleep properly in that uncomfortable bed and fed up listening to some idiot playing an improperly tuned lyre. I had gone out in search of something to drink. Riomandus was walking towards the hill where the grove stands. I greeted him but got no response. He was getting a trifle deaf, so I took no offence. Nobody followed him, though I admit I was not really paying much attention."

"I am quite familiar with Riomandus' insistence that only a willing sacrifice can carry messages across to the Divine Realms. However, I have never heard your views directly, only second hand."

"Oh, right, well..." she seemed slightly taken aback by the change of tack in the gentle old man's questioning, "in my tribe there are certain crimes for which no éraic can be paid. Oh, I know you Iceni demand an honour price for every crime, short of kin-slaying, but that is not our way. Last year an eight-year-old girl was raped in our tribe, and I determined that her own father was guilty of the deed. A depraved creature, I recommended that he be disposed of and the chieftain agreed. He was sacrificed and it wasn't quick, I can tell you that, but it was a chance for him to redeem an otherwise worthless life by doing some small good for the people he should have cared for in life."

"That is certainly one view," Senorix murmured, "the last time I encountered a similar case the man was beaten to death by the father of the child he had abused before any judgement could be passed."

"People like that are better left as wolf-meat than sent to be amongst the Gods!" Luccus snarled, raising an irate glare from the druidess.

"Do you know what this is?" Senorix asked before his fellow philosopher could launch into a tirade.

"Of course," she glanced at the old man's open palm, "it's a finger bone."

"I know, which is all the stranger when we are amongst a people who never go to war and abide peacefully by the law of éraic. Were we up amongst you Coritani, I might be less perturbed!"

The silver-haired Uerdruis sat on the raised wooden bench placed in the sacred grove and surveyed the fifty-odd men and women gathered on benches beneath the trees. For the first time in living memory Esico, the headsman of the Clan Ura, had been allowed to bring two warriors into the nemeton, ready to enforce the law. Luccus himself had insisted on also attending to protect his patron and enforce justice on those who might seek to escape it.

The Uerdruis stood and called for the Sword of Nodens to be drawn. Luccus came forward, and held aloft his own blade – under normal protocol the local chieftain would have used his own weapon, but the headsman possessed only an ill-kempt rusty antique. With due reverence, the bodyguard unsheathed the sword and lay both scabbard and blade alongside each other on the altar.

Only when the god of justice was invoked was a weapon permitted in a holy nemeton. Once all prayers and blessings were said, the Uerdruis turned to face the seated sages and banged his apple wood staff causing the bells on it to jangle melodically.

"We gather before the eyes of our Gods to discuss the heated matter of whether sacrifice of a human life must always be of one willing given, as the late Riomandus and his students contend, or if the lives of unwilling criminals and prisoners of battle may also serve as acceptable offerings to the Old Ones, as Illica and her companions claim. Yet first, before we may come to a conclusion on such matters, we must resolve the brutal destruction of one of our own. The Gods have equipped us with the presence of Senorix, whose skill at untangling such mysteries is well known." He made the gesture of approval towards the thin, hazel-skinned man who sat to his left, hood pulled down. Senorix rose and stepped forward.

"Thank you, learned Dubnos. When searching the body of the

revered Riomandus we found a single bone in his pouch, last of several which Atto says he gave his uncle to replace some dog bones lost en route. I conclude from this that Atto did not inherit his uncle's love of medicine, for this is no canine bone. It is a child's finger bone, which Atto found in this very glade. My old tutor asked his nephew if any battle captives have been taken by this tribe, perhaps following the logic that Trenus, as a follower of Illica's school of thought, might have sacrificed some unwilling captive. Yet the headsman here will confirm that they have had no prisoners of any age, so I ask of the guardian how human fingers came to be within this nemeton?"

Trenus shook with suppressed fury as he leapt to his feet, the young headsman paling before the clouded orbs. "Once again an outsider dares to interfere with our ways! What business is it of yours how we honour the mighty Croucacrumbus?"

"You have slaughtered a child in offering?" Dubnos the elegant Uerdruis was incredulous, and even the bombastic Illica looked shocked.

"Three years past He came to me in a vision!" Trenus stumbled rapturously towards the carved pillar. "Our people have flourished since we gave the Lord of the Mound what he desires. You spoke of Lugus – what did he ever do for us? No, only the lord has granted us what we so desperately needed and he asks so little in exchange. With so many mouths to feed, what cost is it to have a few less?"

The gathering erupted in outrage, and the elderly lady near to the headsman raised her staff as if to strike him for tolerating such an outrage. It was not until Luccus and his fellow warriors hauled the increasingly incoherent Trenus away that the Uerdruis was finally able to restore some order.

"Not only must Trenus account for the slaying of Riomandus," his tremulous voice echoed round the glade, "but Esico must also answer for failing to uphold the duties of a headsman and preventing this madness."

"Trenus is indeed guilty of the sacrifice of innocents," Senorix said, turning his back upon the disgraced headsman, "however, I do not believe it was his hand that struck down Riomandus. The guilt is upon his assistant, the singer Catus. Austere Trenus had been talking to our revered Chief Druid all evening, and I doubt so ill-sighted a man could commit any kind of crime in the dark. Catus, you are his right hand in all things, I say that you silenced old Riomandus when he asked too many questions about the bones. Not only did you fear censure for the unwarranted sacrifices, but dreaded what would happen to the Ura if this insane pact was broken."

Spitting obscenities, Catus lunged at his denouncer with the sacrificial blade drawn from beneath his robes. Luccus was quicker, and a flash of sword severed the murderous arm at the elbow, the blood spouting across the carved pillar in a final offering to Croucacrumbus.

First Story Notes

North Suffolk was mainly under the control of the Iceni, and South Suffolk under the Trinovantes. Exactly where the border between these two tribes lay is anyone's guess, though the River Lark is often cited as a strong possibility. However, it probably fluctuated over time with skirmishes between the tribes. There is evidence of small-scale settlement in the Ipswich area, most notable for leaving behind a deposit of gold torques. It is uncertain whether these were ritual offerings, or concealed to keep them safe during a raid – with the implication that the people who buried them may not have lived long enough to go back and dig them up.

The Iceni (not their actual name, but a Latin approximation of how to pronounce it) left behind coins bearing horse imagery. In a later trend the imagery switched to that of a wolf – this could suggest a change in religious allegiances from an equine to a lupine deity (or, given that they were polytheists, the introduction of an additional deity), or may reflect alterations in a ruling dynasty with new emblems, or merely artistic trends. The wolf images in time gave way to depictions of the wild boar.

Ancient cemeteries have been found in a number of areas around present-day Ipswich, including a major find of impressive gold torques unearthed in the late 1960s from the Belstead area.

Sadly little is known about the nature and beliefs of the Druids and the peoples they served. In a previous non-fiction book, *Old Gods, New Druids,* I outlined some of what is known or conjectured. Caesar referred to the druids of Gaul as having a supreme leader, and this concept is drawn upon in the story through the guise of the *Uerdruis,* or Over-Druid. The story also mentions a *gutuator,* a term translating as 'Father of Song'. The function of the *gutuator* is unclear, but presumably would have involved singing or chanting – something along the lines of a galdr-singer, cantor or choirmaster.

Again referring to our cousins across the Channel Julius Caesar said, "*In fact, it is they who decide in almost all disputes, public and private; and if any crime has been committed, or murder done, or there is any dispute about succession or boundaries, they also decide it, determining awards and penalties*". It was this idea that inspired the idea of Senorix, the Druidic investigator in the story.

The Druids served not only as priests, but also as interpreters and upholders of the law. It was the duty of the chieftains and warlords to enforce legal decisions, but they relied on the wisdom of the sages to inform the judgements that they passed.

Chapter Two

The Fourth Tail

"That's where my poor Appia killed herself." Quintus' mask of the prosperous merchant faltered for a moment showing the grief and bewilderment contained beneath. "Of course this silly temple wasn't there then. The slaves had built a rather charming little bower-seat beneath the shadow of the great oak. Local legend has it that the oak was all that remained of a Druid grove, where terrible rituals took place. Sacrifice you know! Appia was terrified of it."

"Yet you had a bower built here?" Lady Augusta's tone, normally haughty, became positively accusatory.

"Oh, she wasn't afraid of it at first!" Quintus quailed before his sister-in-law's Medusean gaze, gabbling in a way that none of his cowed debtors would have credited. "No, in fact she was the one who wanted the bower. It was only in the last few months of her life that she began to get these sick fancies. She kept saying she could hear the sacrificial victims crying out in fear, howling for justice. Do you remember the letter I sent you, asking for advice about the Lemuria festival last year?"

Augusta did not mention the illness that had prevented her from leaving the Temple of Minerva in far off Camulodunum. They both knew of it, and the guilt that otherwise she might somehow have prevented her youngest sister's suicide weighed heavily despite her own lack of culpability.

"I thought it was all just histrionics, may Jupiter forgive me for my short-sightedness, but presumed conducting the ceremony might have been best – if only to allay Appia's fears. It was that very morning that she sent her slave girl back to the villa to fetch some trifle, and the silly child returned to find her mistress dangling from the branches."

"What became of the tree?" she asked, casting an unconscious glance at Olivia, her own attendant slave, who walked silently behind them.

"Oh, I had it chopped down and the wood burned far from the house lest it be infected. That stump behind the new shrine is all that remains. You know, dear sister-in-law, that when the slaves were digging up roots they came across three small skulls? Well, they refused to dig any further. In honesty, I didn't have the heart to flog them into completing the task. I dare say Mother would have done, but I declared the work at an end and that was that."

"What ceremony did you perform to appease the sacred tree?" The scarlet that infused her brother-in-law's cheeks was all the answer Lady Augusta needed. She rolled her eyes imperiously, and walked into the wooden shrine that Quintus's eccentric mother Clara had demanded. She exchanged a conspiratorial arch of the eyebrow with Olivia, who had been otherwise impressed by the beautiful herb garden that made this dank backwater so pleasurable to visit.

Quintus, sensing the unspoken scorn, harrumphed, "Mother has always had strange fancies when it comes to religion. When she heard that one of her friends from Camulodunum had an Egyptian handmaid, nothing would do but that she should have one too. So I got her one from the Midsummer Market, and have rued the day since Tita came into this house. Mother is completely enthralled by her and had this shrine to Bast built on the girl's guidelines."

"Bast!"

"An Egyptian cat goddess."

"I know who Bast is!" the aged priestess snapped, "Last I heard she was devoting herself to Attis and Cybele – rather appropriately. Still, your mother has always been obsessed with felines, so it can come as little surprise that she has changed allegiances. I always thought Egyptian sacred structures were built of marble or sandstone."

"Oh, well, I refused to provide a marble one." The portly merchant flushed a little at his own daring. "Mother drops religions almost as quickly as she takes them up, and I really didn't want to spend a fortune on some shrine she would lose interest in after a month or two. So it was wood or nothi—–ng."

Lady Augusta gave an involuntary shriek as they entered the gloomy shrine and something hairy thumped against the side of her head. Recoiling, it took the pair some moments to realise what it was dangling from one of the rafters: an overfed dead cat, with a ligature tight about its throat.

Augusta's exclamation was as nothing compared to that of the matriarch Clara, who howled like a beast in Tartarus when she discovered that her beloved puss had been strangled and strung up.

It was many hours before even a degree of sanity was restored to the villa of Quintus Cornelius Britannicus. The slaves desperately tried to conceal their curiosity as they fetched food and drink for their master and the two elderly women. Clara was short and her once plump flesh had started to sag in on itself like a deflated bladder. She had never much liked her in-law, and only tolerated the other woman because of her high standing within the temple of Minerva. The gaunt priestess cast her prominent eyes over her relations, and wished she had stayed in her beloved temple precincts. Clara disgusted her: a stupid and sadistic woman who spread misery wherever she went. Her brother-in-law had never much impressed her either.

"Before I can investigate these claims of a curse, dearest Clara, I would like to speak to this slave girl of yours – the Egyptian."

"She's dead, like my darling little Felicia. It's the curse you know? Bast is vengeful for the desecration of her temple—" The voluble woman was cut off in mid-tirade, as Lady Augusta shot a glare that had been known to make senators quiver.

"Quintus, explain to me precisely what has happened since

my last visit here for the Matronalia. All was peaceful then, and no talk of curses or death."

Looking wistful, the merchant agreed that life had been good the previous spring and told of how it had all gone wrong within a fortnight of Lady Augusta's departure. Ignoring the snorts of derision from his mother, Quintus recalled his wife's gradual descent into madness and fear. At first vaguely anxious, she had become increasingly convinced that spectral voices and restless shades haunted the Druid Oak. Whilst worried about her, Quintus had never guessed that suicide preyed upon her mind and had been shocked when the news was rushed to him as he returned from a profitable trip to Camulodunum. He fretted at length upon the impact that this disaster had had upon their twins, Primus and Prima. The tree had been torn down, and the accursed skulls unearthed. Around midsummer Clara had insisted on the purchase of an Egyptian slave, and almost at once become fascinated by this exotic cat cult. Without saying so outright, he implied that he suspected the slave was making things up to retain a hold over the belligerent matriarch. The wooden shrine had been built within a month, and four months later an exorbitantly expensive statuette of Bast – here Clara burst in to sing the praises of the fabulous antiquity from the tombs of the Pharaohs, formed of ivory and gold, decorated with lapis lazuli – was acquired from a mercantile contact and placed in the shrine amidst bizarre-sounding ceremonies. There the cat had sat throughout the winter, until on the eve of Saturnalia, when it vanished. One of the slaves had been sent out to light some incense, Mother feeling a little unwell that morning. When Mother went to make the noon offerings, the statuette was gone. The girl swore that all had been well that morning.

"She was lying, of course!" Clara leapt in, her face hot with hate. "The procurator flogged her vigorously, but the thieving trollop would not reveal where she had stashed the statuette."

Sighing heavily, Quintus resumed his explanation of how the

villa was searched high and low to no avail. Nearly three months on, and the whereabouts of Bast's idol remained unknown. Quintus had even paid spies to keep an eye on the black market, but none of the usual fences had handled it. None of the rituals performed by Tita, the Egyptian handmaiden, had proved worthwhile. She herself had been on an errand to buy incense for yet another ceremony when some street thug had robbed and strangled her. Mother had been inconsolable. The procurator, sent out to find the missing girl, had fallen foul of the same gang. His corpse had been found stuffed into a midden heap the following day. Quintus's own horse had taken ill and died the week after, then one of his warehouses had burnt down – several costly crates of wine being destroyed in the process.

"I should like," Lady Augusta announced after a lengthy cogitation, "to speak to the girl accused of the theft. Assuming she has not been sold on already?"

Clara dismissed the matter with a wave of her bejewelled hand, "Oh that was not possible. She died as well, though there was nothing sinister to that. She got an infection and died before she could be dealt with. Why are we wasting time talking of her? Someone has murdered my darling Felicia and desecrated the temple of Bast."

"What was her name?" Lady Augusta asked, pushing a stray coil of faded red hair back behind her ear.

Clara sneered and looked away, whilst Quintus looked merely flummoxed and gazed enquiringly at the new chief slave who discreetly murmured the name – Cunsa.

Augusta meandered through the gardens, lost in thought. She came to rest not far from the Egyptian shrine, where the procurator was arranging branches into a small pyre on the path. She wondered why the chief slave was engaging in so menial a task. Upon enquiry the man mumbled, in a thick local accent, that it was for the dead cat – at the order of the mistress of the house. It being a religious ceremony, of a sort, he felt obliged to deal with it in person.

The dear departed lay in a wooden trough to one side of the shrine. Rather gingerly, the priestess examined the stiffened creature. She instructed the chief slave, known by the name of Brocchus, to untie the ligature. It was a long strip of leather with a short shard of bone knotted at one end, much longer than needed to wrap around the feline's fat throat.

At her mistress' side, Olivia murmured one word, "Flagrum."

"Tell me... Brocchus, I understand that since the old procurator died you have been appointed as the new one?" Lady Augusta spoke gently.

The tall man responded shyly that the master had not yet arranged for a brand new replacement as insisted upon by Clara, but that – as the longest-serving slave at the villa, responsibility for maintaining order had fallen to him in the interim.

"How did he die, the old chief slave?"

"Severus was strangled, mistress. I laid out the corpse myself."

Augusta thought he was about to add something, when a squeal and a stream of obscenities disrupted the peace of the garden. A tall dark-haired girl burst through the trees, hurling a few choice insults at the near-identical youth that followed her. The twins came to an abrupt halt, quelled by the austere face of their aunt. Through gritted teeth she informed them that their grandmother's cat had been killed. Prima rolled her eyes and gave a look of supreme indifference, whilst her brother endeavoured to appear sympathetic but ended up looking simply wet.

"You're not actually going to burn the stupid thing, are you?" the young lady demanded to know, nostrils flaring. "Next the daft old trout will be hiring in teams of mourners to wail."

"Caterwaul!" Primus dissolved into snorts of awkward laughter. "Sorry Aunt Augusta...are you conducting the cat's funeral?"

"Certainly not. I have never heard of anything so ridiculous, but I suppose your grandmother will have her way. That is a rather becoming hair comb, Prima."

"Oh yes, that old thing. One of my suitors bought it for me."

"How many suitors do you have, girl?" Augusta asked imperiously.

"Enough to fill an arena!" her brother responded for her, a malicious smirk on his lips. "Well, more than Father knows about anyway."

"Well at least I only accept hair combs from my suitors, not like that avaricious little slut you moon over. How much does it cost to get up Antonia's stola?"

"Shut your mouth, guttersnipe, or I'll—"

Lady Augusta's voice cracked like a whip, "You will do nothing, young man! Such behaviour is extremely unbecoming in those of your station. I shall speak to your father about the pair of you. Have you nothing edifying to occupy your time with?"

The recalcitrant teenagers mumbled apologies and slouched off back to the villa, bickering sotto voce.

Augusta made a brief enquiry of Brocchus, before sending her own slave off on a discreet errand. Olivia scurried away, taking care to avoid the eyes of her fellow slaves as much as possible.

Someone for whom literacy was a chore had clearly written the *defixio*, nailed to the grave marker with enough force to split the wood. The grave made an ill-tended contrast to the neat, flower-decked one further down the plot.

"A cat for a cat?" Olivia muttered quietly, reappearing at Lady Augusta's side with all the stealth of a feline herself. "Have I read that correctly, mistress?"

"Yes, I think that's what it says, though the grammar and spelling are so poor that the author could have intended any of a dozen possible meanings. Though as none of them make any sense, perhaps it is of no significance. Although I am not so sure…oh, of course! How sad. What did you find, Olivia?"

The plump girl produced a wooden rod, roughly the length of her own forearm, simplistically decorated with strips of leather and metal studs, "It was beneath his bed. I also spoke to the house-slaves afterwards as you asked, mistress, and it seems that Severus, the old procurator, was hated by all and sundry for his brutality. None of them would say as much, but I got the impression that the Lady Clara is loathed with a passion. It wouldn't surprise me if the cat was killed just to spite her."

Lady Augusta smiled ruefully, "That much I had already surmised for myself, Olivia dear. Were you able to check the other room, as I asked?"

Beaming, the eager Olivia slipped a hand down her own ample cleavage and produced a small glass vial. Augusta removed the stopper, her face ashen as she sniffed the contents, "It wasn't in the other bedroom at all. I was nervous of going in, in case anyone caught me – even though I was following your instructions, it would still have been difficult to explain. There is a small shrine to the Dioscuri fixed to the wall between the bedrooms, and I tried to make an offering for protection from detection but I'm afraid that I was clumsy, mistress. I knocked over a bottle of scented oil, and when I tried to clear that up the shrine came off the wall. In my defence, it was so poorly attached that it is a wonder it stayed up at all. I found a small niche behind the shrine, dug out of the wall, and the bottle was inside. There is very little liquid in the bottle – is it what you wanted, mistress?"

"It is the last thing I wanted. I rarely wish to be wrong, but this was one of those occasions." She sniffed the contents of the bottle and grimaced. "What in the name of Minerva's owl is that ghastly noise?"

"Oh my! Sorry, mistress, but I forgot to say – that must be the cat's funeral. The lady Clara gave orders…sorry, I mean invited you to attend the ceremony along with the rest of the household. I was supposed to say, but thought that I should attend to your orders first. I think she hopes that a ritual will somehow lift the pall that weighs so heavily over this House of Hades."

"Do stop flustering, girl. Now, if that harridan wants the miasma banished then so be it. Though this is not a task that I relish completing. Be alert, Olivia, I may need to call upon your strong right hook!"

One swipe of Lady Augusta's walking stick scattered the Egyptian artefacts from the altar in the garden shrine. Shock and fury battled across Clara's features, Quintus' jaw nearly hit the ground, and the twins all but squealed with repressed mirth.

"Be silent, imbeciles!" her tone would have had an emperor leaping to attention, and more than quailed the female slaves who had been ordered to serve as official mourners. "This blasphemous nonsense has continued long enough. You wish the misery lifted from your house, Quintus Cornelius Britannicus?"

The spluttering merchant nodded dumbly, and Augusta held out her hand. Olivia placed the wooden rod into it, and the priestess banged it down on the altar. The family all craned to see the item, staring at it in bewilderment for some moments.

"What is it?" asked Prima.

Augusta nodded, and Olivia whispered, "The handle of a *flagrum*, young mistress."

"A what?"

"A whip, stupid!" her brother explained with a theatrically world-weary sigh.

"At my instruction, my slave Olivia searched the villa and found this handle."

"What on earth can this piece of wood have to do with anything, let alone justify your violating the sanctity of this sacred place?" Clara's chins wobbled with fury.

"There is nothing holy here," Augusta snapped. "This leather strip, until recently wrapped around the fat throat of your repellent feline, was once attached to this handle. It is an item that I would have thought you perfectly familiar with, Clara, given that I understand you frequently supervised the brutal floggings of the slaves and encouraged Severus to excesses which, I am quite sure, our new emperor would not approve of."

Always conscious of imperial spies, even the voluble matron paled at the reference to Julian's reformatory zeal, "I...well...I believe in a well-disciplined household," she stuttered.

"Discipline is one thing, savagery quite another. Normally a *flagrum* is only employed for the severest of transgressions. From what I gather, slaves were frequently flogged half senseless with it for trivial infractions. Some even died – the girl accused of stealing your golden statue being one such. She lies buried with the other slaves, though set apart from them. Her grave is well tended with offerings."

"Are you suggesting the girl had an accomplice in her theft?" Quintus tried to reassert his authority within the bounds of his own villa.

"Of course not, Quintus! I doubt very much the girl ever stole a thing in her life, except possibly the odd moment of passion. This golden cat...now, I wonder if we were to send a messenger to the household of this girl Antonia whether we would find that she received some very expensive gifts this Saturnalia past?" Her scathing gaze turned upon Primus who flushed scarlet and began backing out of the crowded shrine, as expletives exploded from his father's thick lips.

"Perhaps Father should take one of these *flagra* to you, brother dearest! But why did the little snot strangle that flea-bitten cat?" Prima positively crowed at her brother's sudden plummet from his pedestal.

Lady Augusta sighed heavily and picked up the whip handle, "He didn't. At this end you can all see where the thongs have been cut. There were once four strands to this *flagrum*. One was used to kill the cat, and of the others I can but speculate. I suspect they were used to choke the life from the procurator and the

Egyptian slave girl. Severus caused the death of the woman you loved, and the Egyptian...did you kill her for the same reason you killed the cat? To make Clara suffer the way you suffered, by taking from her that which she loved, or at least valued?"

Brocchus the chief slave stared at his accuser for a long moment, his eyes misting over, "Cunsa. Her name was Cunsa, and that old bitch couldn't even remember it even after all the years she had served her."

Before anyone could make another move, Brocchus upended the urn of oil he had been holding ready for the funeral pyre. It drenched his own clothing and splattered those near him, who immediately backed away.

"The final tail from the whip, were you saving it for the real thief or for—"

"For that poisonous harpy! I had no notion as to who had stolen the statue, though if I had known I would have wrapped it round his thieving neck. Cunsa deserves vengeance, and I have failed her." He wrenched a burning branch from the brazier and held it to his own clothing. The oil-soaked cloth went up like a candle, filling the shrine with the stench of burning flesh and the screams of the dying and living alike.

In the stampede to evacuate the building the brazier was knocked flying, hot embers igniting the altar cloth, and flames crawling up the walls.

They had sat quietly on the garden bench for an hour. The embers still smouldered, though the twisted corpse of the chief slave had been cleared away. Olivia caught the eye of a villa slave, who signalled that the horses were readied to transport them back to Camulodunum. She murmured as much to the elderly priestess, and helped her to rise.

"Have I done right?" Lady Augusta asked, her voice sharp in the silence. Her large blue eyes searched the slave girl's face, keen for a genuine answer rather than the usual polite platitudes expected of her class.

"In exposing a murderer, my lady?"

"In concealing one." The bewildered expression on Olivia's face prompted the elegant old lady to remove a glass vial from the folds of her dress. "Henbane. They grow it in Rome. Small doses cause terrible dreams and make people see things that are not there. Applied in small amounts over an extended period of time, it can make a person feel they are going mad. Enough of it will kill outright."

Her brow creased in confusion, Olivia delicately reminded her mistress that the slaves had been strangled rather than poisoned.

"It was not the slaves of whom I thought, but my poor sister. Did she really hear the voices of the lemures, unhappy in their graves, or was she drugged with this to send her mad? Or both? Oh, I don't suggest that her death was by any hand other than her own – but if a person is sent mad with potions and takes their own life, is that not also murder of a form, in the eyes of Nemesis, if not the courts of man? Acheruntis pabulum. You said you found this in the wall cavity between the children's bedrooms, hidden behind a shrine to the Divine Twins? I wonder which of them administered it?"

Philosophy was not the forte of a simple slave girl. Augusta emptied the incriminating vial into the ashes of the shrine, and leaned heavily on Olivia as they walked towards the stables.

Second Story Notes

There is comparatively little known about the Roman settlement around the area now called Ipswich (we do not even know what the area would have been called back then), aside from a large villa at Castle Hill, though a plaque dedicated to the god Attis was unearthed from the site. Nothing is known of the family who built it, or even if the same family remained there from the early second until the late fourth century. The villa could have changed hands several times over. All the characters and events of this story are, naturally, fictional.

The majority of the land now called Ipswich was very marshy and of little use for agriculture in those days, which may explain why the Romans had no great enthusiasm for the area. The nearest Roman town of any size was Combretovium (Coddenham) and doubtless the villa would have traded with the people of that community.

For those unfamiliar with the Roman calendar, Matronalia was once the New Year festival in early Rome and held on March 1st. Later the Romans transferred the start of the year to the feast of Janus in the month named after him, which is still the date we cleave to in Europe today. Matronalia, however, remained popular as the major feast of the goddess Juno.

Lemuria was a festival held on May 15th to placate the angry and discontent ghosts. People might become *lemures* by various unhappy means, such as meeting a violent or gruesome end, by committing suicide, or by being interred without the proper and respectful funeral rites. Lemuria was somewhat like Halloween today, and indeed the Catholic Church used to mark All Hallows in May before moving it to the date we are more familiar with now.

Saturnalia began on December 17th and, as the name suggests, was dedicated to the god Saturnus. Much of what the Romans did during this riotous time provided a foundation for our modern Christmas festivities, from the use of decorative greenery to the giving of gifts. It is almost certain that any Romans resident in ancient Suffolk would have celebrated these dates.

This story is set at the start of the reign of the Emperor Julian the Apostate, who in his very brief reign (from 361 to 363) introduced a considerable raft of changes to the way of life that many had become used to – most famously trying to re-establish polytheist religion in a world increasingly under the political sway of often militant monotheism. His reign was one of great upheaval for the Empire, a last surge of hope for pagans and a challenge to the Church's thirst for domination.

The life of a slave in the Empire was hard and frequently brutal, dependent on the whims of an owner – even kindly ones probably came to consider slaves as little more than pets or useful items of furniture. This story reflects a little of what those unfortunate people may have endured.

Chapter Three

The Mark of Cain

It was his own mark upon the chisel; the master carpenter could not deny that. He turned the precious article over with his long fingers, noting the dried blood upon the blade. He looked up at Eafa the tithingman, his bewildered countenance speaking for him.

"There is no accusation made against you, Thrydwulf. I know full well you were snoring like a drunken hog before my own hearth at the time this man was slaughtered. However, someone has laid hands upon your tool to deliberately cast blame upon you it would seem, and I need you to tell me who could have taken it. Have you leant the chisel to anyone, or at least have some notion as to when or where it was stolen?"

Thrydwulf stood silently pondering the weapon, his face darkening with the explosive temper that the tithingman was all too familiar with. The apprentice carpenters, recognising the tensing of the shoulders and the implication of the hand that wiped across the normally handsome face, backed away.

"Yesterday, after lunch, I looked for it and could not find it. Thinking one of the lads had taken it for a jest, or just without thinking. I asked for it back." Three of the carpenters nodded in mute agreement, their fine carving forgotten for the moment. "When it was not returned, and my thinking one of them had broken it, I threatened to leather the arse of whoever was responsible. My lads may be high-spirited and foolish at times, but none would take a life – unless in defence of their own."

Eafa shook his head, "There are no signs of a fair killing made in a brawl. No, this seems something much more sinister. Come with me and see the body, it may be that you know him. My men have been nervous of lifting the corpse, for reasons that you will see for yourself."

"That face scares me to death," young Aedwulf half-joked, indicating the demonic face formed in the chunk of mosaic floor that now stood propped against a mound of disturbed soil. "I wouldn't come here after dark for double my wage."

"What is it?" Thrydwulf asked the tithingman's assistant.

The young man took a step back from the face, and lowered his voice as if afraid the image might be listening. "The workmen unearthed it two weeks back, and I'm surprised you haven't heard. It's caused quite a sensation. Father Roger says it was once part of a Roman house in the old days. The farmers round here are always turning up old coins and things when ploughing. I even found a small bronze figure myself last month, when helping my uncle dig a trench. It looked like an angel, but it still felt creepy. Anyway, the legend goes that the family here were very rich – local lords, or whatever they were called in Roman times. The Malusetne family as you can see from their name written on that building stone over there." He indicated a large slab, jaggedly broken at one side, with badly written Latin scrawled in charcoal up to the break.

"*Malus et nequam homo,*" the tithingman, whose uncle was a priest, muttered under his breath, "an evil and wicked man."

"The foreman wants to use it for the foundations of the castle, but it's stirring up bad feeling amongst most of the workers. They're a superstitious lot and don't want to draw any ill-luck – especially after this. Anyway, the legend goes that the son of this family was monstrously cruel, even by pagan standards. He tortured and murdered many slaves before slowly poisoning off nearly every member of his family, and most of his in-laws. When the authorities finally realised what was going on and came for him, he went berserk and burned the villa down – dying in the flames. That's why these bits of wall and floor are blackened. I think this face is the Roman lord, once his madness and cruelty really took hold."

Thrydwulf stared at the crazed eyes of the mosaic for a few moments, then asked where the murdered man lay. The tithingman's assistant pointed to one of the trenches that the labourers had been digging for the foundations of the planned fortress, informing the carpenter that the body was found in the selfsame hole from which the hideous face and name slab had been unearthed.

Even those who had already seen it approached the makeshift grave with an air of caution. The slim, golden-haired body was quite naked and lay face down, exposing the hole below the left shoulder blade from which the chisel had, until recently, protruded. It had evidently been laid with some care, rather than being simply slung into the hole, for the arms were outstretched like the saviour upon the cross. The hawk-eyed craftsman noticed some small slivers of pale wood lying on the corpse and in the turned soil nearby.

The tithingman indicated that the corpse should be turned, and Aedwulf and a burly labourer tentatively jumped into the trench. After a muttered conversation, they rolled the body. Aedwulf pulled away in revulsion at the sight of the curious symbol gouged across the stomach and chest. Seeing the hacked space where the genitals had once been, the labourer promptly vomited up his breakfast. Thrydwulf buckled at the knees and fell like a sack of turnips into the trench.

An incoherent roar drew Eafa's attention away from the disorder in the trench. A huge bullnecked man, too familiar to the law-keeper from countless pub fights and petty extortions, was thundering up the hill florid with rage. With a sweep of an already stained axe he knocked down one of the labourers, who shrieked with pain. Three others rushed to avenge the fallen man, but were held at bay by wild swings of the weapon. The tithingman bellowed for all able-bodied men to bring this troublemaker low, and a dozen labourers rushed to the brawl.

The mountainous ogre swung seemingly at random, sometimes hacking at his attackers and sometimes slashing at thin air.

Clapping eyes on Eafa, the crazed man stormed towards him screaming about demons. The tithingman fumbled with his sword, and had it but midway from the scabbard when the screaming stopped and the lunatic pitched forward with a gurgle. An arrow, loosed by one of the town guards who had just arrived, protruded from the giant's eye socket. In a state of mute shock, Eafa noticed a spatter of the man's blood dripping down the ancient mad-eyed mosaic.

"You hit your head when you slipped down the side of the trench," Eafa mumbled, trying to avoid any suggestion that the rugged carpenter had fainted like a swooning maiden. The tithingman's wife bathed and dressed the wound, as Thrydwulf sat silent and ashen-faced. "It's hard to tell who it is, with so much damage caused to the face. There was a silver ring on the hand, carved with heathenish symbols which might help put a name to him – if we can find someone that knows how to read them, and perhaps find a family to bury and mourn him."

"A ring with symbols?" Baldith exclaimed, putting her ointments aside. "What symbols?"

Her husband produced the ring from his pouch and proffered it to her. She took it gingerly and looked at the small silver band, passing it in turn to the curious carpenter.

"Those are runes, I recognise it. I don't know what the runes actually spell, but this was the ring that belonged to that bondsman, old Father Roger's man. You know, that corn-haired Danish fellow who was captured during Sweyn's raid last year, what was his name?"

"Oluf," supplied Thrydwulf, "he assisted when we carried out repairs to the church back in January."

"He was a carpenter?"

"No, no – just fetching and carrying, no skilled work. In his homeland he had been an apprentice to a healer. He wasn't a warrior, I think the raiders must have brought him along as a physician. Quite learned on matters of plants, and tended Big Thomas when he trod on a nail. He made an ointment that took away all the aches from my joints as well, would that he had made some more. Oluf talked a great deal – a bondsman's lot is often a lonely one."

"Did he ever mention an enemy, Thrydwulf?" the tithingman asked after pondering for some moments. "There is clearly more to this than some robbery gone wrong – what does a bondsman have worth killing for? I should tell you, my friend, gossip is already spreading against you."

"I have heard talk," Baldith responded to the encouraging glance of her husband, refilling the ale cups as she did so. "Some of the wives are whispering of pagan sacrifice – you must know the old ways of laying an offering beneath the foundations to become the guardian spirit of the new building."

"Animals, yes, but humans haven't been offered for a long time." Thrydwulf shook his head and drank deep of his ale.

"I don't say that you did, my friend, only that foolish people imagine it. I think it is mostly because the corpse was laid in the same trench where that devilish face was found. So violent a slaying speaks of a mind unhinged. Maybe…maybe the killer was simply insane and pounced upon the first person to cross his path? It was full moon last night, and I have often heard that mad people can become much worse at that time of month."

Husband and wife looked nervously at each other before the tithingman broached the subject that hovered over them, "That symbol hacked into the poor man's flesh…it is the same as the mark on your chisel. Some are saying it is a demonic sign, a heathenish bind-rune used by followers of the Old Gods."

"It is my personal mark; you will see it on all of my work and tools. Every master craftsman has his own special mark. There is nothing magical about it, just a pattern made out of the initial letters of mine and Godgifu's names in the old alphabet. If idiots read something else into it then that is no concern of mine!"

"Come to church with us this Sunday, Thrydwulf!" Baldith tried, and failed to make her suggestion sound casual. Seeing the scornful ice in her guest's eyes, she opted to be more direct. "You never go to church, and now people are saying it is evidence that your loyalties lie…elsewhere. Prove them wrong, show them that you have no truck with the old customs."

He paced liked a caged wolf, causing Eafa to question the wisdom of having informed him of the scandalous whispers. "I need prove nothing to fools. My soul is my own affair. Oluf had no enemies. None that I knew of at least, but maybe the priest will know more."

Roger's face was as blanched as his hair when they found him kneeling at the altar. The tithingman helped the stout priest to stand, wondering if the shock of the news might prove to be too much. "The Devil walks amongst us, gentlemen. Your lad, Aedwulf, told me of the disfigurements. And now this Baldwin character, gone berserk. I know of no connection between him and Oluf – certainly the giant never attended my church. It is possible that his mad rampage is just a coincidence, though more likely the Devil has found ingress wherever he may. Such wickedness…poor Oluf, poor foolish Oluf! There are rumours abroad of devilish rituals and blood sacrifice. Too late now but I wish, I do so dearly wish, I could have saved him. It is a failing in me that I should not have been able to help."

"Yes, well, Father," said Eafa, "it's too late now as you say. The watchman swears he passed the trench at midnight and saw nothing, but discovered the corpse on his second sweep some two hours later. Surely Olaf should have been in bed at such a time?"

"He was," the priest nodded distractedly, "at least I thought he was. I can think of no… that is to say, no righteous reason for him to be abroad at such an hour."

"Righteous?" Thrydwulf pounced on the word, startling the old man. "Does that mean you know of an unrighteous reason? Speak priest!"

Embarrassed by his friend's vehemence, the tithingman blocked Thrydwulf's line of sight and requested that the clergyman disclose any details that might bring the miscreant to justice.

The old man was some time in replying, clearly struggling with his own conscience. "It is a sin to lie, but also wrong to speak ill of the dead. I shall tell you, but pray that you hold your tongues and do not sully the name of one who must now face God's justice. Oluf was *earg,* or *ergi* in his own language." Eafa gasped to hear a priest use the sort of language seldom heard outside of the lowest inns. "I do not say it lightly, but of my own knowledge. Once I caught him giving himself to the apothecary's serving man. Whilst Oluf attended church at my insistence, I do not think he truly believed. In fact, though it pains me to say it, I suspect he cleaved to the godless ways of his forefathers. It may even be that his death was part of some unspeakable ritual to honour the demons worshipped by our forefathers. When he came to me he still wore a golden ring inscribed with magical symbols of the old ways. At my insistence he parted with it, and I threw the cursed thing into the River Urewell. I remonstrated with him at great length about his ways, watched him like a hawk to ensure he would not stray into either physical or spiritual degradation again. I even found him a good Christian woman, a wife you understand? They were to be married next month. Somerhild is a good girl, bondswoman to old Roderick the merchant. You may have met her, Tithingman, if you have been to his warehouse to buy a whetstone. Apparently she has quite the mind for numbers, and helps keep the accounts. Roderick agreed that it would be a good match, and that he could easily find work for a willing pair of hands."

Eafa had been to the warehouse, though he could not recall any particular servants, "So you suspect that he may have gone out for a liaison with some lover. Is there any particular man that you have in mind?"

The priest was adamant that, so far as he was aware, the bondsman had given up his lascivious past and could point no finger.

"I have heard that these *earg* will often go with total strangers, to slake their cravings. Perhaps he found some random man, who simply turned on him afterwards. Heaven knows enough prostitutes are set upon by men whom they have just serviced, so why should it not happen to a creature like this too? Though if it is just some passing brute, then we will have scant chance of catching him," the tithingman mused aloud. "I would have thought the docks more the place for that kind of thing than the site of this damnable castle, but there is little accounting for taste."

"Should be easy enough to find," the carpenter growled, "whoever hacked the body like that will be covered in blood. What say you to the claims of blood sacrifice, priest?"

"Well," the cleric eyed the lupine man nervously, "I said he may have harboured faith in the devils of his Viking ancestors. Maybe there are others hereabouts who share that vice as well as his other? Perhaps he crossed them in some way, or was offered up as a sacrifice? Last night was the start of old *Blod-monath*, when our ancestors slaughtered their weak cattle in preparation for winter. It is possible someone thought animal blood just insufficient."

Thrydwulf's sister sat in her favourite chair by the fire, quietly watching him as he in turn watched his young son playing with wooden animals. She hadn't seen him this morose since his wife died three years earlier. Two potential customers had already cancelled, citing implausible reasons. Eafa had not long left, having delivered the news that nobody had been spotted with unaccountably bloodstained clothing. He had also told them that the infirmarian had examined the corpse and declared that most of the wounds, including the unspeakable one, had been inflicted long enough after death for the blood to have stopped flowing. The killer, therefore, was unlikely to have been stained by their deed. The infirmarian was of the opinion that the wound to the chest was most likely the first and fatal assault.

"It is clear you have an enemy, brother. Perhaps it is some rival in the brotherhood. Is there anyone who would seek to displace you as head of the Carpenters' Guild?"

"Who could be foolish enough to break the oaths that bind us…except maybe that pompous little idiot Anselm, or Bernard the timber merchant?"

"Bernard isn't in the guild, is he?"

"No, but since he sold up the pottery and invested the money in rights to logging the West Wood, he's been attempting to bleed our members dry with extortionate rates for timber. From what I hear he has pretty much crippled his former guild brethren, who need his wood for their pot kilns. If he can turn against his fellow potters like that, he'd scarce baulk at undermining our fellowship. He has ambitions to run the Merchants' Guild, once old Robert retires. We need all the wood that can be laid hands to for this castle, and if a gutless fool like Anselm were to run the guild then Bernard would be able to walk all over us. It is only my contact with other merchants that keeps Bernard's greed in check. Now, if you will excuse me I have a few visits to pay."

The tithingman's eyes looked askance at the second, equally rough coffin that the master carpenter hammered nails into.

"The first one was too small," Thrydwulf explained, blushing and causing his friend to speculate on just how perturbed the craftsman must be to make such an elementary mistake. "That sanctimonious crow Roger is refusing to bury Olaf in holy ground, says he must go amongst the suicides and unrepentant sinners in the back field. The poor lad died at the hand of someone who plots against me. He shall rest in my soil, in a coffin of my making. That at least can be done for him."

His friend made a non-committal grunt, "I hear you have been terrorising Anselm the carpenter!"

Thrydwulf snorted in contempt, and explained how he had taken his boys round to discover the depth of his deputy Guild Master's loyalty. They had surprised the tiny gnome of a man on his early morning constitutional. Anselm, his normally rubicund cheeks turning the colour of cold porridge, protested in the strongest terms that he had no dreams of leadership. He had, naturally enough, been at home asleep alongside his wife when the bondsman had met his death. Thrydwulf placed little value in this, however, for cowards invariably pay others to do their dirty work for them.

The same might be said of Bernard, with whom he had failed to secure a meeting. The exhausted-looking servants had barred entrance, claiming that their master was recovering from an illness and not fit to see anyone. Thrydwulf himself had received a visit, some weeks previous, from a toothless knuckle-dragger in Bernard's pay attempting to make an offer that the carpenter was happy to refuse. The scrawny merchant was not a coward, indeed he normally enjoyed gloating in person over those he sought to intimidate, and Thrydwulf was inclined to believe that the man really must be indisposed – or else he would have enjoyed grand-standing in front of him.

Eafa in his turn went on to bewail the lot of a tithingman, faced as he had been with clearing up the mess caused by the lumberjack having run wild. Baldwin had battered his elderly landlady senseless with an ale flagon, before taking an axe to his own dog and proceeding to injure well over a dozen people on his rampage up towards the castle's hill. The man was a notorious thug and a drunkard, but there seemed no reason for him to behave with such insane abandon.

So much time had been spent attending to Baldwin's mess that Eafa had failed to find the opportunity to call upon the grieving bondswoman, whose chance of a husband and family had been so rudely snatched from her. If the tithingman had been hinting about wanting some assistance in the task, it had fallen on deaf ears.

Somerhild was not exactly as grief-stricken as Eafa had feared. A stolid creature with a face like uncooked suet, she sat and glared up at him from her desk, "A sad end for him, but no loss to me. If I am to be married off like a cow put to the bull, then at least let it be to a real man and not some beardless cock-hungry whore!"

The tithingman's mouth gaped open and shut like a fish struggling in the air. It was some minutes before he gasped out a question as to her whereabouts at the relevant time. The diminutive woman's look would have curdled milk, and she pointed out that she slept alone.

"If you are looking for someone who might have cause to kill him, look to the man who gave him that ring."

"What ring?"

"That interfering priest threw away a gold ring that Oluf had from his homeland – he said it was a pagan thing. Then last month he started wearing a silver one, with the same symbols on it. I asked, but he refused to say who had given it to him – but be assured, Eafa, that nobody would spend that kind of money on a mere bondsman without expecting a great deal in return."

The investigator had to agree that such a gift suggested a strong bond. "Speaking of pagan things, word has it that Oluf may have been part of some strange group adhering to the old ways. Did he ever mention such a thing?"

"We never spoke of religion, all that rubbish holds no interest for me. I go through the motions because my master insists upon it, but that is all. That sour hag Ethel, widow of that potter who died last winter, used to buy his potions and was always on at him about magic and all that nonsense. She might know more."

Hard to see so tiny a woman hacking up a corpse and dragging it to the foundation pit, the tithingman suggested to his friend. Oluf had not been a large man, but it would still have necessitated some degree of strength to cause his death – let alone drag the body to its final resting place and desecrate it in such a manner.

"Maybe we're looking for two people? She may have a murderous brother, or perhaps someone willing to kill for what little money a bondswoman can scrape together," Eafa mused.

"Perhaps... I should like to see the place where the woodsman lived. I suspect his madness and this horrible murder may be connected."

Half an hour later the two men stood in the impoverished abode. A brown stain on the floorboards marked the place where the old landlady had nearly bled out her life, the pottery shards of the ale flagon used to batter her still strewn around. Thrydwulf lifted a piece from the base of the vessel and sniffed the dried remains of the ale. Eafa, curious, emulated the gesture.

"A very peculiar smell – what sort of ale is it?"

"Valerian, and something else...not sure what. What is that other smell? Reminds me of whatever my sister uses to scrub the floor." Sniffing like hounds they traced the astringent odour to a clothes chest, which opened to reveal an outsized tunic and some trews, covered in pottery dust. Patches of sticky pine-resin on the seat of the trews explained the strong smell.

"Well, he was a delivery man for the pottery, lugging all those hefty flagons to the brewers – no surprise that his clothes were covered in dust. Will you come with me, Thryd, when I go to talk to the Potter's Widow?" The tithingman pulled out the grubby tunic for a better look, his jaw dropping at the sight of the hefty bag of coins underneath.

Ethel, widow of the previous head of the Potters' Guild sat amidst the drying herbs that festooned the rafters, clearly in the midst of crushing various berries and gums in a pestle and mortar. She offered them cups of homebrewed ale; the aroma was pungent and the taste heady.

She fixed the tithingman with an austere eye upon hearing the nature of his business. "I mourn the boy's loss, gentlemen. For all his humble station in life, Oluf was a friend to me. I had not spoken of it to him, for fear of raising false hopes, but I had thoughts to buying his freedom from the priest and setting him up as an apothecary. His knowledge of herbs was phenomenal for one so young, and I do not doubt that he would have returned the investment."

"Just herbs?" Eafa tried to sound more intimidating than he felt. The ferocious intelligence and unyielding autocratic manner had him quailed, and Thrydwulf was unhelpfully silent.

"No. I cleave to the ways of my ancestors, ways in which Oluf was also very learned. I make no secret of it. I presume you have come to ask if I cavorted naked beneath the moon and slaughtered the poor lad in some gruesome sacrifice? Those rumours have reached even my ears, and I see the fearful glances of my half-witted neighbours. Hopefully, Master Thrydwulf, whom I see has an intelligent eye, is sensible enough to see beyond these wild fears and will point out to you that at near seventy years of age the likelihood of my butchering a vigorous young man are slim, even were I insane enough to dishonour my Gods with such carnage."

"So who hired him?" Baldith asked her husband, laying aside her lucet and two skeins of blue and red wool being woven into a cord. "And why want a bondsman killed in the first place?"

The tithingman ruminated for some minutes before replying, "Someone of means to pay that much, which rules out Somerhild unless she has embezzled a fortune from the warehouse, which seems unlikely."

"And the priest, he isn't likely to have much money either," Thrydwulf growled, emptying his ale cup.

"Oh, but surely you cannot suspect poor old Father Roger!" Baldith looked genuinely shocked.

"Wouldn't be the first priest with blood on his hands."

"Well, anyway," she scowled disapprovingly and went to put more wood on the fire, "have you or Eafa worked out what Oluf was doing up on the hill?"

"Probably going to meet his lover," Eafa opined.

"Not that lumbering ogre, surely?"

"Hardly!" Thrydwulf snorted. "But maybe this woodsman knew of a planned liaison and waited for him there, or more likely just followed the lad when he left the priest's house and pounced as soon as there were no witnesses around."

"Sent by the lover, grown tired of the lad? Or perhaps Oluf was blackmailing his lover, threatening to embarrass him by revealing the relationship? No, that doesn't make sense. It's the *earg* that would get his teeth kicked in, not the man using him. Besides, at the end of the day he was just a bondsman. Father Roger might be a bit shocked by that sort of thing, but as for the rest of us...well, if a rich man wanted to cast aside a dalliance he'd become bored with, then he'd just do so. Hardly any need to pay that monster a fortune to kill the boy, especially in such a horrible way. I don't think it can have been this other man. Maybe a vengeful wife who couldn't bear what her husband was up to, or maybe a rival *earg* who was jealous of the bondsman getting attention?"

Eafa looked at his wife, nonplussed by her deductions. "Why wasn't the lover killed, if he wasn't complicit in the crime?" he asked her after some plodding rumination, the differing gruesome scenarios playing in his mind's eye.

"Clearly he didn't turn up," Thrydwulf piped in, "or we would be looking at another corpse. Maybe the intention was to kill them both? That might explain why Baldwin the potter's man was paid so much. Two kills, and one of them a man of social standing whose death would demand an accounting." Thrydwulf stared into the hearth flames, talking more to himself than his hosts.

Baldith filled their cups, and they sat silently for some time listening to the crackle of burning wood, "Who could afford to hire the assassin, who has reason enough to implicate Thrydwulf in the crime?"

"And why were Baldwin's spare trousers stained with pine resin?" the master craftsman muttered to himself.

"I fear this is all conjecture, my friend." Eafa patted the carpenter on the shoulder. "If Baldwin were still alive I doubt a conviction could be secured on such flimsy guesswork, let alone put a noose around the neck of whoever paid him. God saw fit to strike the oaf down with madness for his wicked deed; perhaps He will punish this other man in his own way too?"

Thrydwulf watched the flame of the altar candle gutter in the draft caused by the opening of the church door. An hour's wait in the freezing mausoleum had finally paid off, and the cryptic message had been answered. "There is blood upon your hands, merchant," Thrydwulf's deep voice echoed round the chamber.

The tall, scrawny man paused as he took in the open casket with the bondsman laid out, made to look as peaceful as possible under the circumstances. Sweat broke out on his brow, enhancing his already unhealthy pallor.

"I told you not to stand in my way, carpenter!" Bernard of Gippeswyk snarled, gesturing towards the coffin with his vicious-looking dagger. "This posturing little sodomite is dead, with your mark upon him. Maybe next it'll be one of your own apprentices, or that sister of yours. How long is the guild going to want you running the show, with the tongue of every gossip in town wagging against you? The tithingman may not be able to put a noose around your neck, but you'll be as good as dead in this town if you don't stand aside."

Thrydwulf poured himself a generous cup of mead from a flask; he glared at the timber merchant for some minutes before grudgingly offering him some. Never one to pass up anything free, the other man snatched the flask and swallowed the remaining liquid before slinging it to one side with a contemptuous sneer.

"Was it necessary to hack him apart in that way?"

"Baldwin always did go too far!" A mirthless chuckle echoed in the emptiness. "He laughed about it afterwards, when he came to see me. Said the filthy little *earg* was practically a woman, and now had the gash to prove it. All I wanted him to do was put your mark in the flesh, the rest was…let's call it as close to artistry as that lumbering cretin ever got."

"Artistry." He spat the word out like it were venomous. "You are right to call him a cretin, for he gave you away. The pine resin from where he'd plonked his fat arse on some fresh cut timber whilst visiting you…maybe some secret discussion in one of your workshops? For a moment I thought it was that old herbwife Ethel that had hired him, what with all her potions and unguents. Doubtless she uses resins, but scarcely a puddle of it for Baldwin to sit in. You would have known him, of course, from your days as a potter. Though I should have known the instant I saw him roaring up that hill – what on earth would a delivery man be doing with an expensive axe like that? A payment from you I expect, no doubt for some past service."

"He was useful for a while, but be aware Thrydwulf that there are plenty more like him willing to do anything I ask for the right sum."

"Did you enjoy Oluf's ale?" A look of surprise weakened the merchant's arrogance, and Thrydwulf took a step forwards as his opponent glanced confusedly towards the discarded flask. "I expect your hired thug considered it an added perk, to snatch the jug away from Oluf's dead hands. Guzzled most of it himself no doubt, but I bet you had a tipple too? Ironic really, because that ale was genuinely meant for you."

"What do you mean?" The blade clattered loudly on the stones, as it slipped from Bernard's grip. He tried to pick it up, but swayed like a drunk as the floor reeled away from him.

"Oluf made himself a little ready money with his herb lore. Love philtres, basic medicines, that sort of thing. He tried to give me one of his potions, something he said would unhinge the mind of an evil bastard like you. I'd told him about your attempts at intimidation. I was meant to meet him that evening, but lost track of time drowning my worries at Eafa's house. A shame you suffered so little – the Devil's own luck let you elude the worst of its effects by only having Baldwin's leftovers. I wasn't sure the potion would work, but it certainly did for that bloated savage. Know this, Bernard of Gippeswyk, my Oluf taught me many things, including just enough of his knowledge of herbs and potions."

A predatory smile crossed his lips as he watched the merchant, pallid skin streaming sweat, topple to the floor. His own cup of doctored mead lay untouched on the pew.

"At least there has been justice of a sort, even if we may never find out who hired that towering brute. I must go, my friend, I cannot bear this place and that cursed mosaic scares me almost as much as it does young Aedwulf. Call me fanciful but it is almost as if I can hear the dead crying out. Please do not stay here too long…such an atmosphere can do you little good." The tithingman stood awkwardly, and patted his old friend on the shoulder in an embarrassed manner. He mumbled a few more words, expressing his relief that the master craftsman had been exonerated of all suspicion, and bade his leave.

Thrydwulf sat on the foundation stones in silence throughout, head turned away from Eafa. Tears trickled unnoticed down his unshaven face, coldness raging in his heart for the man who had ordered the murder of sweet, beautiful, sensual Oluf. Bernard of Gippeswyk's screams went barely heard in the wooden coffin beneath the very stones on which Thrydwulf reclined. The air would not last much longer.

Third Story Notes

A tithingman was the local agent of law enforcement in the period when this story is set. They were answerable to others with wider-ranging briefs, all the way up to the reeves. In pagan times the chief agent of law was the *gerefa,* who held a position midway between barrister, investigator, and religious exponent.

The motte-and-bailey castle which Thrydwulf is helping to construct lasted until the 1100s when it was torn down. One argument suggests this was done around 1153 after it was besieged by King Stephen during his interminable war with the Empress Maud. An alternate suggestion is that the castle was torn down in 1176 on the instructions of Henry II. There is some dispute as to where exactly the Ipswich castle was located, with archaeologist Keith Wade suggesting it was in the town centre, roughly where the police station is currently located. However, for the purposes of this story the older notion that Castle Hill derives its name from the presence of the castle is being adhered to!

Exactly when the castle was constructed is uncertain, though prevailing evidence suggests sometime early in the reign of William the Bastard. This tale takes place in 1070, though there's no certainty that this date is a probably one from an historical perspective, a year after Sweyn of Denmark and his Vikings pillaged the town. Sweyn was defeated by a force led by Robert Bigod, whose descendants remained a considerable influence in the area. Indeed, it was their involvement in seditious upheavals that finally resulted in the castle being destroyed as part of a punitive retribution.

The early guilds, such as the one to which Thrydwulf belongs, had been in existence in one shape or form for several centuries and combined the functions of trade unions, business cartels and religious brotherhoods. A number of churchmen complained about the rather pagan, esoteric nature of guilds and the strange rituals they carried out. Whether they really were in any way pagan is a matter for some debate. All-male groups seem to have a predilection for engaging in somewhat peculiar rituals and etiquette regimes, so the guilds may have been indulging little more than that.

Thrydwulf's craft mark, hacked into the victim's chest, is inspired by a real symbol found only (so far as anyone knows) on a decorated house timber now attached to the wall at the back of the Tourist Information Centre in Ipswich. The timber features a shield with the letter R inscribed, and is commonly believed to have come from the house of a local 16th-century politician and friend of Cardinal Wolsey, Sir Thomas Russhe. It is probable that the symbol was his merchant's mark, though it may have been the sigil of the architect who designed the house.

This story suggests that the symbol is a runic one, made out of initials – which is somewhat fanciful. Some merchant marks were just random designs, whilst others had specific meanings. If the Ipswich one was just an abstract arrangement, or if it had some deeper significance, remains a mystery.

The old Norse term *ergi* (and its Anglo-Saxon equivalent of *earg*) was, at least by the Christian period if not earlier, a term of grave abuse used to imply that a man was both the willingly passive partner in homosexual sex and also "unmanly" in general. More than that, the concept carried with it notions of sorcery. Partly, it is argued, this may be because attacking by magic (rather than with an axe or sword) was deemed a womanly, or rather a cowardly act in keeping with the implication of effeminacy. Partly it may be because of a tradition, implied in the pagan mythology of the Northern tribes that *seidr* (a form of trance induced mysticism taught by the goddess Freya to womankind) was, in some way, inappropriate for men to practice – though Odin used it.

Some modern rightwing Heathens swallow the Christian perception of homosexuality without question, doubtless because it serves their political preconceptions. Whilst there is no evidence to suggest a radically positive approach to gay men (and even less evidence for the treatment of lesbians) amongst the ancient polytheists of Scandinavian and Germanic lands, there is equally little reliable evidence to support the homophobia espoused by a vocal minority of modern Heathens.

Chapter Four

The Fricwebba

I dreamt of him last night. Such little sleep I get as it is, and his grinning, bloodstained, wolf-eyed face is the one that comes to me in the hours of darkness! It must be the new oblate, Simon, who has unwittingly conjured these memories. When first I clapped eyes on the boy, my heart nearly stopped. When the lad smiles, which he does often, the very likeness of my long-gone lord and one-time ward lifts from the grave. He threw my mind back so many decades that my head was awhirl. The prior rebuked me for daydreaming, when I failed to heed his constant petty queries. He probably has little past worth remembering, nothing to distract him from the trivia of his office.

Sherwood encompasses most of my dreams, but last night I flew back even further. Beyond the great forest to the days when I was a young man, fresh in the cowl and appointed tutor to a lord's son. Oh, not my Robin! No indeed, for the tales of his blue blood are of recent coinage, doubtless told to appease those high-born Norman audiences who could not abide to be bested by a mere commoner. He would have laughed at that, to be considered to have perched his arse on a cushioned seat. Though, in fairness, there was at least some blue in him, even if it were from the wrong side of the sheets.

Being a by-blow of the old baron, the lad found himself considered something of a pet and called upon to serve as a servant-cum-companion to his older legitimate half-brother, who was my proper charge. Though similar of appearance they were quite different in temperament. As so often happens with opposites, they got on well enough with each other.

I remember well once, the boys could scarce have been more than twelve winters old, that the baron took it upon himself to make a pilgrimage to the shrine of Our Lady of Grace in the town of Gippeswyk amongst the South Folk. His new wife, who had been born in that town though she had left it when but a girl, had taken seriously ill, and the pilgrimage was to petition for a cure. The boys were to accompany him, and naturally I went to supervise them. It was an arduous journey, all those countless miles down south, and as to the mayhem that befell us on the stopover in London – well, that is a whole tale in itself, but not this one.

We were to stay in the Manor of Mallory, which was owned by a cousin of the baron's first wife. The manor was on a hill a few miles outside of the town walls of Gippeswyk, and a relief it was to be so far away from the stench of mud and marsh. Our Lady chooses some most peculiar places to make her presence known. Mayhap the town was in greater need than most for her gracious presence?

Upon our arrival at the stead the boys and I, naturally, were ferreted out of sight whilst the grown members of the family became reacquainted with each other. There were four children already in the house; two motherless infants, whose names I do not recall, the heir of the house, a rather self-important boy called Aldwyn, and an orphaned cousin on the verge of womanhood, Eadgyth. My primary pupil, Renweard, formed an instant friendship with the other boy, though I could sense a reticence on the part of young Robin. He never did have much patience with boors.

Eadgyth offered to show me around the salient parts of the house. She told me a little of her adopted family. The head of the household was a nervous creature called Brand who leaned heavily on a silver-headed stick, in listless mourning for loss of his third wife to a riding accident several months earlier; Brand's rather austere silver-haired father Gyric was retired from running the household and content to potter in his beloved herb garden; and finally Brand's widowed older sister, a joyless harridan by the name of Emma. Grief seemed to weigh heavily upon the household.

Eadgyth, who I suspected rather wanted for friendship or warmth, bustled me from the house and into the garden and surrounding lands. I remember the beautifully fragrant roses, and an unusually shaped fish pond. There was an orchard too, though rather unremarkable. She led me to some derelict, ivy-clad walls and the scattered remains of some ancient building. A large wooden tower cast a shadow across the pungent herb garden, and I felt my guide shiver a little as we paused before it.

"The dead are restless here." I remember her words still quite clearly. "Sometimes I can hear them sobbing. Mistress Emma says I am filled with foolish imaginings, but what I have heard is as I have described."

I enquired what the structure was, and was informed that it was all that remained of an old wooden fortress that had been torn down on the orders of King Stephen. The door was boarded up and smothered in impassable ivy, apparently most of the internal stairs having long-since rotted away making it a danger to adventurous children.

"The castle was held siege before being torn down. There are all manner of stories about the deprivations the men were driven to, and the butchery visited upon them when the fortress finally succumbed. I think the ghosts must be those of the soldiers slain during that siege."

A crow lowering at us from a pear tree chose just that moment to rasp unnervingly, I crossed myself and rapidly changed the topic to discuss some of the plants and flowers. Oddly she seemed to know little about gardens, though most well-born girls are schooled in the subject. Old Emma, I gathered, had scant warmth for the girl – some old family grievance connected to the man her mother had married. It was to become obvious that the Mallory household fostered hatred like a spectre, long outlasting the demise of the person prompting it.

In the centre of the herb garden stood a stone replica of the famed Gippeswyk statue of the Virgin cradling the baby Jesus. She pointed it out to me with pride, and I was about to genuflect before it when I registered the cloud of flies around the Holy Mother. Peering closer it became apparent that a quantity of blood had splattered up the statue's dress and onto the hand that held the babe. Eadgyth was as puzzled as I, and summonsed the head gardener – so deaf that he talked loud enough for the birds in the trees to hear – who was equally at a loss. He went off in search of the head steward, whom he clearly regarded as the font of all wisdom.

The diminutive steward, who had a face like a deflated jester's bladder, appeared clucking and tutting. Some hours later I was to learn from one of the gossipy housemaids that the steward was utterly flummoxed. Not a single servant or family member had a wound, not so much as a scratch, to account for the blood. The livestock were equally unharmed. However, the gardener's boy had vanished – probably as irritated by the old man as his predecessor had been – and, perhaps, the blood was either his…or maybe he had run off because he had in some way caused some as yet unknown person or creature an injury. The quantity of blood suggested a painful wound, but certainly not a fatal one. It was a mystery, and one that some of the servants clearly associated with the talk of ghosts in the old ruins.

"I am to be married soon," Eadgyth announced when she joined me later that day for a bite to eat. Her tone was not that of an idealistic maid, "I come of age in three days, and am to be wed some ten days after that."

My lord had spoken of a family wedding on the journey down, though I had given the matter little thought – being quite preoccupied with managing two boys bent on mischief. Further enquiry revealed that Eadgyth was by way of a *fricwebba,* a peace-weaver; she was to be married to the youngest son of a hated rival family, the union intended to finally end the generations-long feud and bring peace. Clearly she had no love for the acne-scarred Osgood, but was resigned to her fate for what she considered the greater good of her adoptive clan. Doubtless the fact that she would have been given little choice in the matter also contributed to her despondent mien.

As is so often the case nobody seemed entirely sure when the feud had started or what over. I mentioned it later to two of the older servants and each gave a differing account.

The steward, when I asked him later, opined that it was down to an allegation of embezzlement made decades earlier – Gyric had displaced some now long-dead member of the minting family as head of the League of Grace, whose reputation had been besmirched in the process. Some toothless harridan recalled how she had once been lady's maid to Brand's late mother, a woman of unsurpassed beauty. After her fourth child this veritable Venus began to gain weight and a few wrinkles, leading to some rather catty and very public comments by Seaxburg. The following day the maligned woman had hanged herself. An extreme reaction, it seemed to me, but mayhap she suffered from the instability of humours common to many women after birth. The mortified Gyric had never remarried, a widower of over thirty years standing now, nor had he ever forgiven Seaxburg for her vinegar tongue.

I asked Eadgyth what her future family was like. She took some time to form a reply, clearly trying to think of a politic way of answering. The groom's sister and her husband lived in a grand house in the heart of Gippeswyk, he being a leading luminary in the Mint. Indeed, the whole family had been tied up with coin making in one manner or other for generations. Little Eadgyth was marrying into money, but I had no sense that she was an avaricious person for whom the prospect held any great allure.

There had been another sister, but she had died some years

ago in the same plague that had carried off the patriarch of the clan. The mother of this brood still lived, and Eadgyth was clearly in fear of her vitriolic and domineering ways. The prospective husband she described as devoted to his mother, though her expression clearly indicated that this went beyond the bounds of any natural obedience. My attempts at reassurance were of scant avail. A woman's lot is seldom a happy one.

The days passed pleasantly enough, and we all visited the shrine of Our Lady in the parish of St Mary, just outside the walls of Gippeswyk, to seek the Virgin's healing grace. The boys' natural ebullience calmed once we all left our shoes at the Slipper Chapel and made our way barefoot down the rush-strewn path to the shrine amidst the hundred or more other pilgrims. The wooden statue of the mother and child was truly inspiring, and the church billowed with clouds of incense that made a welcome haven from the noxious odours of the town and its surrounding marshlands.

The boys and I sat behind my lord and his kin, even the normally restless Robin gazed in reverent awe at the beneficent gaze of the statue. The spill of light through the vivid stained glass created an aura of wonder that I have rarely experienced since. My mind floated away on the cadences of the hymns. Deep in prayer, I heard a clear, deep female voice. It said to me, "This wickedness must stop." I looked around, but no woman sat close enough to have whispered in my ear. To this day I am certain that it was the voice of the Mother of God.

After the service, whilst my master spoke to the priests about endowing a new window in exchange for a month of prayers for his wife's recovery, I was bewildered to watch the lowering stand-off between the silver-maned Gyric and a hideous toad whom I later learnt was the matriarch of the clan into which young Eadgyth was marrying. The two engaged in a stilted conversation with one of the priests, endeavouring to be polite to the cleric whilst shooting daggers at each other.

Eadgyth informed me that the old man had, since his retirement, become a leading light in the League of Grace. The organisation consisted of many of the well-heeled members of Gippeswyk society who tried to help the poor and destitute in various practical ways. The batrachian matron had been striving to push her son, the soon-to-be groom, on to this august body. Reading between the lines it seemed that this had little to do with any charitable feelings on his part, but rather that his mother saw it as a social stepping stone. Clearly old Gyric did not welcome this move on the part of his future in-laws.

I was permitted a few hours to visit the monastic houses, which Gippeswyk seemed to have in abundance. Though a Cistercian myself, the Augustinian brothers made me most welcome and, after so long in the company of the young, it was a pleasure to converse as an adult upon matters of faith and doctrine.

The sub-prior of that house was a gentle soul of such obvious kindness and wisdom that I confided in him my mystical visitation. He assured me that I was neither the first, nor likely to be the last, to be touched by the Madonna. As to what the wickedness might be, he agreed with me that it was unlikely to be any childish mischief on the part of my wards – anything they could get up to would hardly warrant so weighty a warning. Likewise the portly brother agreed that my own minor vices could not bear the descriptive of wickedness. However, he informed me a little of the history of the town and it struck me that such a den of iniquity could have any number of scandals that might offend the Lord, or his revered Mother. We both prayed that the Mother would make it clear in due course what she wanted me to do.

My visit over, I bade my farewells and accompanied my lord's party across Gippeswyk to the *haligwille* at Stoke, where my lord wished to draw the holy waters and bottle some to take home to his wife. Whilst the waters at the shrine were sacred, it was curious that it was only the smaller well on the outskirts of town that was famed for its healing and restorative powers.

The household was naturally much occupied with the wedding preparations, and on one occasion Robin and I were privy to a visit by the groom-to-be and his monstrous mother Seaxburg, whom I had previously seen at the Shrine. He was an unprepossessing thing, simpering, rather greasy, and clearly under his mother's thumb. I do not think I have ever met so rude and high-handed a woman as the dwarfish Seaxburg, as she barked orders at all and sundry. It became apparent that the death of her husband, and several other family members, in a plague the previous year had precipitated the decision to sue for peace with a family she clearly still held in utter contempt. The sour expression upon her face when she glowered at her surviving son suggested to me that perhaps she did not consider him a worthy inheritor to her husband's belligerence. The dithering Brand seemed at a loss as to how to deal with her, flinching when she snarled demands at his own servants. I could not but wonder how long this uneasy reconciliation would last, for it seemed to me shifting sands upon which to build. It was a terrible burden to place upon the shoulders of so tender a blossom as Eadgyth, the healing of a wound that showed all signs of still festering.

Watching from the shadows, it struck me that Osgood had as little enthusiasm for his future bride as she had for him. He twitched every time the dragon snapped his name and had watery, ill-focused eyes that wandered all round the room. A young man in love might be expected to make puppyish glances to his beloved, but this creature could barely focus on the woman with whom he was to share his life.

The venerable Gyric entered the hall with young Robin to whom he had been explaining medicinal herbs, handing the lad his heavy leather gardening gloves and packing him off with them when he caught sight of his future in-laws. The look of distaste that flitted across his face in the moments before he composed a friendly mask to meet with Seaxburg did not escape my notice.

Utter hatred danced briefly across the troll's face as she approached the silver-haired patrician. Civility masking their mutual contempt, a stilted conversation ensued concerning the choice of music at the wedding breakfast.

Once again the topic of the League of Grace was broached, Seaxburg leadenly prompting her son into announcing that they had take on two housemaids, formerly paupers who had been retrained by the League. My interest in raising funds to retrain paupers was minimal, and I wandered off to check upon my wards.

Renweard and Aldwyn had become as thick as thieves and Robin, a mere peasant in the eyes of the snobbish heir to Mallory, was rather shunted to one side. My perambulations were blocked by the house steward furiously announcing that two swords were missing, as indeed were Renweard and Aldwyn who had failed to return from running what transpired to be a non-existent errand for the heir's grandfather. The possible consequences did not bear thinking about. The venerable Gyric, who looked desperate for an excuse to escape the conversation, smiled wryly at my vexed state and, in a moment of thoughtfulness seldom encountered amongst the wealthy, offered to take my ward off my hands for an hour and show him the orchards and fishponds. Greatly relieved, I was freed to become a bloodhound and track down the disobedient boys.

Having searched the grounds to the point of exhaustion (I never was built for such exertions), I returned to the manor for advice as to other possible hiding places. The servants I passed were of varying degrees of help.

It was on the way to the far paddock when I spotted the gaunt figure of Osgood. He was, and I blush even now to think of it despite a lifetime amongst the Brethren where I have seen all manner of things, quite naked and in a state of obvious enjoyment. He appeared to be either holding on to a branch, or possibly tied to it – it was too distant for me to distinguish – of an oak tree whilst some young man whom I think was a servant from Mallory laid about him with a birch rod. The hysterical giggling emanating from nearby bushes revealed the hiding place of my quarry. Whilst I was mortified for them to be witnessing so perverse an act, and indeed threatened to turn them over to the manservant for a thoroughgoing whipping of their own, it may have been some small relief that they had fallen upon this distracting scene and so didn't manage to disembowel one another with the pilfered swords.

The walk back to the manor was one long scolding from me, and I insisted that they swear an oath of silence before the statue of the Madonna in the herb garden. Yet boys will be boys, and it came as no great surprise when they could not resist making supposedly naïve double-entendres during the sumptuous meal held that evening. I sat discreetly in a shadowed corner of the great hall. Osgood looked uncomfortable and not just for the obvious reasons. Old Emma, sour as ever, began to rail about the general laxity in society – a wave of petty thefts in Gippeswyk having triggered her ire. Seaxburg was in favour of horse-whipping the miscreants, which induced the most ill-mannered sniggering amongst the boys, soon quelled by authoritarian glares from Gyric and my own lord. Brand appeared oblivious to, or disinterested in, his son's rudeness, and announced that when he took over his father's place on the League then he would extend the work of that august body to providing new recruits for the Town Watch. He glanced for approval at the old patriarch, who gave the notion a fleeting smile of approval.

My own lord tried to lighten the conversation with discussion of various criminal cases from our own manor in the north. Gyric suggested that poverty was the greatest driver of such deeds, which Brand echoed in a manner that curiously reminded me of Osgood's tendency to agree with every word that fell from his parents' lips. The seeming sycophancy of her brother provoked Emma to recommend stocks, birching and all manner of gruesome cures for the deeds. Eadgyth, who had a face like stone and had barely spoken a word all night, stated coldly that she could never see a justification for cruelty under any circumstance. I wondered at the time quite what she might have heard from her young cousins.

When I retired to bed that night I could not shake a horrible sensation of being watched, though there was nobody else about. The tales of the restless dead shadowed my thoughts, and it shames me to say that I was almost as skittish as some silly young maid walking down that darkened corridor – and was quite relieved to pull the blankets up over my head and be saved any unsought glimpses of figures that ought not be there.

It was young Robin that found Eadgyth dead the following morning. She was sprawled awkwardly in the herb garden amidst chunks of rotted wood and shards of a broken urn jabbed into her back from where she'd fallen on it. The shadow of the tower fell across that fragile corpse, its neck snapped. Three parallel gashes ran across her left cheek, not deep enough to kill but certainly painful and liable to have left permanent scars had she lived. We both wondered what sort of animal must have inflicted such marks. I sent the lad to fetch help whilst I stood guard over the dead. As I said prayers for her soul, I kept my eyes wide lest the thing attack me too – regardless of what I had said to young Robin, I could think of no normal animal whose claws could inflict such an injury. My thoughts returned to what she had said of weeping spectres, and I wondered if some hellish beast had ripped at her flesh. Scarce did I realise then how right I was.

As surely as I had heard the voice of the Virgin at the Shrine, so then I swear I heard the rattling of chains that brought to mind poor Eadgyth's account of the restless spirits of slaughtered soldiers. I was shaking with fear and grasping the replica statue of the Madonna for protection by the time that the family and servants came pouring out.

Old Emma's hatchet features dissolved in a flood of humanity when she saw the corpse, pushing past Brand's ineffectual attempts to shield the womenfolk from what they all knew was in the herb garden.

As the only religieux on the scene, I was directed to sit with the body once the women had cleaned and properly dressed it. Sitting there with the poor girl I reflected on her mode of dress when we'd found her in the garden. Despite the grubby blanket pulled round her shoulders, underneath she had been dressed for bed. The body had been quite cold and stiff, suggesting she had died when she ought to have been deep asleep. Had someone managed to abduct her, dragged her outside to kill her without raising the notice of anyone in the house? Though if he had, I could not imagine the villain that would take the kindness to wrap his victim in a blanket first. If she left of her own volition, what could have led her to wander outside without taking the time to dress properly first…a secret assignation?

"What caused the cut on her hand?" Robin's voice startled me out of reverie, and I made to push him from the room – but he dodged me and repeated the question. I had noticed the wound on her right palm earlier, and we looked again. The dried blood had been washed away, of course, but the scars of two parallel lines, about three finger widths apart, with the lower one having a diagonal nick in, remained. Neither of us could work out what might have left such strange scars.

Brand naturally raised the hue and cry, though to little effect. What few neighbours they had had seen no strangers, the Town Guard could report none of the usual dubious characters leaving or returning at untoward hours. The women of the house had already announced that poor Eadgyth had died a virgin, which scuppered the common view that she had been ravished by her murderer. In due course her maid informed Brand (and then all the servants) that the poor girl's humble collection of jewels was all accounted for.

My vigil over, an idea came to me as I took an exhausted turn round the fishpond in a successful bid to clear my head – many a person has been driven to mad deeds by thwarted love. Love may have been too dignified a word for whatever occurred between the sweaty Osgood and the bondsman, but fear of losing his whipping boy could have driven the man to murder. A difficult thing it is to question a man on his private peccadilloes, especially when natural shyness about such matters makes even naming the deed impossible. He was a handsome sort of fellow, in a thuggish way and I found his forceful manner quite flustering – perhaps exacerbated by knowing his propensity for harshness. I questioned him along with a number of other servants, to avoid appearing to single him out. His manner with the female servants was leering and forward in the extreme. It may have just been a mask, but I began to suspect him one of those tom cats who will go with practically anything, provided with enough beer or maybe more sober incentives. Try as I might I could not see the brute as having great passion for Osgood, beyond whatever coin might be provided him…and, really, would merely getting married be likely to stop Osgood pursuing his interests with the bondsman, or anyone else that might draw him?

Robin had not my romantic streak – as poor Marian was oft to complain in later years – and when we had finished our evening prayers and Renweard retired to his cot in his cousin's room, the lad cut to a point I had not considered.

"If any of the family had found out about the carryings-on in the paddock then they would have got shot of the bondsman. Not there and then, lest word get out about the real reason, but after the wedding, some trumped-up charge to dismiss him on and drive him out of the district, stop any gossip spreading locally. A servant might well kill to keep a roof over his head and three square meals on his table."

As well as speaking to the bondsman, I had also discovered that Eadgyth's final day in this world had been spent initially with the seamstresses in Gippeswyk, before being entertained by her future sister-in-law to lunch in town, and then collected some ledgers from the League for her adoptive grandfather to peruse back home. The remainder of the day had been spent at Mallory. As near as could be established from questioning the maid who had accompanied Eadgyth to town, the lunch conversation had been vacuous in the extreme and focused largely on matters of fashion and how the mistress was finding the new servants.

It seemed I would have to pursue other avenues to find the truth of the matter. I sat in the herb garden and prayed before the replica of the Virgin, my mind returning to the mystery of the blood that had besmirched her stone garments even as I recited the words.

I have already sworn that I had heard the voice of Mary in the shrine, and I will oath again now that I heard a voice right then pleading for help. A voice so low as to be barely perceptible, but the suffering in that whisper was palpable. Suffice to say I was alone in the garden. Alone, that is, of the living…what else might have been in touching distance of me, yet unseen by mortal eye, I cannot say to this very day.

"It was Gyric's mother-in-law who started it many years ago," Emma said in response to my question after I had finished reading to her from the family Bible that evening, "she was a formidable woman and quite the beauty too, just like her daughter. They started out just feeding the destitute, but then became more pragmatic and started helping the poor get work and take care of themselves – paying craftsmen a small stipend to take on board additional apprentices, or households to train up servants. We have several here – housemaids, gardener's boys, kitchen skivvies and the like. The idea being that the households take them on in knowledge that they are new to the work and so won't be very good at it, but once they are trained up they can move on to get a full wage in some other house."

It seemed that the League paid a small monthly sum to craftsmen and householders for each apprentice or servant that they took on; these details being logged in the ledger.

Unbidden, young Robin slipped up to the scribe's room and retrieved the ledger for me. More than an hour I spent by candle-light that evening searching through eighteen months' worth of records of assorted craftsmen and householders around Gippeswyk, the paupers they had taken on, which placements had been successful and which beyond training, and how many months' worth of payments they had received. There were even sad little notations concerning housemaids thrown out after falling pregnant, boys running away after tiring of the work, and a few acts of petty theft. Such troubles had even befallen Mallory. If anyone were guilty of fleecing the League then I could only think that it must be for such niggardly sums as to scarcely be worth murdering for.

Robin and I took a turn around the fish pond whilst Renweard and Aldwyn ran on ahead, re-enacting some battle with their wooden swords. My youngest ward was a better swordsman, even at that age, than either of the older boys and besting them in combat the previous day had not gone down well with the petulant heir of Mallory. Sagely, he had decided to sit out of the game by feigning a sore arm.

Robin repeatedly asked about the League servants at the manor, which I confess rather annoyed me when I was busy pondering possible motives for sour old Emma and her twitchy brother. Rather snappishly I informed the lad that Mallory had taken on two pauper women as housemaids and five orphaned lads in various menial capacities within the preceding two years. Emma had made her disapproval of the marriage known, but I really couldn't imagine her killing anyone, least of all her own kin, just to stop the union.

Renweard's squawks broke my reverie, and pulled me into a trot. The old gardener lay sprawled outside the shack where all the gardening equipment was kept, the back of his head cracked open by the wooden shovel that now lay beside him. I dispatched Aldwyn and my ward to summon the house steward. Young Robin, never one to shy from blood even then, found a cut upon the man's hand identical in shape to the cut we had seen on Eadgyth.

He wasn't dead, but insensible. Given his age and frailty I held out little hope of his recovering from such injuries. The cawing of a crow flying out from the leather curtains at one of the tower windows sent a shiver down our spines. Though Christian born and raised, I also knew the old stories and omens, and felt the presence of cold Hela in that moment.

To say the sour Emma beseeched me to lead the house in prayer for the poor gardener's recovery (and freeing Mallory from whatever malice stalked it) would mislead; rather she ordered me with all the imperiousness of a papal emissary. Beneath her iron manner a genuine dread lurked. Though she cared nothing for the elderly gardener whose name I can no longer recall, it was blood upon blood and the doom of her family was writ large in it.

We all gathered, servants and family alike, in the great hall and I led them in prayer, beseeching God for his mercy and that an end should be put to the madness that plagued the house upon the hill. As all knelt, heads bowed, my eye roved amongst them and my mind speculated. Emma and her brother side by side, her stoic and he twitching and ashen; grotesque Seaxburg oozing malevolence, next to her son who kept trying to catch the indifferent eye of the manservant; my own lord portly and weather-beaten next to the tall, aristocratic Gyric; the two boys between them with young Robin stood betwixt the maid servants and the house steward, who stood behind the half-dozen servants under his yoke, and looked more shaken than any of them.

Our prior says it is a sin to dwell upon the outer world when one is meant to be praying, but I think God has long since forgiven me. What I thought of then, when I should have been thinking of God, eventually helped me to solve a far greater sin.

Once the servants were dismissed after the prayers, the stiff-necked Emma approached me to express a form of gratitude. I asked her then, trying to make it sound innocuous, what had led Mallory to accept the overtures of peace from Seaxburg's brood. It wasn't as if they had much money or advantage to gain from the allying of the houses.

"Brand decided it was time to end the feud," she said simply, and swept on. I ponder his possible motives for this, but could only really think of one reason why Brand appeared to do anything.

I woke up in the dark hours thinking of crows, of gloves, and of the Virgin Mother. A flood of thoughts fell one upon the other, and with a terrible certainty I knew. Not the reason, I confess that eluded me beyond the realisation that a terrible madness was at the root of it, but the neck that deserved a noose placing about it; of that I was certain. "The crow," I muttered aloud and near jumped from my bed shrieking like a maiden when a quiet voice answered me.

"That's where he keeps them," wraithlike Robin spoke from the gloom. The last three nights he had taken to pulling his cot into my chamber, unwilling to sleep alone. It was only later that

I was to realise that he did this for more than a natural and childlike fear induced by the terrible crimes.

"It's not the money; it's the amount this place gets through. She probably didn't even read the ledger, she wouldn't have needed to. I think she had already begun to understand the true nature of the ghosts." I could but concede that he was correct, perspicacious even then.

The hours until dawn dragged with a necrotic slowness. We needed light to see what we were about. Truth be told, I was also scared to face what was to come without the goodness of sunlight.

For the best part of an hour we searched round the statue of the Virgin Mother in the herb garden, and I prayed for forgiveness as I pushed and tugged on parts of the statue and its plinth in hope of finding a hidden lever. Robin it was who eventually found it, hauling aside a heavy herb-planter a foot from the statue. He had already rummaged through the soil, before shifting the whole pot aside to find a small pit beneath. Amidst the leaf litter I caught a glint of metal, and reached in to find a handle. Stiff with age, it grated as I pulled and yelped at the same time. Snatching my hand away, I saw that the rusted metal had cut my palm in the identical manner suffered by Eadgyth and the old gardener. Doubtless like them, we watched with amazement as the statue and plinth rose a little and shifted aside enough to reveal a hole beneath. We were able to push aside the Mother of God to reveal a shaft and rickety wooden stairs leading down into the dark.

We had no oil lamps, and I agreed with Robin that it would only attract unwanted attention if we returned to the manor to fetch some. Fortunately the light coming down the shaft was just enough to help us blunder down the grubby wooden-walled tunnel. Blessedly the trip was short enough and we emerged inside the boarded-up tower. Contrary to what we had been told, the stairs were intact – though I wondered if they were strong enough to bear my weight. Footprints in the thick dust as we mounted four flights of stairs showed the passage of a number of people, at least some of them seemed to be small and feminine to me. Almost all the footprints seemed to head up, few returning. Some would say I was mad allowing a boy that young to accompany me on the trip through the dark, that I was irresponsible to a criminal degree. My lord certainly would have thrown me from his service had he ever found out. All I can say is that the madness which seemed to emanate from the walls of that damnable place had unhinged my reason.

The sight of that accursed room has haunted my memories for many years. The stench hit us like a wind from hell, before our eyes adjusted to the gloom and saw a world to match the odour. Piles of bones caught my gaze first, all that remained of so many of those orphaned boys found work at Mallory by the League. All those supposed runaways vindicated of dereliction in the worst possible way. Then our gaze fell upon the instruments on the stained table. Ill memory it is, and I will not give them further garment but suffice to say that they were the tools of the torturer's craft and carried the stains of long use. One instrument had three vicious prongs that reminded me of the mutilations on sweet Eadgyth's face. The broken boards across the curtained window suggested where she had been pushed, or perhaps staggered backwards, to her death.

The rasp of a chain made me cry out the name of Jesu, I am ashamed to admit it. His eyes fixed on mine, at once alive with terror and yet deadened by an excess of it. Horror rendered me stupid, and it was some moments before I realised that the thing before me was actually a boy, little older than my wards, gagged and chained to the wall. Welts, burns and scars distorted his grimy, half-starved flesh.

I can scarce put words to the feelings that filled me. It took some moments to master my tongue and ask the terrorised lad where the key to his manacles was to be found. Still gagged, he could make no reply, but those eyes saved my life, for I realised only just in time that he was staring over my shoulder with cringing dread. Turning I saw the boy's tormentor, and the monster responsible for the dozen or more skulls that littered the charnel house, emerge from the shadows holding one of those lethal instruments of suffering. That he had been about to use it on me was clear, as he hefted the wicked device in his gloved hands.

An unholy hunger twisted those patrician features into something demonic. "The keys are about my belt, Brother, and it will cost you a deal of blood to wrest them from me!"

In retrospect I know that he was an old man and doubtless he would have been easy enough to subdue, but the knowledge of what he had done made him seem far more of a threat to me than he probably was. I cowered, and tried to splutter something about the impossibility of his crimes going undiscovered – foolish given that he had clearly been perpetrating his wickedness unchallenged for a lifetime. Dear God, what canker of the soul could lead someone to relish tormenting and violating children in such a manner? How many had suffered? These were questions that were never to be answered. I wondered aloud if discovery of his vile nature had been the true driver of his wife's suicide those many years ago, and the old man's reaction at least confirmed that sudden suspicion.

"Is that the window you pushed her from?" little Robin asked as he hovered at my elbow, discreetly pushing something wooden into my hand. A look of such lascivious yearning came over Gyric's face as I imagine must be seen on the fiends in Hell. Bile burnt my throat.

"Nosy little bitch should have left well alone, as should you fools!" the maniac snarled, inching closer to us and weighing up the best place to land a killing blow. My own death seemed less a threat than what would happen to my ward after.

"When you showed me the fishpond that day I saw that look

upon your face, reflected in the water as you stood behind me. I knew then that you were unnatural, a beast in human skin." The old man faltered at the strangely forceful tones from the little lad beside me.

He lurched towards my ward with such alacrity that I instinctively brought up my hand to swipe him away, the snapped stair rod that Robin had given me cracked him under the chin and knocked the old man backwards against the smouldering brazier. As he fell awkwardly the iron basket emptied its bitterly hot branding irons along with its coals. Gyric hollered as one of the torturing irons rolled against his own flesh, but fell silent when Robin snatched the stair rod from me and broke it across the old monster's head. He ripped the keys from the belt, and minutes later my shaking hands had succeeded in freeing the poor captive.

"Hurry!" my ward hissed, as smoke billowed from the filthy pile of discarded clothing. Barely had I picked up the weakened lad in my arms, when the scattered embers caused the rags to burst into flame.

We were scarce more than a dozen steps down the stairs when we heard the murderous old man howling with pain and stumbling about. Evening knowing what I did, still I found myself about to turn back up the stairs when I caught a glimpse of the devil flailing past the open door with his silver hair and tunic ablaze. It was Robin's insistent tugging at my sleeve that drew me back to the task in hand, and I kicked apart the boarded-up tower door mere moments before black smoke and red flames began to pour from the uppermost windows of the accursed tower.

Servants and family members came rushing from the house in due course, but there was nothing anyone could do except stand and watch that unholy monument reduce itself and its contents to ashes.

The tortured boy was tended to and passed into the care of the priory. What became of him after that I do not know, but pray the Blessed Mother was able to salve the wounds done to his mind as I had salved his body. The family put it around that old Gyric had grown frail with age and dropped a lamp, causing the conflagration. A lie, but who would willingly own to a demon amidst their own kin?

Fourth Story Notes

It probably seems a little contrived to have a story of Tuck and Robin taking place in Ipswich – largely because it is! I have written a number of short stories featuring the Merry Men tackling crime and disorder in Sherwood Forest and, whilst this story could have featured one of the countless other monks in Holy Orders in Ipswich, the temptation was just too great. Plus having a group of outsiders visiting the town was a good way to emphasise the importance of Ipswich as a site of pilgrimage for people from all over the country.

So important was the shrine that, in 1297, a royal wedding took place there between Princess Elizabeth, daughter of King Edward I, and the Count of Holland. The father of the bride stayed in the town during the wedding. It could be that the king or his daughter had some especial devotion to the shrine, maybe having benefitted from it in some way. Following the royal seal of approval numerous visitors went there, including Henry VIII and Catherine of Aragon, as well as the locally born Cardinal Wolsey, and Thomas More.

The popular image of Robin Hood as a loyal follower of Richard the Lionheart is one not created until the later literature, and much-bolstered by film and television. The earliest mention of the forest rogue goes back to the Middle English ballad *'A Gest of Robyn Hod'*, probably printed somewhere around the late 15th century though believed to have been written originally around 1450. In this romance the king is not Richard, but Edward, and scholars believe it refers to Edward III who attained the throne in 1327.

In creating my tale of the Hooded Man, I have opted to follow the *Gest* and set his life during Edward's reign. Historians have placed the ballad's events somewhere around 1340 and, assuming Robin to be a young man at that point, his childhood trip to the

Shrine of Our Lady of Ipswich takes place roughly a decade earlier (at least two years before the founding of the Cistercian monastic community of Fountains Abbey, home to the aged Brother Tuck – who would not have been a friar, that Order not having them). In the earliest recorded tales, the only Marian that Robin is devoted to is the Virgin herself. Later authors seemed to reinterpret this as a human love interest.

The Ipswich shrine first appears in written records in 1152, and was a major site for pilgrims, including the aforementioned royal devotees. Exactly when the shrine was first constructed, and what miraculous events drew the faithful there, is lost to time. Unusually the waters of the shrine were not considered to have healing powers, so perhaps the shrine was sited there following a vision or some other miraculous event. The statue was eventually carted away to be incinerated at Chelsea in 1538, though some small degree of mystery hangs over its exact fate. There is a fair chance that it was spirited away to the city of Nettuno in Italy, where it may well remain.

How sad that these days the local council cannot be bothered to offer more remembrance of this site than a grubby little plaque on a featureless wall in Lady Lane, which these days is really no more than a place for drunks to pee in of a Friday night. A humble recreation of the statue, however, can be found in St Mary Elms church not too far away.

As just noted, the waters of the shrine were not considered to be efficacious in the treatment of disease, but an old healing well is mentioned in the area near Stoke Bridge. Whether this was associated with a particular saint, or dates back to pagan times, is uncertain. Visiting that well seems to have formed part of the pilgrimage trail, but not so major a part as to have resulted in any impressive and lasting structures being erected. Possibly the power of the waters was relatively low key and only treated minor ailments.

Chapter Five

The Golem of Ipswich

"Isaac is dead, Father!"

"Isaac has been dead for over a year now, child."

"Then the man he had become had died, if you wish it thus. Brother Paul has been killed."

"Then Brother Paul shall be given a Christian burial, as befits his status. What a tragedy that Isaac could not have been given a proper funeral as befitted his status."

"Don't you even want to know how he was killed, Father?" Beatriz's voice grew shrill as she fought to keep the tears from her eyes. The burly, grizzled man turned his back to her and picked up the sheaf of notes concerning the amount of stone required by the architect. "He was murdered, Father; your son was beheaded by some maniac with an axe! *Mas vale vergüenza* en cara que *dolor de corazón*."

"I have no grief in my heart, girl. All my mourning was done twelve months ago, and any shame that was on this family has now been washed clean."

"Washed in my brother's blood?"

The older man leapt to his feet and raised his fist as if to strike her, his face flushed and furious. She bellowed at him, inarticulate with grief and stormed from the room. Only then did he sink into the chair, knees buckling and chest heaving with dry, silent horror.

Dwelling in darkness was no barrier to finding her as he merely had to follow the enchanting aroma of almond and vanilla oil. As his fingers found her shoulder she glanced up at his gentle face and, once again, found herself raked with sobbing though her throat was raw with it already.

"Isaac has passed beyond contention now, my child. As a novice they will give him Christian burial. I do not know if he would truly wish it, but I have been thinking about saying Kaddish for him. That little woodland glade along the banks of the Gipping, where you took me for the picnic last month that might be private enough to pray without fear of being overheard. Will you take me there, Beatriz?"

The beautiful young woman stood and wiped away her tears, offering her elbow for her great-uncle to take. Slowly they passed out of the courtyard and made their way down to the river, where donkeys and boatmen made their way up and down the walkways, hauling the laden vessels along on hefty ropes.

After a while Uncle Zeevi asked to sit and rest. They found a wooden bench set back from the river for the very purpose, and the frail old man eased his bones down. The two sat a while in companionable silence, Beatriz nodding a greeting to the occasional boatman.

"Tell me, my dear, what you know of Isaac's murder. Has anyone been charged with the deed?"

"No, the priory is in uproar. Nobody knows who struck Isaac, or Paul I suppose we ought to call him now, nor do they know why it was done. One of the old monks has a grown daughter, from before he took holy orders, and I met her coming out of the church this morning. She could barely contain herself. Paul was beheaded at some time during the night, they found him when they awoke for matins – his headless body on the steps of the church." She fought to retain control of her emotions as she described the gruesome fate of her younger brother. "They hunted for his missing head, but it was not found for some time."

"And where was it when they did find it, *presiado*?"

"In the workroom at the priory, where Isa—Paul, rather, was creating his statue of Saint Botolph. Bess said the head was cast at the feet of the unfinished saint, amidst the stone chips and dust."

"The head at the feet, a world turned upside-down. You fear that you will have to mourn twice do you not, my child?"

She weakly protested that she didn't know what her great-uncle was talking about.

"Once for Isaac and again for either your father or brother if they are found to have blood on their hands."

"Papa would not..." she tailed off, unwilling to voice the possibility.

"I hope he would not kill his own flesh, but he has a terrible temper – as does Felipo, and both of them have grown iron muscles from years of hauling great blocks of stone about. It is no easy thing to take a man's head off." Beatriz sobbed again, though the elderly man's voice was gentle. "In Spain I have seen botched executions. Even a supposedly professional headsman may need to take three or four swipes."

"It was a single stroke. I heard the infirmerer talking to Prior Felix. The prior said they should never have accepted a *converso* into the Order and that the taint of Judaism was still too strong. It had let the Devil into the cloister. He also said that there was some sort of message left on the body, but I do not know what."

The two of them sat in resigned silence for a while, both thinking that it might soon be time to move again. At length Beatriz spoke again, "The family will have to attend the funeral, Father cannot afford for the prior to know that he did not approve of Isaac's decision to convert for real. Not with the fortune that will be spent on building Wolsey's new college."

"The building contracts have been signed? Nobody told me."

"Not yet, Uncle, but Felipo said the prior has all but confirmed that we will be a major supplier, especially for the decorative stone. Assuming that they will still want to work with us after this! The Sacristan has been against us since the day we arrived here ten years ago, a veritable Thaddeus."

"Then we must find the killer, and pray that he is not one of us." The frail man stroked his long beard, a gesture of reflection, before reaching for his stick and signalling that it was time to find the still glade and recite the prayers for the dead.

Brother Malachi stood in his infirmary watching the two visitors as they looked at the headless corpse. At least the beautiful raven-haired girl looked, the old sage at her elbow wore a strip of cloth to cover his empty sockets. Malachi had been told that the man's eyes had been gouged out on the orders of some Spanish grandee, leading to the family fleeing that accursed land many years earlier. The two spoke to each other in their mother tongue, and whilst the monk did not understand it he gained the distinct impression that the woman was describing the corpse in response to old man's questions.

"The identity of the killer remains a mystery, Master Cazalla but the Justice of the Peace has been notified and will be here by tomorrow. He is currently attending to a case some miles away, on behalf of the cardinal. He will want to know if the novice had any enemies."

"None that we are aware of," Beatriz answered on behalf of her great-uncle, "though as he has been a member of your priory for the last year with scant contact with the outside world, surely an enemy is more likely to be located here?"

"We are men of God, child!"

"Men are still men, Brother," Zeevi pointed out, "and subject to the same passions as those who do not wear the cloth. My great-nephew was always a dreamy child, not of this world. He had little interest in money or status, so I find it hard to imagine him becoming embroiled in some bitter rivalry."

"I assure you, sire, Paul was a novice – there was no status to be wrested from him, nor any wealth or power. He had nothing worth killing for, least of all in so gruesome a fashion."

"To behead a man seems almost judicial." Zeevi stroked his beard in thought. "Is there someone who considers himself a law? Who punishes the monks when they transgress?"

"Brother William the sub-prior deals with the imposition of discipline, but the novice was something of a favourite with him. He is a very stern man, true enough, though not the kind of tyrant who would slaughter someone for being disobedient!"

"I have heard it said that a message was found with the body, is this true?"

"Yes, it was fixed upside down to Paul's chest with a sharp pin. Here…sorry, Mistress Cazalla, would you like me to read it for you?"

"I can read, Brother." She took the small blood-spattered sheet of parchment. In a rather poor hand were scratched the words: 'Behold, I was shapen in iniquity; and in sin did my mother conceive me'.

"It's from Psalms, 51:5. Quite why it was put there I really cannot imagine."

"I want to see the place where my brother's head was found," Beatriz cut across the infirmerer's protests. "I want to see for myself, to help understand why this monster felt the need to carry Paul's head there."

Some minutes later the three stood in the mason's workshop, and Beatriz described the drips of dried blood leading to the blackened pool at the feet of the statue of the saint. However, it was the statue itself that drew attention even more than the signs of murder. Unable to credit his guide's description, Zeevi ran his fingers across the stone. Just above life-size, the habited figure held a stone candle in one hand, an open Bible in the other and did indeed have the face of what might have been either a dog or a wolf. The base of the statue had the legend 'L.L.I.T.' inscribed in it.

"The head of a hound! Is that not blasphemous, Brother Malachi?"

"Well," the tall monk scratched his sandy beard, clearly uncertain what to say, "it is strange but not without precedent – Saint Guinefort is cynocephalic. Though this devotional work has created much discontent in the priory, there are those who see it as an affront to the saint's memory. Brother Christopher, the precentor for one. He believed that your great-nephew was trying to create a golem."

There was an awkward pause in which Beatriz glanced nervously at her elder, aware that the monk was watching them intently. At length the old man answered calmly, "Our family converted to the True Faith two generations ago, Brother Malachi, we no longer have any truck with the magic and superstition of our ancestors."

Malachi appeared far from convinced by the protestation. "Being foreigners, you may not know, but Botolph was a Suffolk man one of whose legends does involve him mastering the wild beasts of the marsh where he dwelt for a time and calling upon them to defend him in his battles against the pagan marsh demons. In one account it is a wolf, in another a great dog. Either way the usual custom is to show the saint as a man with a loyal beast sitting at his side – certainly not to give him the head of a beast. Yet Paul said this was the vision he received which led him to dedicate his life to the cloister."

"And leave his family traditions behind," the old man murmured sadly.

"Oh!" Beatriz clamped a hand over her mouth, eyes wide at the sight of the stained axe placed on the dusty table amidst the carvers' tools and now being crawled over by half a dozen flies. "Is that…?"

The infirmerer nodded, and told them how it had been found alongside the severed head. He noted that the girl was close to fainting, leaning heavily on her white-haired relative. "I was going to clean it, but the prior said I should change as little as possible until the Justice arrives and sees everything for himself. Curious thing is, it's not one of our axes, which are all accounted for. The weapon was from outside and the killer must surely be too."

"If the precentor thinks the statue is blasphemous, why was Paul allowed to make it at all?" Beatriz asked, clearly trying to change the subject.

"Because the sub-prior shared the vision, and what he says goes, regardless of what the precentor thinks. I don't mean he had the same mystical experience as Paul, but rather that he sees our little priory becoming a great monastery, a place of pilgrimage. He was at Bury St Edmunds for many years, and I think was much taken with the tale of the wolf that guarded the king's head."

"And wants something of the sort here?" Zeevi was familiar with the rivalries and grandiose ambitions that filled men of the Church. Indeed, much of his family's wealth came from fulfilling such dreams.

"The body was cold and stiff, Brother Malachi. What does your knowledge of physic tell you of his death?"

"That he died not too long after the midnight office, though quite where he died I cannot say."

"What do you mean?" Beatriz asked.

The infirmerer ran a hand across his tonsure. "Cutting a man's head off causes, and forgive me for being so graphic, a great outpouring of blood. There was blood upon the church steps, certainly, but nowhere near enough if he had died there. As you can see from the floor here, again there are small splashes but that is all. I have searched all over the Priory grounds but found no unexpected bloodstains."

"So he was killed somewhere, then his body taken to one place and his head to another?" Beatriz spoke softly in a voice shaking with grief. "Why would anyone do such a thing? This is the deed of a twisted mind."

"Maybe one that wishes to make some sort of declaration to the world, or at least to the Priory."

The door banged open and a large, awkward figure filled the entrance. They were all familiar with the sight of the simpleton

Adam Brandon, who lived with his widowed mother immediately outside the priory gate. He grunted at them and made a rapid series of hand gestures which Brother Malachi interpreted, and announced that he was wanted by Prior Felix in the church. As the monk walked his visitors out, followed up by the mute, he explained to Beatriz that the gestures were a form of finger alphabet, similar to that used by Cistercians though much simplified, which he had taught to Master Brandon many years earlier to overcome the loss of speech inflicted by a particularly savage childhood beating from Brandon's late and unlamented father. Beatriz had often noted the old scars and dents to the giant's shaven skull and wondered how he had come by them.

"Could anyone have broken into the priory last night?" Zeevi asked as they reached the gate.

"No, Adam says not."

"Adam? How would he know?"

"Ah," Malachi blushed, clearly finding the topic awkward, "well since our last porter absconded from his vows we have been rather short-handed. Strictly speaking only a brother of the Order should serve as porter, but it is a simple job and Prior Felix has given special dispensation for Adam to step into the role until such time as our membership has grown. We asked Adam shortly after the murder was discovered, but he indicated through signs that nobody had passed in or out of the gate during the night."

Beatriz and Zeevi thanked Brother Malachi, and agreed to return the following day when Sir Rupert Newbury, Justice of the Peace, was expected to arrive.

As Beatriz passed out of the priory gate she saw the silent Adam emerging from his humble home a few yards away, carrying a chair for the diminutive form of his crippled mother who hobbled along, severely hunched and leaning on a staff nearly as gnarled as she was. Adam deposited her in a chair in the sun, and she eased herself down. Beatriz felt a pang of sympathy that the poor woman's back was so hunched she could not relax with any degree of comfort. However, the sympathy evaporated when she realised Mistress Brandon was glaring daggers at her and snarling something unintelligible.

"I beg your pardon, did you say something, Mistress Brandon?"

The hag looked shocked to be spoken to so directly, "I have never spoken to you in my life, yet you are so bold as to know my name!"

"I know nearly everyone in Castle Hill by sight, having lived here for ten years. I am Beatriz Cazalla, my father…"

"Yes, I know full well who you and that old swine are!" The tiny woman made it sound like the vilest of accusations. "I also know about the stone merchant and his tribe of *conversos*. If my son were still alive, there would be no Christ-killers allowed in this holy place."

"What?" Beatriz was momentarily shocked. Such sentiments were far from unusual, but they normally echoed from the empty heads of the young and belligerent, "how dare you!"

"I remember your son, he was a gentle, tolerant soul. He would be ashamed to hear such bile from his own mother." Zeevi's tone was as gentle as ever.

"Shut your mouth!" She edged forward in her seat and Beatriz felt sure that, were it not for her twisted back, she would have leapt up and struck at Zeevi. "My son was weak, too damned tolerant of the likes of you. This whole priory has become a godless den of depravity, and none of these weaklings will stand up for what is right. Boy! See them off."

Adam came lumbering out of the house, making inarticulate grunting noises and flapping his arms at Beatriz as if shooing off geese.

Beatriz made it round the next corner with her head held high before she felt the tears spilling down her cheeks, a mixture of anger, shock and fear. They stood, invisible to the people passing by whose innate Englishness insured that public displays of emotion deterred them even more than the effluent flowing down the street.

"Are you in need of help, Mistress Cazalla?" Beatriz looked up to see the familiar and jovial face of Brother David the cellarer, whom she had often seen distributing alms amongst the poor, and the stranger sight of a monk she had never before met inside or outside the walls of the priory. "We do not wish to intrude upon your grief, but…"

"No intrusion and thank you for your kindness, Brother. Grief and anger are poor bedfellows, that beldam Brandon has touched upon a raw nerve with her foul mouth. On a different day it would wash off me."

"I have a wonderful new recipe…"

"Avice Brandon is a monstrous woman, eaten alive by hatred and resentment," the unknown monk cut directly across the cellarer as if he had never spoken. His legs seemed little more than wizened sticks, poking from beneath his rucked up habit, and sat upon a low wooden board to which small wheels had been attached. Brother David held the rope that pulled the board along as if it were some strange kind of child's toy. "I offered to give that poor child shelter in our priory after he recovered from the injuries done to him by that devil of a father, but she insisted on taking the boy back knowing his days were numbered. God's justice saw to him though when that hell-bound sinner fell drunk into the Orwell and drowned."

"Many women become enraptured by terrible men, Brother..?" Zeevi tilted his head this way and that, trying to work out why the speaker's voice had come from so low to the ground.

"Oswald, Master Cazalla, I used to be the infirmerer until I fell from the priory roof and ended up as I am now. Now I am nothing."

"Brother, let us not revisit this old wound." The cellarer's normally jocular manner faded and he spoke as one who has heard the same bitter diatribe time and time again.

"Tell me, Brother David, what do the letters L.L.I.T stand for?" Beatriz stepped in, sensing a degree of tension between the two monks.

"Lux Luc…"

"Brother David!" the crippled man's voice cracked like a whip. "I find myself in urgent need of the reredorter, perhaps we could return to the priory now."

"Oh, yes, of course, Brother Oswald. Mistress Cazalla do stop by the kitchens sometime soon, and I shall teach you a recipe for a pheasant pie which I think you will find well worth adding to your repertoire." With that the two men headed off to St Botolph's with a turn of speed and the *conversos* ambled home.

Felipo sat across from his sister, sharpening his stone-cutting tools and refusing to utter another word upon the subject that has evoked such voluble passion from him minutes before. The bitterness of the argument hung between them as surely as the ghostly presence of Isaac. Her normally olive-skinned brother was pale with fury at the implication of the statement that had sparked it all off.

He had not been able to account for how their own wood axe had been found in the priory, stained with the blood of their estranged brother. The axe had last been used by Felipo himself, some four days before to chop up a large pile of logs.

"Do you really think I would describe our mother as conceiving in sin, or whatever that vile piece of parchment said?"

Beatriz had to admit she could not conceive of him writing such a thing. Nor could she see him dragging Isaac's headless body about, even if he had killed him accidentally by lashing out in a fit of temper.

"Father was snoring all night long, fit to deafen the neighbours as usual, but I heard someone going downstairs in the night. I don't remember hearing them return. Was it you or Sarah?"

"Sarah went to check on the children in the night, and I got up for a piss!" he declared angrily. "If you didn't hear us return it was probably because you fell back to sleep. By all that's holy you cannot imagine that Sarah or I would do such a wicked thing?"

"You were always so angry at Isaac." She felt as if her world were falling apart.

"With good cause!" He thumped the table. "To make a show of Christianity is one thing, to survive amongst these savages, but to actually throw away his family to embrace that madness as fully as he did is beyond forgivable. He chose to swim with sharks, and now he has been bitten. There is nothing more to be said."

The light from the window was suddenly blocked and the siblings turned to see the cumbersome figure of Adam Brandon looming there staring at them. He uttered some strange croaking noises and thrust a beefy arm through the open shutters, presenting a mismatched posy of flowers to Beatriz. She tentatively took the offering, and ignoring Felipo's contemptuous snort went outside into the sun to thanks her strange admirer.

"Thank you, Adam, did you pick these for me?"

He nodded, a lopsided smile lighting his coarse features.

"Would you like a drink?"

He loitered outside whilst she fetched a cup, and downed it in a single gulp. Beatriz tried to engage him in conversation, but was unsure of how much he could understand. He pointed to the flowers growing round the courtyard, and Beatriz named them for him.

"Do you remember Paul, the novice?" she asked, and saw his face fall immediately. He coloured, looking almost as if he might burst into tears. He gesticulated a cutting motion across his own throat.

"Did he argue with anyone?"

The simple-minded creature nodded and made some strange mewling, almost infantile sounds and repeated a couple of hand gestures several times that meant nothing to his hostess. Eventually he gave up and sat heavily on a wall, sighing despondently. Beatriz sat by high and held his hand in what she hoped was a consoling manner. He looked at her with a sense of wondering devotion that reminded her of nothing so much as a small dog she had owned as a child. A lump rose in her throat and she could think of nothing useful to say, but was saved from further inarticulate silence by the eruption of her young nephews and nieces from the house. At once Adam jumped up and joined them in their various games of quoits, skittles and whatnot. With the way of children, they rapidly accepted the ungainly hulk as one of their own.

"Ipswich cake!" Brother David declared proudly, as his visitor took a bite and complimented him on his baking. "Mostly almonds and breadcrumbs, very easy to make. Whatever other madness occurs round here, food always brings us back to normality."

"The infirmerer said he had searched in vain all over the priory for the bloodstains from where the murder occurred. Maybe Sir Rupert will have more success when he arrives."

"Oh, he is here already. I have already pointed out to him where the crime must have taken place."

"What?"

The rotund black-robed monk led her out of the kitchen and into the sun-baked yard between the refectory and outhouses. He pointed towards a stone trough set into the ground with a large wooden tripod arrangement set over it. She glanced tentatively at it, but could see no blood and said as much to him.

"This is where we slaughter animals for the table and butcher the meat afterwards. This must be very distressing for you,

Mistress Cazalla, I'm sorry. Yesterday this was covered in blood, but it should not have been because no sheep has been prepared here in over a week. I always scrub the trough clean after an animal has been dealt with otherwise the flies become terrible, especially at this time of year. If Brother Malachi looked here he may have assumed the blood was from an animal and paid it no heed. I explained all this to the prior and the Justice this morning."

"This takes us closer to the truth. Do you understand the finger language used by Adam, Brother?" When he assented Beatriz replicated the two gestures that the mute had made the day previously.

"Well, that one means wall, and the other is the letter W which Adam uses to represent sub-prior William. It doesn't make much sense…in what context was he trying to communicate with you?" Beatriz fudged her response, feeling that events at the priory warranted caution although she felt the cellarer to be a kind, trustworthy man, "Well…I'm not sure what he might have meant. Were you being summonsed to a meeting with the sub-prior outside the priory wall maybe?"

"Possibly…when I couldn't understand him we just sat a while in the sun and then he wandered off home. The infirmerer did say someone from my family might be required to speak to the Justice of the Peace when he arrived today, though I would have thought he would speak to my father first."

"Well, the best thing is that we go and find Brother William and ask him if he sent Adam to you with some message that he managed to garble."

Brother William, however, was unable to explain whatever he may have said to Adam, for they found him sprawled dead in his cell. A meat cleaver remained buried in the sub-prior's forehead, and Beatriz's involuntary scream of horror brought a clatter of footsteps – two sandaled and the other booted.

"Christ preserve us!" Prior Felix gasped before clamping a

hand over his mouth, a look of quite genuine shock fixed upon his normally bland face. The flamboyantly dressed man accompanying him could be none other than Sir Rupert Newbury. He looked suspiciously at Beatriz and Brother David before going to check the corpse, whilst the mortified prior made stumbling and ineffectual introductions.

"What is that Jewish dog doing in this holy place?" the one-eyed Sacristan lowered at her.

"My family are converted as you full well know, Brother Martin."

"You killed the sub-prior, you filthy…"

"Enough, Brother!" the Justice snapped. "The blood is starting to congeal and the corpse is cooling. I think this man can have been dead for no less than an hour, but probably not more than two. Clearly a girl as slight as this could not bury a cleaver so deeply in a man's skull. Let us have no more foolish accusations."

"He was with us at prayers and that was, what, about an hour and a half ago. What maniac has done this terrible thing?" The prior could not take his eyes from the corpse.

"That's my best cleaver!" Brother David whispered, and then looked shamefaced for having mentioned such a triviality in the face of such wickedness.

"What's this?" Sir Rupert held up a small white clay ball, no bigger than a pebble that was on the floor near the corpse. Then his eyes alighted on the strip of parchment held in the dead hand. Beatriz saw the same quotation that had adorned Isaac's corpse – 'Behold, I was shapen in iniquity; and in sin did my mother conceive me'.

The pages of the *Zohar* were exquisitely illustrated, and just gazing upon the play of colours, diagrams and lettering struck Beatriz as a mystical act in itself, let alone reading the text to Great-Uncle Zeevi. She sat close to him so that she could murmur the words, always fearful of being overheard although they were in an upstairs room.

"Why do you stop, child?"

"It's getting dark *tiyo*, I just need to fetch a candle to read by." She slipped out of the room for a few minutes and returned to find him stroking his beard in thoughtful manner whilst the other hand caressed the wooden box that the *Zohar* was normally hidden inside.

"Lux lucet in tenebris," he muttered when she asked him if he was alright, "sorry, child, I am thinking aloud. You have just now drawn a link, like a path between the sephirah on the Tree of Life. The letters you told me inscribed on the base of that strange statue of the dog-headed saint, LLIT, which Brother David began to explain to us before Oswald cut him off. In Latin *lux lucet in tenebris* means light shines in the darkness. Along with the candle and open Bible, such as those held by the statue, it is the motto of the Waldensian heresy."

"I've heard of them, they are condemned as heretics are they not?"

"Very, though I thought they had all but died out. They preach a path of poverty, and the need for clerical purity in order to make the sacraments valid – neither of which are at all popular in the Vatican, as you may imagine."

"Why would heretics kill poor Isaac?"

"The Waldensians wouldn't!" He sat stroking the book box for some moments. "They are adamantly against capital punishment. It seems madness that one of them would strike a man down with an axe…though fear can tear people away from their ideals. If it were known that a Waldensian were worshipping in Ipswich then Wolsey would burn him at the stake without a second thought."

"So maybe Isaac stumbled across a secret heretic and threatened to expose him, and so was silenced?"

"Perhaps, but it was Isaac who carved those letters on to the statue. Though maybe he was simply following a commission and didn't really understand the context of what he was making."

"The sub-prior! I remember the infirmerer saying that Brother William shared the vision of St Botolph and that Isaac, or Paul rather, was a favourite of his." Her enthusiasm for the train of thought tailed off as she recalled the sight of William with a cleaver in his head.

"If William killed Isaac to silence him, who then killed William and why? Besides, if the second death were wrought by a different hand why then place that same Bible quote on the second body? The significance of that line needs to be accounted for. A similar choice of weapon too, I cannot but think that one person is responsible for both crimes. I do not like what you told me of the way Sir Rupert questioned you and the Felipo, he seems determined to find a connection to our community. It doesn't bode well."

"Why don't you consult the book?"

A gentle smile lit up the old man's face at her suggestion and, with help from Beatriz, he positioned the *Zohar* on its spine and began to recite a Hebrew prayer over it. At the finish of the prayer he allowed the tome to fall open, raised a finger and let it fall upon the revealed page. He asked his great-niece to read the passage out.

"It is a passage which you have underlined already, with a line pointing towards the sephirah of Binah on the Tree of Life. It says – 'And when they came to Marah, they could not drink of the waters of Marah for they were bitter: therefore the name of it was called Marah'."

"Ah, I see…oh, but surely that cannot be possible?"

"I remember you telling me that Binah, on the Tree of Life, is the Mother of Understanding. What is Marah?"

"The salty sea from which all life emerged, but whose waters are so bitter than none can drink them without becoming ill. The darker side of understanding, if you like, that the nature of mortal existence is to experience loss and grief. My old rabbi used to say that that was the reason why tears are salty, to remind us of the power of Binah."

Beatriz mulled upon this for some time, but could not see how it took them any further forward. "Oh, I quite forgot to tell you something with all else that has happened today. Sir Rupert found a little white clay ball next to the corpse of the sub-prior. It was like, well really more like a child's marble than anything. It may not be significant, but I thought it worth mentioning."

"Sad to say it makes a form of sense...yes, particularly if it actually was a child's toy and not merely like one. I think I see what the *Zohar* is pointing us towards, but I need you to be my eyes once again. Tomorrow we need to go and stand in the place where Brother David butchers the animals and said that Isaac must have died."

"What can you see, Beatriz?" They stood by the inset stone trough. Feeling queasy, the young woman described the surrounding buildings of the priory – the kitchens, one of the outhouses where the animals were kept before slaughter, the refectory off to one side. Zeevi asked her if she could see the outer wall and anything beyond it, though all she could see was the tops of two birch trees, the attic window of Mrs Brandon's house, and the roof of the apothecary's shop.

"There's Prior Felix and Sir Rupert." Beatriz spotted the community's leader and a small body of black-robed monks heading for the priory gate. Brother David bustled across to hail them, whilst Beatriz guided Zeevi. They caught up with the band just outside the gate. "My great-uncle wishes to speak with you regarding the death of my brother."

"God be with you, Master Zeevi." He gave a brief aside to Sir Rupert explaining who they were. "Do not think me harsh but we are due at a meeting with Cardinal Wolsey in town to discuss our role in the creation of his new school. The cardinal does not like to be kept waiting."

"I understand the nature of the crimes that have plagued your house, Prior Felix. These deaths will not stop until you choose a path." The aged sage felt tired and breathless.

"Path? What are you talking about?"

"The Pillar of Mercy and the Pillar of Severity stand before you. The Pillar of Moderation is, I fear, long since closed off to those who live upon this hill."

"This is nothing but the superstitious ranting of an unrepentant Jew!" the Sacristan spat, his one good eye blazing hatred.

"I knew it! I told you all that those filthy foreigners were unbelievers, defiling the sanctity of this parish!" The deluge of vitriol surprised them all, echoing from the disregarded corner of the garden wall where Mistress Brandon was ensconced on a chair basking in the sun. "That dog-faced golem came to life and killed its creator, mark my words!"

"She is right." Zeevi spoke quietly, but silenced all, including the old woman, with his remark.

"The…the statue killed our novice…are you sure?" The prior crossed himself at the alarming thought.

"Not the statue, but a golem nonetheless," Zeevi corrected, "a half-formed creature bereft of speech and carrying out its creator's bidding, with only the most basic understanding of its own actions."

"Uncle Zeevi means Adam the mute," Beatriz explained to the bewildered faces, eliciting squawks of protests and derision.

"He may have the muscle to wield an axe," countered Brother Malachi, "but the boy is simple in the extreme. I tell you, I have known Adam all his life and he hasn't the wit to plan such a crime as this. Nor could he write that biblical quote found on the bodies – the boy is without letters."

"I do not say he planned it, only that he executed it. The planning, and the writing of the passages, was done by the golem's maker, for does not he act upon his mother's every command?"

"Me?" the accused woman shrieked. "Shut your blasphemous mouth, you old devil!"

"Yes, you – you who are so utterly consumed with hatred of my people that the very thought of a *converso* joining the Brotherhood filled you with such a blind rage that you sent your creature out to slaughter that naive young man before the final vows could be taken. Adam carried out your will as he has always done, barely understanding the nature of what you asked him. What hope has Adam ever had, raised on a diet of bitterness and brutality? You sit up there in your attic window watching Brother David slaughtering animals – enjoying the blood and the fear, I do not doubt, and dreaming of spilling some yourself though your body is too crippled to carry out your will. Did you sit in the attic window watching Paul's beheading, inciting that speechless creature to be your hands?"

"The hand of God!" she hissed, a look of insane hatred twisted her already haggard features. "The Lord smites the wicked and sinful. A Jew and a heretic purged from this holy place, the first of so many that need to be cleansed from this Augean Stable – Prior, you ought to be praising God not standing by listening to this pig."

"Two deaths are upon your hands, old woman," Beatriz cut across the harridan's incoherent shrieks of outrage, "and a third will soon follow – for you have surely condemned your own son to the hangman's gallows."

Avice Brandon blanched and attempted to swing her stick at them, but her hands were too arthritic to do the job. Apoplectic with rage she hurled herself out of the chair and seemed intent on biting her accusers. The monks backed away in mixed horror and disgust, only stepping forward when she collapsed spluttering and spasming like a fish out of water until she fell still. Brother Malachi gingerly stepped forward and examined the prone form, pronouncing her alive but paralysed by the seizure.

An enormous paw shoved the infirmerer aside and cradled the twitching, dribbling form. Adam emitted a disturbing infantile mewling that made Beatriz's skin crawl.

"The golem is broken *presiado,* but our days here are numbered. When Wolsey goes on his way there will no longer be any reason for the Sacristan to keep the peace. Come, it's time to plan our flight from Ipswich."

Fifth Story Notes

This story is set in 1528, three years before Henry VIII made the first formal invite to a group of Jews (musicians in this case, along with the Christian-convert Marco Raphael, who acted as an adviser on Talmudic law) to enter the kingdom since their expulsion by Edward I in 1290. This invite was a small-scale one and it would not be until Cromwell that the banishment would be formally lifted. However, Britain had been home to small numbers of Spanish and Portuguese merchants and their families who had, at least officially if not always in private, converted to Christianity. The language sporadically used by Beatriz and her relatives is Ladino, the Sephardic equivalent of Yiddish.

The description of the Sacristan as a 'Thaddeus' refers to a character in European Jewish folklore of the period, a monk who constantly whips up anti-Semitic feeling and is an embodiment of all that is wrong with bigoted Christians. A number of golem legends present the man of clay defeating Brother Thaddeus' schemes. Folklore portrays the golem as a sort of prototype robot, a creature made out of clay and brought to life to carry out the will of the magician creating it. Various rules limit the uses to which a golem can be put, and flouting them traditionally leads to the golem running amok.

Ipswich has its own tiny walled-in Jewish cemetery, still standing down near the docks. The cemetery dates from a much later period than this fictional tale. Some headstones are now illegible through erosion, but the earliest readable one is 1797 (or the year 5558 if we follow the Jewish calendar), and the last is 1850. There are thirty-six headstones altogether, which can just about be glimpsed amidst the overgrowth if one peers like a deranged schoolchild through the iron gate.

In 1528 Cardinal Wolsey (by then also Lord Chancellor and Bishop of Bath and Wells) had not long missed out on pushing his own influence to the ultimate level – the papacy. His aspiration to replace Leo X on the Throne of St Peter had come to nothing. The visit of this enormously ambitious man back to his hometown in 1528 is a matter of pure fiction; indeed he seems to have been an infrequent visitor to Suffolk. He did, however, finance the creation of a school in Ipswich on the site of a priory dissolved specifically to provide the money for the project. When Wolsey fell from grace and was arrested in November 1530, dying of somewhat uncertain causes by the end of that month, the project was abandoned with the building works still incomplete.

A notoriously ostentatious voluptuary such as Wolsey would have had scant sympathy with the poverty-loving Waldensians. Not long after this story is set, in 1545, many Waldensians were massacred during an act of religious persecution in Provence. Yet more were slaughtered in 1655 in Piedmont.

The Benedictine Priory of St Botolph is entirely fictitious, though their patron saint was real enough and regarded as a great exorcist of marsh and bog demons. He was also associated with lupine and canine iconography during the first few centuries after his canonisation.

Chapter Six

Suffer a Witch

Castle House, Ipswich
24th June 1645

My Dearest Lady Ursula,

I write to you with a heavy heart to inform you of the tragic death of my beloved John. Three days past the Lord took him from me. We buried him this very morning, and I write now by the dying light of evening as much a means to marshal my thoughts as to pass on the melancholy news of his passing. I know that you will remember him in your prayers. Will you light a candle for him in that beautiful little chapel of yours?

John's departure from this world was quick and utterly without warning. In my last missive to you I mentioned that my husband had interests in purchasing a new house with an inheritance which he had recently come into, so that we should move away from the town and those dark forces of temptation. Castle House is an impressive structure, though much in need of repair. John was very keen due to the low price, though I mentioned before to you my reason for uncertainty on the purchase was the very cause for the low price. The owners of the house died of virulence some quarter of a century ago, one so bad that it is said the town authorities boarded up the doors and windows with the entire household – family and servants alike – shut inside to die. It is told that the miasma which spread amongst the Brady family came back from Africa, either with the eldest son or with one of the slaves whom he had brought with him as a gift for his parents.

All inside that house died and lay there rotting for over a

year, for nobody dared risk opening the house nor even setting it to fire for fear that the poisonous miasma escape and spread amongst the populace. I remember how terrified the locals were when the youngest son returned from the plantations in the Caribbean and insisted that the house be opened and his family given decent Christian burial. He brought with him his own slaves, and as well it is that he did for not one local man would help with the moving of the bodies regardless of how much money was offered. Those poor Negroes had to wrap up and carry out the bones, risking who knows what fate. Two of them were even shot and killed by a fearful soldier, worried for what else they might have brought out the house with them.

None of the local churches would permit burial, lest their soil be tainted and the plague spread to the living. Since those days the house has stood unoccupied. Some local people were paid a stipend to act as caretakers, but it appears they have done precious little to earn their money.

The youngest son saw to the proper disposal of his family and the servants, and then returned to the distant plantation. His own daughter and her husband now have ownership of both Castle House and the Caribbean lands, though I believe they have never set foot in this country and have no interest in doing so. They are keen to sell the old family seat, and instructed their agents to sell at as best a price as could be managed. Hence the niggardly sum demanded of John.

Though he goes to church like any other man, it is but for form's sake and, as you well know, he believes in nothing but cold hard coin and the power of luck – alas he has succumb several times since last I wrote to the terrible vice. It was only some game of chance that enabled the proposed purchase of the house, and it is always hard to argue with a betting man when he is winning. A less superstitious or imaginative man would be hard to find. All the talk of curses and miasmas meant nothing to him, especially when faced with so good a business proposition. My concerns about the plague were laughed at, and being a surgeon I could but assume he knew better than I as to the real risks posed by disease.

My conditions for the move were spelled out in my last letter, and I wish to all the saints that I had held to my first thoughts and refused the move. Yet what is done is done. I said that John should rent the place for a week, that we might live there and put the rumours of dark spirits to the test. After much argument he agreed, though I think he could also see the practical benefit of not forgoing our home in Ipswich until such time as we were quite certain that living on Castle Hill was suited to our needs.

We gathered there for midsummer week, taking three servants with us. The owners had, with some resentment I gather, permitted that we stay there the week in exchange for a nominal sum. From the very first day there ill-fortune followed our footsteps. My hand rushes to tell you of John's horrid demise, but I feel that I should tell you first of the death of another poor man, though I barely knew him. It seems to me that this first loss foreshadowed what was to come.

We met the house agent, a Mr Smallpiece, quite literally as he stepped off the stagecoach from Norwich and crossed the road to the door of his office. He had been away on business for a fortnight, and the poor gentleman was obliged to attend immediately to our needs before even being able to return home and change his clothes or dine. There had been some accident upon the road that had delayed the coach's arrival in Ipswich by almost three hours.

He was an odd thing, white-haired and florid-cheeked with an unfortunate stutter that made his speech difficult to follow. Once he had collected keys and papers from his office, John hired a carriage to take us all across to Castle House. At some considerable embarrassment he explained to us that he had returned to his office before the letters of instruction to his clerk had (I often find the post quite slow too) and that no preparations had been made with regards to the house.

John was most annoyed, and I confess that my spirits fell at the thought of having to stay in some filthy ruin with slates off the roof and rats in the wainscoting. However, we tried to not vent our spleens upon Mr Smallpiece.

We arrived at Castle Hill and it was indeed the very image of a haunted house, the new caretaker having failed to live up to his title. The fool was nowhere to be seen as the agent showed us through cobwebby rooms, the thick dust showing the passage of the old man's boots and his wife's daintier shoes as they ranged around the place.

I fear the caretaker must have been asleep in a drunken stupor on one of the beds, for he only appeared as we made our way upstairs. The servants were carrying a few boxes upstairs when Rackham staggered out onto the landing, looking more like a tramp than a working man in an ill-fitting coat and ridiculous hat. He reeked of alcohol and seemed utterly bewildered as to who we were, indeed he barely seemed to know who he was himself. Mr Smallpiece had some sharp words with the taciturn fellow, as I did myself, and set him to sweeping up and being generally useful.

That very evening Esther, my maid, gave a shriek that brought us all running. She had gone to clean one of the smaller bedrooms and found what for all the world looked like a great splatter of dried blood up one wall. Not one of us had a wound to account for it, and John assured us that it could scarce have been left there from the days of the plague. Poor Esther was convinced that the Butcher of Ipswich had returned to claim another victim, though I pointed out the foolishness of this.

My mind was made up to give that useless Rackham a boot up his broad fundament, and to have strong words with old Smallpiece about the quality of his minions – especially after what had happened with the last one.

The next morning I had just finished giving the house agent a good rollicking when, and may God forgive me for the quickness of my tongue, Esther set up with shrieking again. Up we all went and found her pale and shaking by the attic steps. In the attic itself we found Rackham, quite cold, nearly naked with his wrists savagely cut with a broken bottle. A hefty bruise on his forehead was the only colour upon his pallid corpse. Strange that in death he seemed much diminished, like an inflated bladder that had punctured.

John and one of the male servants carried the limp corpse out of the house and laid him in an outhouse, until the family could be summonsed. I could have sworn that I had seen him walking down the garden path towards home late the previous evening, but he must have sneaked back in sometime after midnight. We knew nothing of his life or of the causes that could have driven him to so sinful and despairing an act; even Mr Smallpiece was largely in the dark having but hired him a month previous. All he knew was that the old man lived in a tiny house several streets away with his wife, whose job it was to keep the house clean (clearly a job she had not troubled herself to do). The corpse reeked, and it was the stench that had drawn Esther to check upon the attic, which otherwise we would have had no need to use during the course of our week's sojourn.

Smallpiece set out to find the wife and give her the bad news, returning minutes later having found her walking up the garden path with bucket, broom and mop ready to cover her previous slackness. The hefty woman, who was much younger than her husband, looked somewhat shocked to see the body, as well she might, but far from heartbroken. I confess I felt much the same when my first husband died.

I had assumed the blood in the bedroom must have been the caretaker's, though on suggesting this John said no – had the man ripped open his veins in the bedroom and then staggered down the corridor and up to the attic, we would have seen great gouts of blood all over the place. So the mystery as to whose blood stained the bedroom wall remains.

I must get to telling you now of how I come to be widowed now for the third time. Truly Castle House is a cursed place. John has always had a passion for Shakespeare and it has been a tradition of his, since before our marriage, to entertain friends with readings from *A Midsummer Night's Dream* upon that very night. As a distraction from his incessant gambling, I heartily encouraged it. There were five guests to table. An unusual number, you will say, but young Oliver Denham was too unwell to accompany his mother, my dear friend Alice whom I have written to you about on numerous occasions, on the visit. The Reverend Fairclough and his wife Emily came, as did our house agent Mr Smallpiece and his widowed daughter, Goody Phillips, who lives with him since her husband drowned in the Stour some years ago.

There would have been several others, but each made various excuses – I fear the reputation of the plague house dissuaded any of them from wishing to set foot in our temporary abode. John may not believe in curses, but many do. Cook, beleaguered by the filthy and ill-equipped kitchen, insisted on a collation of cold meats, breads and cheeses rather than a formal meal to table.

As soon as my afternoon visitor had departed, we all set to making the house presentable whilst cook prepared the meal. Even the dour Widow Rackham pitched in, though I said she really had no need to so soon after her bereavement.

John returned late from his barber's shop, I think in part because something had been weighing heavily on his mind for several days. I recognised the signs, and knew better than to prompt him before he was ready to speak. It seemed to me then that he was concerned over the death of the old caretaker, though in what way I cannot say for he never lived long enough for me to ask him. All I do know is that on several occasions he muttered to himself about the reek of the dead man.

The guests arrived, the food was served and the atmosphere was strained. Smallpiece gushed effusively, as a man who knows that his hired services have not been all that they should be and his hoped-for commission from the sale may yet be snatched away upon the wind. His gaunt daughter alternated between dour and garrulous moods, clearly uncomfortable though whether due to the house or to some private matter I could not tell.

Dear Alice attempted to be her usual jovial self, but clearly had other concerns weighing upon her and often seemed to drift off into distracted thought. We spoke of her herb garden, and exchanged brewing receipts, and began to speak of some of the religious contentions that are rife in Ipswich, but this so incensed the vicar that the subject was rapidly dropped.

The vicar, who feels it beholden upon him to keep in favour with increasingly Puritanical fervour of the Ipswich authorities, has decided to disapprove of theatre, an entertainment he was more than happy to indulge in during years past. Mistress Fairclough flows wherever her husband leads. You will not think me churlish, I hope, when I say that often times that dread evening I began to wonder why that pious pair had deigned to attend an honouring of Shakespeare if they were intent on being so unrelentingly sour about it.

John and I read sections, and Goody Phillips obliged in stilting manner, for she does not read well. Her aged father could barely see the words, having left his spectacles at home. Alice performed with gusto, all the while our reverend couple glaring on with sour faces. We had not progressed through more than three Acts when there came a thunderous hammering at the front door. The servants attended the visitor, and were swept aside by a drunken and belligerent Henry Reade. In a previous letter I told you of how Master Reade, formerly engaged to my granddaughter, had been cast aside by her some months previous after an incident involving one of the harlots who frequent the Ipswich docks. I am pleased to say she is now entertaining approaches from the son of a successful farmer out Hintlesham way, having been introduced by Cousin Susan. We have hopes that an offer of marriage will soon be forthcoming.

Reade forced his way into the dining room and abused both John and myself for interfering in his life. I could almost have believed that he had indeed loved my Annabelle, had it not been for his bilious and vile accusations that I had cursed him with some pox or other! No doubt whatever vile infestations or disfigurements he has are the remnants of his visitations with the dockyard trollops. Never have I seen anyone so drunk, the fumes were so strong it was almost as if he had bathed in the foul stuff.

John was all for striking the man down, despite the ship's captain being less than half his age and a deal fitter. However, the vicar and his wife sought to calm the man down, and themselves become the target of highly personal remarks as he became increasingly vicious. The menservants arrived and bundled the fool out of the house, and gradually the guests settled down though they were at first all for leaving.

After some extensive bewailing of the lowering of standards amongst the young and the generally disreputable character of merchant sailors, Mistress Fairclough announced she preferred hearing stories from the Bible to wicked fancies about fairies. John, eager to re-establish the peace, went to fetch the family Bible from the otherwise almost empty library, where one of the servants had deposited it on our arrival. I understand from Smallpiece that most of the original books had been ferried to the sugar plantation, those that were left behind were in so mildewed a state that I had them all taken out to the compost heap by the caretaker.

The rest of us drew closer to the fire and talked of favoured parables – strange as it may seem to say of high June, but that building was unaccountably cold. We waited and waited, until at last I went to see what was keeping him. I found John writhing on the floor of the library, barely able to do more than croak and gasp with pain. The family Bible lay carelessly upon the floor, soaked with most of the contents of a brandy decanter that lay shattered on the floor besides it.

He had always seemed in such rude health. I can but think it must have been a seizure or something of the sort. Certainly he showed no signs of illness beforehand and there were no injuries upon his person – not that anyone was in a position to have inflicted any. None of the guests left the dining room, and all the servants were fully occupied in the kitchen. The brandy was something of a mystery, for we had not been drinking any in the dining room. On questioning the servants later, I learned that a bottle had been decanted and left in the library preparatory to serving it to warm the guests when they were ready to depart into the cool evening.

Though no physician, the midwife was able to apply her basic medical knowledge to tending to John whilst a doctor was sent for. Grief it is to say that he died quite suddenly in the small hours, just as the medical man arrived at the front door. Those last hours had been terrible ones. Alice, the midwife and the vicar had remained with me to assist in varied capacities whilst the others had departed home with promises to pray for John. Had he been capable of knowing anything, he would have scorned such offers. They gave me some small comfort, however.

It weighs heavily on me that John died in the few minutes that I left his bedside. Alice and I had gone to fetch some cool water and towels, whilst the vicar prayed at the end of the bed and Goody Philips applied pungent mint compresses to the burns upon John's skin. As the manservant returned with the medic and met us upon the stairs, poor John's groans of pain and the creak of the bedsprings from his convulsions suddenly fell silent.

The doctor declared him dead, but it was hardly necessary.

My question as to what had caused such an ending resulted in the usual vague humming and evasive dithering.

I should like to tell you of the funeral, but it is so late – I have written far more than I intended, and find that tiredness is now overwhelming me. I shall write more of it next time, when I have moved back to my town house for I have no wish to spend any more time in this accursed place than absolutely necessary.

Your most humbly affectionate, Mary Lakeland.

-0-

Crowbridge Manor, Exmoor
Friday 30th June 1645

My Very Dear Mary,

I have prayed for you every day since receiving your sorrowful news. How may I express my condolences for you? Whilst I only met John on the one occasion, the news is hard for me to believe. He seemed so vital a man, so energetic that the thought he could have just died in such a manner, without warning is hard to credit. I would say that the Lord moves in mysterious ways, but not all that happens in this world is down to the hand of God and I wonder from reading your letter over again if there is more to this than meets the eye?

Please be careful, my dear friend. At this time you doubtless have so many other heavy weights upon your soul, that caring for your own safety is unlikely to be foremost amongst such concerns. It strikes me that John's death may not have been natural. Did you personally wash and prepare his body? Though it may distress you to think of it again, pray tell me of anything you noticed about your dear husband's body. Had he any rashes or strange marks upon his skin?

The letter also makes mention of an afternoon meeting on the day of your husband's death in which you partook. Was this held at Castle House and, if so, I pray that you would you oblige me by telling me who was in attendance at this gathering.

The bloodstain upon the wall gives me cause for concern, for if it is not the blood of anyone in the house at that time then some unknown person must have been in that room of recent times and come to some serious injury which has gone unmarked by the local gossips – for surely you would have heard of such an oddity from the neighbours? To create a high spray of blood such as that, an artery must have been severed. Too often men die of such wounds. My man Jared, who has seen a great deal of battle, confirms that such an arc of blood signifies a dangerous injury.

This Master Reade you have mentioned in previous letters, and I recall that neither you nor John were not enamoured of the idea that your granddaughter should marry him. Was there not talk that John had some especial reason to oppose their union, though you did not tell me the specifics? I took it at the time that he knew some ill of the man. Now, tell me if you or the servant who admitted him to the house recall if Master Reade entered the library at any time in his uproarious presence at the gathering. Indeed, did any of your other guests go there at any point, and in this I include whosoever attended the afternoon convocation.

Reverend Fairclough you have also referred to previously, something connected to an amount of money that you had borrowed from him a year or more ago to pay off one of John's gambling debts. Or do I confuse him with another, for I know you have confided in me that you have had to approach several local worthies to address those debts?

Your missive mentioned a butcher of Ipswich, though I confess myself confused as to what involvement a tradesman has with the terrible events that have befallen you whilst sojourning at that accursed house. Why did your maid fear this butcher, was he some scorned paramour of hers intent on violent revenge?

The midwife's use of mint compresses bemuses me, for I can see no reason for them. Was there some aspect to poor John's illness that you have not mentioned that would necessitate such a treatment, or is it rather that she is ill-trained and just used the wrong simple? Whilst I keep a close eye on our own town here, I have heard tell some awful stories of incompetent self-declared healers in the villages further down on Exmoor. Too little knowledge is indeed a dangerous thing.

So many questions with which I bombard you! Please be assured, my dear Mary, that I only do so out of my very great concern for your personal wellbeing.

Life here continues on much the same as ever it does. The only real change since last we wrote before this tragedy is the curious behaviour of the publican at the Stag's Head. I shall tell you my theories as to what drives him to act in so peculiar a manner in my next letter, though it is such a trivial matter I fear it inappropriate to parade it before you at such a time as this.

May God be with you, Ursula, Countess of Exmoor

-0-

Lakeland House, Ipswich
Sunday 16th July 1645

My Dearest Lady Ursula,

Your letter has given me grave cause for concern, though I cannot ascertain what it is that leads you to worry – is it fear that the malign influence of Castle House should follow me home to my little house in Ipswich?

The Butcher of Ipswich, of whom you asked, is not a tradesman or purveyor of meat! My dear friend, he is – or rather was – one of the more ignoble sons of our town. In April of this year a simple-minded giant by the name of Atkins, who had served as caretaker to Castle House, went insane and slaughtered his family. They all lived in a tiny tithe cottage adjacent to the garden wall – Atkins himself, his second wife, mother, and two children from his first wife.

According to the accounts the neighbours heard a terrible and unnatural moaning through the walls, and then smoke was noticed billowing from an upstairs room. These same neighbours found Atkins sat crooning over the headless corpse of his aged mother. Upon the staircase they found one of the children, the daughter I think, also brutally killed. The fire became too bad for any further incursions to be made, though the charred corpses of the rest of the family were later recovered from the embers of the cottage. Just as with the current situation, this Atkin's wife (I do not recall her name, though I think it was a biblical one) served as cleaner and general domestic for the house. As I understand it, the charred bodies were also dismembered, hence the appellation of Butcher given to him by the town criers.

It was this Atkins that was replaced by the ill-fated old man who killed himself in the attic on the night we moved in. One might almost think that the job itself is cursed, or maybe that the house drives mad all those that stay there. I tell you without any jest that I have suffered the most terrible dreams about that place, even though I have not set foot there since John was carried out on a bier.

The half-witted giant ended his miserable life upon the gallows several weeks ago. I hear he was gibbering and incoherent till the end, wailing about a witch. John went to watch, though I was unwell at the time. Perhaps he imagined that his mother was a witch? I hear tell she was a shrewish, ugly old harridan. Rumours of witchcraft have dogged this town since before I was a little girl, and have disturbed wiser minds than his. My maid tells me that there is much talk within the taverns about hiring in a witch hunter to find if there is any truth to the Butcher's ravings. There was some such nonsense over in Essex no more than a year ago, and I swear that some of our citizenry will not be happy but that they should have a scandal of their very own.

To the matter of tending to poor John, naturally I prepared his corpse myself. Goody Philips and Alice were good enough to come to my home in Ipswich to assist me in this – the former being a midwife she is used to death and Alice would never let me to suffer alone. Though we were not searching for strange signs, I recall nothing more unusual than a small crust of dried blood at the top of his neck. John's convulsions were so violent that he may well have banged his head against the bed frame. There was a small rash about his mouth, is it that you suspect some manner of poisoning rather than disease? The food and drink served at the dinner all came upon collective platters and decanters, such that I cannot see how anyone could have slipped some noxious substance into his meal or drink. If the brandy had been poisoned, I cannot imagine by whom. The servants opened a new bottle and decanted it in the library only after we had all sat to eat. Not one person left the dining room till John himself did, and I refuse to believe that any of our servants could possibly have contrived such a thing.

It is not unknown for an outwardly healthy man or woman to be struck down with a sudden seizure. You will not, I hope, be offended if I suggest that you see a sinister mystery where there is only tragedy.

Your question about the mint compresses is odd, for the doctor also asked the very same when he arrived too late. I have told you all that happened to my husband, and know practically nothing of Goody Philips to speak to her medical expertise or lack thereof.

Would that you were the only one to think the death suspicious! Rumours abound in Ipswich that John's death was brought about by unnatural means. Several of my old friends have started to avoid me.

This may be in no small part due to the vitriolic gossip of Emily Fairclough, who had come round to help select hymns for the funeral. Though John had no time for religion, I felt unable to stand against the tide of Samuel Fairclough and his frightful wife in their presumption that not only should my husband be given to God's care – a notion that I cannot fault in itself – but also that my own belief in the True Religion should be swept aside in favour of their conventions.

My maid and I were just tidying up the pile of clothes that Alice had helped remove from dearest John's body, when out fell the most peculiar and revolting thing. It was a cloth doll, crudely made and transfixed with three pins. Emily positively shrieked when it landed near her feet, and I impaled my hand trying to pick it up. Two of the pins were actually darning needles, whilst the third was a thicker spike with a rough end and nowhere to place the thread.

What this was doing amongst my husband's clothing I cannot begin to imagine. I have, of course, heard of such things but had never till that moment seen one of these tools of the witch's craft. After I managed to deal with Mistress Fairclough's concerns and push both her and Goody Phillips out of the door, I searched through my own sewing box and then John's surgical kit – yet all the needles were accounted for.

I had always understood that poppets were meant to resemble the person whom they were intended to effect for good or ill. This one does not look like anyone, so I am at a loss to know if it were used to harm my dear John or if it were maybe directed towards myself, or even perhaps one of my children or grandchildren, by some hateful creature. All that can be said of the revolting thing is that the stitching was well done!

My guest on the afternoon before John's death was Cousin Susan, whom I think I may have mentioned to you before – a relation of my first husband, with whom I have remained in close touch. She and I are sisters in the True Religion and meet often to discuss what may be done to keep the Faith until such time as England throws off the shackles of False Religion and returns to the Old Ways. We are far from alone in this cause, and there is a small but growing coterie of us covenanted to the Truth. We are of all levels of society but I fear to put any of their names to paper, lest this letter may fall into the wrong hands and their lives become endangered.

As you say, my concern over my granddaughter's engagement has been expressed to you before. Sailors, even ship's captains, are seldom known for their continence, and have many opportunities to contract many odious illnesses. Indeed, John is often called upon to treat them, as well as providing minor surgical operations. Even before my granddaughter caught him *in flagrante* John had voiced his concerns over Reade and his suitability.

The town council meets tomorrow to discuss the problem of all the beggars on the streets. Most of the poor souls are only in that state as a result of the war; widows, orphans and crippled former soldiers. There is also a motion to bring a Witch Finder to town, some creature from Essex. I cannot think that any good will come of it, for these people are more interested in money than justice. The ravings of Atkins the Butcher have clearly set weaker minds to fervid imaginings.

Your most humbly affectionate, Mary Lakeland.

-0-

Crowbridge Manor, Exmoor
Tuesday 25th July 1645

My Very Dear Mary,

Oh my dear, this situation worsens with every letter I receive from you. I fear to think of what may befall you next.

Mistress Fairclough witnesses the poppet roll from your husband's clothes, and shortly thereafter the town council elect to invite a Witch Finder to attend upon them? Again I beseech you to come and stay with me, the instant you receive this letter pack your bags and take a stagecoach. Do not remain in Ipswich a day longer.

It seems unlikely that you would have kept so grotesque a thing, but if you have indeed retained the doll will you examine the pins for me and tell me which have blood upon them? Better yet, bring the wretched thing with you when you come to stay, that I might see it with my own eyes.

The story of this man Atkins is a nightmarish one, and it is strange that two men associated with that house should come to so dark an end in so short a space of time. There is more at play here than is obvious. I wonder that you might not send someone to check upon the family of the most recent caretaker to ensure that they too have not met with an untimely demise.

Thinking more upon the bloodstained bedroom of which I wrote at some length, I draw a conjecture from the tale of the Butcher. No injuries to any persons have been remarked upon, except for the terrible violence visited upon these neighbours. May it not be the case that one of those poor people – the wife, mother, or those ill-starred children – may have been set upon in Castle House and their body, dead or insensible, carted across to the adjoining hovel by the monster Atkins? If the wife with the biblical name was employed to clean the house, as the current one is, then she would have perfect reason to be in Castle Hill with her husband. Mayhap an argument started, and he did some terrible injury to her in the bedroom then lost his mind and set about the rest of his family?

Tell me again of the people you dined with that fatal evening – had any of them cause to quarrel with John, or resent him for any reason? I find it hard to shake the sense that John's death was the result of malice, not from some spectre within the house but of someone all too human. The semblance of illness can easily be brought about by mortal agency.

I must confess that I thought a solution to the crime, for such I am convinced it is, apparent. However, the issue of the poppet has quite thrown my ideas into disarray. I must reconsider. If only I were in a position to visit you and look at these matters in person.

When you tell me of such spites as may have existed against John, I pray you include your Cousin Susan. Doubtless you will fume at this and say I am impugning loyal relations (albeit by marriage and not blood), but trust that I do not ask out of idle gossip. Someone who has been in that house has ill intent, and I worry that more mischief may yet be intended. Tell me also which of these people had access to the brandy bottle earlier in the afternoon or to the decanted drink during the evening.

This covert campaign you have to re-establish the True Faith is most ill-advised. We live in difficult times and, whatever ideals burn in one's soul, it is only prudent to move with extreme caution. It is not so very long since people were burnt in Ipswich for cleaving to a religion which those in power disapproved of.

There is no reason of which I can conceive for your cousin to wish harm to your husband, but it is best to eliminate all possibilities by careful consideration than mere sentimental unwillingness to weight the evidence.

May God be with you, Ursula, Countess of Exmoor

-0-

Ipswich Gaol, Ipswich
Wednesday 2nd August 1645

My Dearest Ursula,

I write to you from the Ipswich gaol. The worst possible news – I stand accused of bringing about the death of my own John through the use of witchcraft. The whole thing has happened so quickly that I can scarce believe it. The Witch Finder arrived in Ipswich in the morning, with an ill-tempered assistant. By that very afternoon this creature, a man by the name of Master Hopkins, had come to interrogate me in my own home!

He knew all about the poppet and asked me at length about John's death. His implication was clear – he suspects me of making away with my own husband by means of spells and magic. Not only that, but he has all but accused me of making away with a moneylender by the name of Lawrence who succumbed to one of the fevers that regularly sweep round the docks. It is certainly the case, as Hopkins somehow knew, that John had an outstanding debt to the man from one of his many card games and that he had been pressing me for payment. I wonder if he will try and lay all the deaths in Ipswich at my door?

He asked at length about my visitors in the afternoon, and of course I denied all knowledge. A foolish move on my part, I fear, for after several hours of berating me he mentioned my cousin as part of the covenant. Clearly someone had seen who attended Castle House and has told Hopkins with immodest haste. My denial was used against me, to suggest that the nature of our meeting was something worthy of keeping secret. Which of course it was, though not in the way which that posturing fool imagines for he openly implied that our pact was with the Devil himself! You would, I think, despise this man almost as much as I do. He is a strutting popinjay, behaving like some third-rate actor reciting his set pieces and pausing as if to receive the applause of an audience present only in his mind.

I am entrusting this letter to my maid, that she may get it past the gaolers and out to you. If she fails in this task and it falls into the hands of my accusers, well – I already fear that I am beyond your power to help. Now that Cousin Marchant is known to the Witch Finder, I wonder how long before she is pressured into naming other members of the True Faith? She is a woman of limited mental powers, though kind-hearted and unlikely to be able to resist Hopkins' wiles as well as I have. There are several others both in Ipswich and in Hintlesham, a hamlet some few miles from here. I pray that they have the wit to hide themselves off to whatever distant relatives or kindly friends they may have to grant them sanctuary.

If only I had taken your advice and journeyed to Exmoor when I had the chance. Yet done is done, and if the worst happens I ask you to see that justice is done both for me and, more importantly, my children and grandchildren. Whatever insult is hurled at me must not adhere to them, or mar their chances in life.

If I am forced into a corner and all else is lost I shall pull down the roof upon myself and shield them as best I may. At least I have no sons to be haunted by a name that incites suspicion and gossip.

Master Hopkins' parting shot was to announce that tomorrow I am to be searched for witch marks and third teats. He intends to hire a woman for this intrusion, to spare my modesty, and yet in the next breath he announces that he and at least one of the judges will be present to supervise. Pray for me in my darkest hour.

Two questions you asked in your last letter, and I rush now to answer them. I burnt the accursed poppet the very afternoon that I found it, but recall that when I examined the evil thing two of the skewers driven through it had dried blood upon them – though I had but one puncture mark in my hand. One lot of blood was my own, as to the other I am at a loss to say. The wound upon my hand was a small one, and I think it must have been from the darning needle rather than the thicker spike. What cause had you to ask this question, or to suspect some oddity in regards to bloodstains?

As to the question of enemies, it is hard to think of any reason why our guests of that night might have wished ill to John. The house agent has lost a good profit from my husband's death, and his surly daughter was unknown to us before that night. The reverend has, it is true, become increasingly cantankerous in his faith of late and had had some heated disputes over matters of religion with John in the past – but surely people do not murder each other over such things? Fairclough had been a customer of both my husband's surgical and barbering skills, and so must have trusted him regardless of their spiritual differences. His shrewish wife presumably shares her husband's zeal.

Master Reade had much cause for complaint that night, though I cannot see how he could possibly have done John to death. He went nowhere near the library after the brandy was decanted, the servants have sworn to this. Even if by some improbable means he was able to return to the house unseen, how could he have possibly known that John would be the first to drink the lethal brew? What advantage could there be to him in accidentally poisoning the vicar's wife or the house agent, or do you suggest that one of my guests was so mentally unhinged that they did not care who they poisoned?

There is talk that the day after tomorrow I am to be moved to the gaol at Bury St Edmunds, where my trial is to take place. Sir Harbottle Grimstone, who was known to my first husband, came to see me yesterday. He is to sit upon the bench. Any hopes of good sense from him that I might have harboured were dashed upon seeing that glowering toad-like countenance. Whatever tenuous link there was between us, it clearly means nothing to him and he made it clear that I am not merely to be charged with being a witch, but also with having procured poor John's death through use of that blasted poppet.

The charge is to be one of petty treason, a burning offence. I can scarcely believe it. How can anyone imagine that I would have harmed the man that had made me so happy? For all his gambling and taste for the bottle, I still loved him. That shrill harridan Fairclough has doubtless spread word of the doll all over Ipswich, likely enlarging on the tale until it is sinister beyond all reason.

Do you hold any hope that common sense will prevail and the truth of this matter come to light? With each hour that passes I find it harder and harder to hold on to my faith that goodness will prevail over ignorance and wickedness.

Your friend in despair, Mary Lakeland

-0-

Crowbridge Manor, Exmoor
Tuesday 15th August 1645

My Very Dear Mary,

Everything that I have most dreaded from the first mention of John's death has come to pass. Would that I were able to journey up to Suffolk and address the court upon your behalf, but the Fates turn against us for two days ago I fell from my horse and broke my leg. The physician has me laid up. The suggestion of jolting about in a carriage for several days sent the old fool into virtual apoplexy.

However, I shall not leave you unaided and instead send to you my man Jared Penderow to do what he may in this time of need. Be assured that many who stand accused of witchcraft are acquitted, and I pray that you will soon be free – and when you are, do quit Ipswich at least for the winter, until memories have shortened. I have shared with him my thoughts upon this matter and given him letters of introduction, one of which is for your maid that she may also act at my direction. I only pray that he makes good time and gets to you before the court passes judgement.

As caution stayed your hand in mention of the True Religion in your last letter, so it now restrains my own. I cannot guarantee whose eyes will fall upon this page, and so most of my thoughts are to be passed to you via Captain Jared. Though you have met him but the once, I trust that you will recall him and know him as a trustworthy and clever man.

I will say that I can but see that only three people had the opportunity to place that vile poppet in amongst John's clothes: one very close to you, of whom such disloyalty is difficult to imagine; the wife of the Reverend Fairclough; and the midwife who aided you in washing the corpse. That dried blood was found on two of the barbs driven through the doll speaks volumes to me. The solitary wound in your hand accounts for the blood on one, and I strongly suspect that the blood on the thicker of the implements was from your husband and the ultimate cause of his death. In the letter you mentioned a small crust of dried blood at the top of his neck.

John always had a thick head of hair, and I fancy that a needle-like weapon could have been driven into his brain. Had the handle snapped off and the spike lodged in the wound, then it would have served as a plug – very little blood would have escaped. So little that possibly the weapon would have gone unnoticed without a very careful search, with the fact of murder going unnoticed.

If my imagining of events is correct, I can but see that only one person would have had the opportunity to remove the spike and use it to impale the poppet. Yet I cannot see how she could have delivered the deadly brew in the first place. Though the most obvious solution to that difficulty could also provide some form of motive, although the precise details of it mystify me at present.

My mind returns to that arc of dried blood that your maid found in a disused bedroom at Castle House. Would I be wrong to surmise that this neglected room had not only a bed in it, but blankets upon the bed?

May God be with you, Ursula, Countess of Exmoor

-0-

The Sun Inn, Ipswich
Monday 21st August 1645

My Dear Lady Gyre-Carlin

Mistress, I write to you as instructed. I have made contact with both your loyal friend, Mother Lakeland as she is called in these parts, and her maid. Following your guidance, I have passed myself off as a distant cousin to gain admittance to the prison cell. She is in low spirits, and has been roughly treated – though not as badly as the other women with whom she shares her dungeon chamber. The search made of her person seems to have broken her resolve; not only was it of a brutish nature and done in front of the vulgar eyes of a magistrate by the name of Grimstone and this shard-born oaf Hopkins (give the word, and I will gladly deal with him), but it was also conducted by some midwife that Mistress Lakeland says she has already written to you about. It is said that the clergyman Fairclough is to sit upon the judging panel, despite his presence in the house of death, along with some other divine called Calamy who is unknown to me.

I have searched Castle House and found all to be much as you described. I had ascertained ahead of time that the old house agent had yet to find anyone fool enough to employ as replacement caretaker – yet, exactly as you predicted, I am certain someone was in that property. I heard footsteps in the upper storey, and quick as could be mounted the stairs to search for the intruder. Yet, whoever it was, they either made their escape or had some hidey hole into which they secreted themselves before I could find them.

However, whoever it was they left behind some half-eaten bread and cheese...and ill-washed feminine undergarments. These were of poor quality and some girth. The revolting things are now in my saddlebag should you wish them to be offered up in court as proof of a crime.

From all I have been able to ascertain, the description of the slaughter of the Atkins Family by the half-witted caretaker was exactly as described. I have spoken to the men paid to clear up the ashes of the house, and they found the charred remains of the two children and their stepmother. The headless body of the old grandmother was taken out when the gibbering giant was led from the house. They say he was quite docile, more frightened child than raging monster.

The neighbours were quite shocked at what happened, saying they had always considered the giant to be a gentle creature. Though, by all accounts, the household was a tumultuous one with constant loud arguments between the wife and mother-in-law. Mayhap he simply snapped after one row too many? I have known many a man to be driven beyond his wits end by the tongue of some female relation.

The popular word in the inns is that Mother Lakeland is a

pawn of the Devil and in league with a dozen others of her kind. Few publically question the truth of the accusations against her. Several times I have heard it said that her first husband was the brother of some Catholic prelate, and that she has strong sympathies towards popish ways. To bend the knee to the Man in Rome is, in so many eyes, little more than to submit to Satan himself. It would seem that she has made too many enemies with outspoken partiality for the royal cause. I have questioned Mother Lakeland's servants, and can see no way for anyone to have guaranteed the poison would have been drunk by John Lakeland.

Master Henry Reade is widely hated in the docks, notorious for his violent temper and reluctance to pay his gambling debts (this latter fault also being much said of the late John Lakeland, though I have heard no other stain cast upon his character). The vicar seems little more than a contentious fool eager to ride whichever bandwagon will keep the vicarage roof over his head. His diminutive wife is widely held to be a shrew and a gossip-monger, but no more ill is said of her than that. As to Smallpiece the house agent, I can find no ill word said against him bar that he is not very good at his job. His daughter likewise is deemed a rather poor midwife of the sort only hired by those who can afford no better, and something of a sour-tempered baggage. I can find no reason for any of them to wish harm against Master Lakeland, nor do any of them appear to profit from his death in any way.

The best I can suggest at this stage is that slowness in paying gambling debts may have offended some dangerous character. Though it seems to me poor business to kill a debtor before the money is paid.

I await your instructions, but advise you to hold little hope that your friend will emerge from this unscathed.

Your loyal servant, Captain Jared Penderow

-0-

Ipswich Gaol, Ipswich
Friday 25th August 1645

My Dearest Ursula,

I fear my days are numbered and that even someone as resourceful as you may have difficulty in extracting me from the web that is being spun around me. I do not even know the identity of the spider that hunts me. To fight against an unknown enemy is to flail in the dark; pointless and exhausting. At first I had considered Master Hopkins to be the instigator of the plot against me, but sitting in my wretched cell with the other accused women with naught to do but think…well, I can but speculate that Hopkins is but one cog in a much larger machine.

My Sister in Faith has been accused and incarcerated with me, along with three of her neighbours from Hintlesham who were unknown to me. Why anyone should wish such half-witted old widows on the end of a rope, I cannot imagine.

The cockroaches have flooded from the woodwork in the last few days of this trial. Hopkins and the fat buffoon that works for him gave their evidence as to my alleged *maleficium*, of how my dear little Elemanzer is actually my familiar spirit, and so forth. Between me and the other women in this cell, we are meant to have a veritable menagerie of creatures and spirits.

So convinced are they of the demonic powers of a harmless little dog that I am now claimed to have caused a tumour in the shape of Elemanzer to deform the leg of Henry Reade. I know full well that he sought John's skills for the treating of unnatural lesions upon his body some nine months back, and made no claims then that they were induced with magic. A far more prosaic cause, I fancy. Indeed, Master Reade has even had the gall to stand up in court and suggest that I have hexed his ship and caused it to catch fire whilst at sea! Were I possessed of such impressive talents, would I now languish in my present condition?

Now not only am I the purported killer of my husband and that fool Lawrence and his child last year, but now also am charged with sending imps to lay low some maid of that bombastic cretin Jennings and his sour troll of a wife. It might seem laughable were it not me it was happening to. Really, they seem to think me a more prolific murderer than the Butcher of Ipswich, and I quite expect to be accused of somehow casting spells to send that poor devil off his head as well!

There is no end to the number of wicked deeds that I am meant to have done. The accusations come thick and fast, and even Master Hopkins seems to find the volume disconcerting. I fancy he is one of those idle sorts who wants the greatest results for the least effort, and takes little pleasure in being called back and forth investigating quite so many bizarre claims. I wonder if the town council's fear of the Devil will match their fear of Hopkins' bill?

The bedroom in Castle House did, exactly as you imagined, have a bed in it made up with rough blankets. Do you suggest that this bed was in use? I had suspected that the filthy old caretaker had been inclined to use the place as a flophouse, probably for when he was too drunk to return home to his shrewish wife. Even if he had died in that room, though John thought it impossible, what difference could it make to what befell my husband?

Your friend in despair, Mary Lakeland

-0-

Crowbridge Manor, Exmoor
Wednesday 6th September 1645

My Dear Jared,

A hurried note, but I urge you to go to the home of the Widow Rackham. It is my belief that you will find the caretaker's widow is herself dead and will have been that way for some period.

You must also return to Castle House and lay in wait for the miscreant who lives there in secret. She has killed at least twice to protect her sanctuary, and will do so again at the slightest provocation – so be careful. If she can be taken alive, so much the better for then she can be forced to give evidence before the court and so prove my dear Mary innocent of slaying her husband. When that charge falls apart, it is my hope that the other ridiculous claims will also be dismissed.

My prayers speed you on your way.

Your mistress, Ursula, Countess of Exmoor

-0-

Crowbridge Manor, Exmoor
Wednesday 6th September 1645

My Very Dear Mary,

The bed had been in use, though I fear not by the caretaker or his idle wife. You mentioned once how grubby and dust-laden the house was when first you arrived, and yet there were the footprints of a woman in the dust. If Mistress Rackham had not been cleaning, then it is hard to conceive of another reason for her to be there. It seems to me more likely that the footprints belonged to another woman. It may be that the old man had some life left in him after all, though he scarcely sounds a romantic proposition.

I fancy that few people would have wanted to conduct an

illicit liaison in a filthy house widely believed to be cursed. Except maybe those already very familiar with it, and who had nowhere nicer to meet. My man Jared has found a woman's undergarments in the room at Castle House and I fear they belong to one half of this murderous tryst.

A great spray of blood up the wall suggests to me a serious injury, most likely an arterial wound. I have seen soldiers wounded in the war that gouted blood over considerable distances. Almost all died from their wounds. Yet there seems to be no account of anyone killed or gravely injured in Castle House, but there were terrible deaths only a short distance away. May it not be possible that one of the Atkins family may have been slain, or at least wounded, at Castle House before fleeing or being carried back to their own hovel? There is, I feel sure, a connection between these two dark crimes.

I also ask myself why the caretaker never reported the stains upon the wall. Was he so incompetent an employee that he never even ventured into the room to see the blood? It seems hard to believe that anyone could be quite that incurious. Though I think your husband may have marked what had happened, for did you not say that he commented several times upon the stench of the old caretaker's corpse? You said yourself that the body laid limply in the attic. A newly dead man should not smell so strongly, and had he died roughly when you thought he had, he ought to have been showing the rigidity of death. It may be that John had realised that Rackham had been dead considerably longer than he theoretically could have been. Had he been dead long enough to pass through rigour and become limp again, then whoever it was that showed you around the house when you arrived could not have been the old caretaker you found dead in the attic the very next day.

You wrote to me that the corpse seemed much deflated, and I say that the reason for this is that the live caretaker was a different, more heavily built person than the old man whose place they had taken.

May God be with you, Ursula, Countess of Exmoor

-0-

Lakeland House, Ipswich
Sunday 10th September 1645

To the Lady Ursula, Countess of Exmoor

I hope you will pardon my writing to you, for you do not know who I am. My name is Esther and I have had the honour to be lady's maid to Mistress Lakeland these many long years now. My heart weeps to tell you that they executed my mistress yesterday. On the eve afore she died they let me see her one last time, and she pressed upon me your last letter to her and asked that I write and tell you what she cannot.

The trial was a terrible thing, with lie told upon lie. I could wish a gruesome fate upon half the people I once called neighbours. This dashing soldier who arrived a few days ago, saying he was your fellow, says that if you but give the word then he will happily bring some real justice to these false witnesses.

They burnt her. The stench is still on me. I thought to show your letter to one of the magistrates, but know they will not listen to one as low born as me. It is only thanks to my mistress that I have sufficient letters to write to you at all. It has been said that the executioner will sweep up the ashes and throw them into the River Orwell, that the waters shall wash away all wickedness.

They have washed away one wickedness at least, and I am proud to have played at least some small part in that. My lady gave me all the letters what you sent her, and I read them as best I could. Your man and I went to the hovel where old Mistress Rackham dwelt and, just like you said, she was dead and stinking. Weeks dead from the look of the poor hag, with a cord still knotted tight around her throat. The stink must have got so bad that the woman as was playing her part must have given up living there and gone back to hiding in Castle House.

Captain Penderow reasoned that we should go and keep watch on Castle House, as that was where you had told him you thought some miscreant had been hiding beforehand. Seven hours of waiting it took before we spotted her moving about. She was hiding in the attic, and when the captain slipped in (and I followed) and cornered the ugly great mare she tried to pass herself off as the Widow Rackham. When we confronted her with what we had discovered at the Rackham house, she went berserk and tried to kill us. If your captain hadn't been as quick with his sword, I don't doubt that I would be as dead as my poor dear mistress. Her end was quick, mayhap too quick for one who had killed so many, including her own stepchildren, poor mites. But it is justice of a sort for them and for the master.

Jared, if I may be bold to so call him, says you reckon that she had been using the deserted Castle House as a trysting place with the house agent's daughter, and that it all came to a head when someone – most likely the mother-in-law – grew suspicious and caught them in their unspeakable act. Having killed the old woman, Jared reckons the two succumbed to a bloodlust as foxes will in chicken coops and laid waste to the whole family before burning the hovel. That half-witted giant really was innocent of the terrible crimes for which he hanged.

I have known men who found a ghoulish pleasure in hurting others, perhaps these two were as much drawn together by a love of causing pain as by anything romantic – if I can call it that and still be a good Christian? Master Jared reckons they killed the new caretaker when he chanced upon them in the house, on one of his rare calls of duty, but I am minded to wonder if it was more for the joy of killing. Or perhaps Goody Rackham saw my mistress's carriage drawing up to the house and panicked, killing the drunken old man and stripping his corpse to provide a disguise to explain her presence? With old Master Smallpiece returning late from Norwich, like as not he hadn't had time to mention to his daughter that Castle Hill was being occupied so it all came as a shock to the murderous pair.

Jared doesn't know whose body it was that the neighbours pulled out the ashes, but since the war there's been no end of paupers living on the streets. Easy enough to kill one of those poor souls off and let the corpse get buried under a false name. I wonder if she'd have gone on hiding out at Castle Hill forever, or if they had a plan to run off somewhere and be together? If they did, I suppose it was one that needed time to pull off; else they would not have turned to more crime in order to drive the Lakelands out of their dusty sanctuary.

Master Jared searched the awful creature's possessions and found a small bottle of tansy oil, which he says proves your suspicions that the midwife probably left it somewhere for her fricatrice to find. The captain says there's no way Atkins could have known who'd drink the brandy first, and maybe she didn't care who did. So long as someone died, or leastways drunk enough to get ill, then perhaps they hoped that would have been enough to put the Lakelands off wanting to stop there. When the doctor arrived at the door, he says maybe Phillips panicked that he would recognise the smell of tansy and too many questions would have been asked. So she polished the poor master off quick with some tool of her trade whilst the old vicar was busy praying.

I watched her give evidence against my mistress in the trial, and that wicked, terrible woman was glowing with pleasure. Such as her love to torment others and watch them suffer; made me feel sullied just to watch it.

We raced as quick as could be to the gaol to say that we had new evidence, but the wagon had already left to take my mistress to the stake. The gaoler tried to delay us with endless questions and threats of what would happen to us if we were to interfere with the course of justice. Justice! He so delayed us, and I wonder now if that were a deliberate ploy, that by the time we got to the place of execution the fires were already billowing.

There was no screaming, and I have heard it said that the executioner accepted a heavy sum of money to strangle her first and spare my dear lady the agonies of the fire.

Jared was all for vengeance dispatching Mistress Atkins' unnatural lover to the same fate, but Mary Philips had already left Ipswich in the company of Master Hopkins; she has become his creature now and much good may it do her. She had gone with him before she could have heard that that fiend hiding in Castle House was dead. Mayhap her perverse passion had run its limit.

I have a letter from Mistress Lakeland and a bag of coin, instructing me to book passage to you in Exmoor bearing certain items that she does not want to fall into the hands of her enemies. Though the good captain says I can ride back with him. After that, I do not know what is to become of me. There's nothing in Ipswich that I want to come back to now.

Your servant, Esther Brock

Sixth Story Notes

Most of the characters appearing in this short story are based on real people, with the exception of the sleuth herself. The accused woman, Mary Lakeland, lived and died in Ipswich. A woman of considerable wealth and several times married, she was accused of murdering her barber-surgeon husband after he keeled over dead rather unexpectedly. Exactly where and when he died is unknown – quite possibly at their home in central Ipswich, not far from a charming building known as the Ancient House that was built in 1567. However, for the sake of this story, the death occurs at temporary rental on Castle Hill a few months before the trial would have taken place.

What distinguished Lakeland's trial from countless other mariticides is that she was, as per the story, accused of having disposed of her husband by means of magic (from which we may deduce that there were no more obvious causes of death).

The chances are that John Lakeland died of a heart attack or some similar cause, and various historians speculate that the real reason behind the accusation was that Mary may have been using her wealth to bankroll the Royalist cause in an otherwise staunchly Puritanical area.

I have often wondered if this dour Puritanism persists to the 21st century and is the underlying reason for the town's unwillingness to celebrate its previously mentioned (in *The Fricwebba* story) colourful Catholic past as a major pilgrimage site, drawing in tourists the way nearby Colchester does with its history.

After the initial accusation was made various other people came forward, whether off their own bats or with encouragement is unclear, to add the secondary charges mentioned in the story – killing her granddaughter's ex-fiancé, sending a spirit dog to attack Mr Lawrence, and a spirit mole to assault Mrs Jennings and her maid etc.

The records indicate that Mother Lakeland was tried alongside a number of other women and (according to the research done by Malcolm Gaskill in his interesting and useful book '*Witchfinders*') one man, though the details as to who these people were proved elusive. However, other records report that four women from the neighbouring village of Hintlesham were also accused in the summer of the same year – one of them also a supposed husband-killer, though Susanna Stegold did not receive the same punishment which may mean she was acquitted or died in prison. It is speculation on my part to make the Hintlesham women the ones alongside Lakeland in the dock (but not, I think, an unreasonable speculation). History places Alice Denham as jointly accused of malignant magic with Mother Lakeland, though the accounts do not make it clear as to the nature of the women's relationship or of Alice's place in Ipswich society – so I have shamelessly embroidered the details.

The notion that John Lakeland was murdered is an even more lurid example of literary license! British witches were normally hanged or sentenced to a lesser punishment. Mary Lakeland was burned at the stake specifically because the court deemed her guilty of murdering her husband, which was classed as petty treason – an attack upon the monarch's representative in the home. Of course, by the time Mary was convicted of such a crime the country had just gone to war in order to get rid of that very monarch, but old habits die hard.

Ipswich has a monument to those Catholics slaughtered by intolerant Protestants, and one to those Protestants done to death by equally unyielding Catholics. We have no monument to any of the people killed by the fanaticism of courts convinced that they were in league with Satan on trumped-up evidence and the histrionic claims of malicious neighbours.

It is recorded that Mother Lakeland was convicted at the Bury St Edmunds assize and sentenced to be executed on Saturday 9th September. It was common practice for women convicted of petty treason to be strangled to death by the executioner shortly before the flames reached them, in a small act of mercy. The exact dates of the trial have proved difficult to find, and so I have distributed the other dates in this account to suit the narrative structure.

The magistrate Grimstone (there was also another called Bowes) is historical, as are the Reverends Samuel Fairclough and Edmund Calamy, and Robert Rich, the second Earl of Warwick. As many readers will already be aware, the Witch Finder General Matthew Hopkins was only too real and is the topic of a number of books by other authors. The real Hopkins was much younger than the delightfully sinister Vincent Price, who portrayed him in the film *Witchfinder General* (called *The Conqueror Worm* in America). At the time of his death, two years after this story finishes, he was about 27 years old and a remarkably rich man as a result of the amount demanded off those parish councils who called in his services. His right-hand man, John Stearne, survived his master long enough to write a pamphlet in defence of him. In this text Stearne claimed that Hopkins had sent some 200 supposed witches to their deaths.

Elemanzer, incidentally, was the name of an alleged witch's familiar spirit from Hopkins first and most infamous trial. It makes a great name for a pet, and one well worth reviving.

A wide variety of modern writers have seen the witch hunts as evidence to support their pet theories – be that of patriarchal sexism, plutocratic oppression, or whatever else. Without going into a long treatise, it is fairer to say that the various outbreaks of persecution that took place over many centuries and in a wide variety of different countries had many causes converging, rather than one neat, easy interpretation.

As far as the East Anglian outbreak goes, we must bear in mind that most of it took place in the interval between the end of the first phase of the Civil War (which, for contemporaries, would have been taken as the complete end) and the flare up of the second phase. In a country where neighbours, and even families, had been killing each other just a few months beforehand, tensions must have been extremely high. Many of the people that Hopkins 'discovered' were elderly and poor, with few friends and no resources to defend themselves in court. It takes little imagination to see this as a case of a cynical man making a fast profit and indulging a sadistic streak in terrorising the weak.

The chaos caused by a weakened judiciary, a disoriented church still reeling from the execution of Archbishop Laud, and in the grip of low-level paranoia made an ideal arena for exploitation by a cunning, ruthless character like Hopkins. Though what led him to make his very first accusation of being attacked by a magical bear conjured by a gang of illiterate old women (before it was apparent as a means of gaining money and status), is open to a deal of debate.

Towards the end of his short-lived career, Hopkins began to accuse educated people from the middle classes. This may have been simple ambition and greed getting the better of him, or he may (as some have postulated, such as Richard Deacon – who was not above embroidering his account even more than I have mine) have been acting with some political agenda. Hopkins was a Parliamentarian and it is possible that at least some of his targets were suspected, rightly or wrongly, of having a Royalist involvement or being Catholic sympathisers. To many Puritans at the time Catholicism was tantamount to sorcery, with its black-robed priests, Latin services, magical acts of transubstantiation, and so forth. The accusation of witchcraft may have been more a thinly veiled accusation of Roman sympathies.

Whatever else was going on, it is profoundly unlikely that the so-called witches were practitioners of an ancient goddess-worshipping mysticism, as suggested by Margaret Murray (and still echoed by the more wistful sections of the modern pagan community to this day). Rural areas were replete with people making or using love charms, herbal medicines, curses, fertility spells and the like, but these were practiced within the context of a confused, unorthodox (one might say heretical) form of Christianity, rather than as an underground polytheist cult.

Chapter Seven

Angel's Blood

Ipswich? Don't talk to me about Ipswich! Now don't get me wrong, dear boy, at first I loved the town. Well, it was the site of my theatrical debut and who could hold a genuine grudge against the birthplace of one's career? However, I cannot hear the name these days without the picture of poor old Gabriel Dean sprawled quite dead in front of that demon from the dark continent. Stage blood is one thing, darling, but the real thing – such a stench as you cannot imagine (one doesn't like to talk of such things, but he had, well let's just say parted company with continence!). 'Poor' Gabriel indeed! How time does eulogise the dead. In truth he owned half the slums in Ipswich, yet fancied himself cultured despite having the charm and visage of a bullfrog. His temper was equally vulgar. At his first meeting with the troupe he bent over to pick up a fallen walking cane, splitting his breeches right up the seam. Naturally most of us laughed, but he took it so ill that he stood up and punched the nearest fellow and broke his nose. Our actor-manager leapt in to escort the wounded chap off stage, and calm him down a little – but what could any of us really do? Dean held all the purse strings.

It was back in that lovely summer of '41, when I was still plying the vintner's trade in London. Always been partial to the odd tipple, as you know when darling old Henry Giffard offered me the chance to join his theatre company. I'd already penned a play for him, which went down marvellously well, and assisted as prompt and stand-in during rehearsals for whoever was too drunk or otherwise indisposed on any given day. So off to the provinces we all went, with that torrid old pot-boiler *The Royal Slave*. Ever seen that? Frightfully overwritten of course, but then

Southerne always was. I had a small part, but very sympathetic: Aboan, the chap who helps the star-crossed lovers to escape from the wicked king. Not that they escape for long, but audiences do warm to the role, and if I say so myself I positively made the part my own.

Dear Giffard had some tie to the theatre proprietor…a cousin, or brother-in-law, something of that sort. Helped secure the booking anyway, and of course the fellow was able to secure us lodgings too. Some frightful harridan with teeth that could uncork a wine bottle, and a wall-eye. Fortunately she was deaf as a post, so I could slip out of my room in the attic and test the bedsprings with Lily Cattermole on the first floor. Lovely Lily I called her then, though looking back now and comparing her to my wonderful wife Eva-Maria, well I can scarcely recall what I saw in the blowzy old trollop. Still, I was a mere 20 then and my passions were raging, and they do tend to blind young men to the flaws in the objects of their desires.

Anyway, Aboan was my first taste of the stage, and delicious as it was I had to sup from the cup of Thespis incognito. My blessed mother had died not long before, God rest her, and in deference to her and the rest of the family I didn't want to embarrass them by having the family name appear on the playbill. So I called myself Lyddal as far as the bill went instead of Garrick. Damn silly it seems now to hide so illustrious a cognomen, but as I say I was young. Poor mother was of the opinion that all theatricals were whores and sodomites. In fairness, the lovely Lily was more than ready to trade her charms for the chance of a good part, if you'll pardon the pun. Our leading man, Jake Barrow, was indeed rampantly uranian. "David, how's my beautiful wee man?" he used to ask me in that Glaswegian burr, which rather unnerved me until I was finally reassured that he could (eventually) take no for an answer.

I do miss that darling boy, he was always such delightful company, sober or foxed. Jake was the leading man, Oroonoko the African slave, which naturally required him to use blackface. It was the morning of the dress rehearsal and half of it was wasted standing in the wings listening to Jake and Giffard thundering at each other. That saucy young devil was handsome as Old Nick, and made his fortune from his face (though his understudy, a catty little snipe called Hazelton, whispered that he earned far more money with the opposite end of his physiology). Well, by the time that Giffard had smeared enough pancake on the lad to choke a horse, even his own mother would not have recognised him. In Aphra Behn's book both Oroonoko and the girl he runs off with were Africans, but the dreadful Southerne fancied himself in the shoes of the Bard and turned the book into a play in pale imitation of Othello, and made the girl Imoinda as white as milk. So there was Jake trying every trick in the book from fluttering his eyelashes to pouting and throwing the props about the stage to get Giffard to make Oroonoko pale skinned too. All just so he could flash that winning smile at the old dragons on the front row. The flat-nosed stage manager, some haughty local called Brooks, leapt about trying to catch the flying décor and save further breakages.

As may be supposed, we'd all grown a tad weary of the histrionics. Mister Dean, who had been watching from the stalls, leapt on to the stage. Well, as close to leaping as a creature with the physique and complexion of a Dutch Edam cheese may get. I swear he was nearly as fat as the then Prince Regent, whom I have heard needed to be lowered onto his mistresses with a harness (those unfortunate damsels must have been in mortal dread of it snapping.) Whatever money they made from such ghastly endeavours they certainly earned.

But I digress; Gabriel Dean bellowed that Giffard should sack that "posturing catamite" for Dean's own nephew could act the part better. The youthful relative in question dawdled in the wings chewing tobacco, looking for the world as if he had more hair than wit. Jake hurled his spear and palm-frond hat at Brooks and stormed off stage. Well the rest of us breathed a sigh of relief and got on with our lines. I adjusted my grass skirt and dashed on stage to ply my art before they could change their minds.

It was then that our backer made his ill-fated announcement that he intended to hold a garden party at Castle House and expected his paid-for cast of thespians to perform short excerpts from the play to entertain his crippled child and a few select guests. He made it abundantly clear that a certain sodomite was emphatically not invited to partake and that the gormless nephew Ralph would be taking the part for those scenes.

The date was set for some ten days hence and Giffard, for which transgression it took a considerable quantity of gin to forgive, visited the burden of preparing the gormless Ralph for his theatrical debut upon my shoulders. This, I have no delusions, was because of my junior status within the troupe. Anyone else would have told him what to do with such a suggestion; I alone dared not.

The ten days simply dragged. Ralph was not blessed with brains or the sensitivity needed of an actor. He worked for his uncle as a general factotum, gathering rents and dealing with whatever trivial issues arose amongst the poorest tenants. From Ralph I gathered that Uncle Gabriel owned some two dozen squalid dives in the filthiest part of Ipswich, each more tightly jam-packed than the average rabbit warren. However, the old toad also had some rather more desirable residences dotted around town and Ralph aspired to service these properties (though I suspected that he was more interested in servicing the bored wives of Ipswich's industrious gentry). Whilst he had the brain of a carthorse, Ralph had a pleasant enough face and (without wishing to be vulgar, but with the fashions of the day it was hard not to notice) bore a resemblance to those hardworking equines in other regards. I fancy that, had circumstances turned out differently, he might have been quite popular in the theatrical walk of life. In minor roles, you understand?

He squeezed rehearsals in around his other duties, thereby doubling the length of my working day. Though remembering where to stand and which props to hold in any given scenes, the lines eluded him and I had to resort to writing them on paste-boards. Alas he was no great reader, and even with the lines before him he still managed to mumble and stumble like some slovenly schoolboy reciting his Latin prep.

Truly I came to despair of Ralph, news which caused Giffard to sigh deeply and mutter darkly of misguided angels, and simultaneously made naughty Jake laugh up a gale. Well, who was to blame him for rejoicing in the incompetence of the man who nearly came to replace him?

Whatever his mental shortcomings, Ralph was eager to be liked and rewarded my endeavours with a goodly supply of alcohol and cake from a very talented baker. His capacity for consuming both led me to wonder if, whilst having dodged his uncle's visage, he might inherit that man's girth in the years to come. Through our chats I learnt that Uncle Gabriel and his wife were not locals, but hailed originally from the far side of Cambridgeshire. They had arrived in Ipswich many years earlier as newlyweds and sat about transforming a small fortune into a considerably larger one. In other regards Fate had been less kind, with only one child surviving to that present day, and she crippled in body and mind.

For all his brutishness towards the rest of the world (Ralph himself alluded to having suffered the wrong side of his uncle, though he did not go into details), Gabriel Dean doted upon his unfortunate daughter.

The dreaded day of the garden party rolled around and, again as junior member, I was delegated to assist the stage manager in transporting a few of the more impressive props and set dressings to create our select scenes. Between us we managed it all in one trip, each supervising a laden cart. The rest of the cast went up in Giffard's better-appointed transport, arriving in full costume to avoid the nonsense of trying to change at Dean's abode. I must say that owning slums was clearly more lucrative than I had imagined given how well Gabriel had done for himself on the proceeds.

The house, which one of the servants told me later, had been in wrack and ruin when it had been purchased for a song a couple of decades previous was now an impressive pile. The gardens were ornate, as a casual glance as we rode through clearly showed, and the walls were lined with the sort of fearsome spikes that suggested the owner had plenty worth stealing and was serious about keeping the hoi polloi out.

I spent most of the morning flapping around fetching and carrying for Mister Brooks, who made the inspired suggestion to Giffard that we create two stage areas in the garden for the different scenes, so that the audience need but shift round in their chairs to see the on-going action.

I was dimly aware, as the afternoon rolled around, that assorted bigwigs were gradually arriving and being ushered into the house. I had also become conscious of a small and curious face watching us, seemingly for hours on end, from an upstairs room.

A doddering old servant who had earlier been setting our chairs summonsed me and Brooks to carry out the orders of the lady of the house. It's a wicked thing I'm sure to laugh given what was shortly to happen, but it was only with the greatest difficulty that I avoided corpsing at the prospect of Mrs Magnolia Dean. I swear by all the saints that it looked to me as if Gabriel had a twin brother who'd taken to cross dressing! I've heard it said that a woman's face is her destiny, and one can but feel sorry for a creature with so grim a fate as that poor thing must have been made for.

She announced that "the other one" was to be carted out to our makeshift stages and, she was most insistent, that it absolutely had to go on the back of our cart and be taken to Tankard Street at the end of the day's entertainments. Of course neither I nor the stage manager had a clue what she was on about as she babbled away. We merely followed in her wake into the hallway of Castle House.

As my eyes adjusted to the gloom of the house, I glanced up and saw the most hideous, demonic visage glaring down at me and...well, there's scant point in denying it, squealed like some scatty milkmaid.

It was explained to me later that the grotesque wooden statue that dominated the hallway was some African antiquity that had belonged to long dead former owner of Castle House who had possessed a plantation and slaves. Dean had purchased the place lock and stock, one of his servants eventually finding the glowering oddity in a back cellar.

My instinctive revulsion to the thing immediately made a friend of me to Magnolia, who took my unmanly response as proof that I too shared her paranormal sensations of malice emanating from the carving. At tedious length she regaled us with accounts of the many bad dreams she had suffered, plagued by the sound of jungle drums and visions of the two statues coming alive and devouring human sacrifices.

It would appear that this icon of some nameless heathen deity had been the very inspiration for Mr Dean becoming a backer to our play. Though actually I heard some variations on that theme; Giffard claimed that he had been trying to touch the old toad up for some funds to stage *'Tis Pity She's a Whore* when, whilst dining at the house, he had seen the carving and immediately decided to put on the African play (on the assumption, false as it turned out, that Dean was some passionate collector of art from the dark continent) given Gabriel's overt hostility to Webster's play.

Mrs Dean gave the alternate account that, as soon as she heard that a play about slaves was being staged at Tankard Street, she badgered her husband into patronising it purely in an attempt to convince him to loan (permanently if she had her way) those wooden creations as props – we had quite a selection in the play: the large statues, several hefty spears, assorted native drums, some small carvings of demons and animals, and a couple of masks used by witch doctors. She was far more terrified of the statues than I had been, though in her case she had lived with them longer and developed a more deeply rooted superstitious fear of their demonic influence.

It's ridiculous really that I should have been alarmed by the sight of this idol, given that I had already seen what might be called its twin sister (it looked vaguely female in a peculiar sort of way) back at the theatre. I gathered later that Mrs Dean had been pushing her husband to take this last article to the theatre but that he had been holding on to it for some obtuse reason. Possibly just to annoy her – he seemed to be the sort of person who enjoyed making others squirm, even those closest to him. Maybe especially those closest to him.

We had already nicknamed the idol at the theatre Man Friday, so it seemed only right to christen this new addition Woman Saturday. With a great deal of heaving and sweating from myself, Brooks and one of the servants we hauled the dusty monstrosity out onto the lawn and sat him to loom over the secondary stage.

As we were adjusting the angle of Woman Saturday I spied the lovely Lily giggling coquettishly in the shadow of a tree, whilst our bloated hog of a host pawed at her. Though I did not wish to admit it at the time, she certainly seemed neither unfamiliar with his touch nor unwilling.

A few costume repairs and a swift drink later, and we were all ready to earn our keep. The cast loitered behind an erected sheet strung between two trees, our very own 'green room'. About a dozen guests (local worthies whose names were pointed out to me, though I can recall none of them now) were seated in the sunny auditorium, with servants loitering behind them. Dean and his wife were seated, like shorter versions of the looming Friday and Saturday, either side of a wizened figure on the front row. I recognised the smiling face as the one that had been watching us from the upper storey. The poor mite had legs so diminished as to be unable to support her weight, and one arm that ended at the elbow. Despite the mangled state of her body, she was blessed with an angelic face quite unlike the bulbous, florid features of the relatives gathered around her.

I enquired of Ralph which of the guests were his own parents, to be left feeling somewhat gauche when the poor lad told me that he was an orphan since infancy and had been raised by his uncle and aunt at Castle House.

Giffard stood and made an ingratiating speech, transmogrifying Dean into some sophisticated patron of the arts. Judging from the expressions on the guests' faces a few could barely contain their hilarity at Henry's unctuous eulogy. The cultural icon in question stood to say some words of benevolent patronage, but thankfully we were all saved from yet more blather by the clearly unexpected arrival of a late carriage. All heads turned to witness a flunky assisting an ancient simulacrum of Gabriel Dean descend from the carriage. Quite as ugly, but deflated by immense age and with dewlaps flapping from the momentum of the journey, the worthy and our host stood gawping at each other. Backstage as I was, the conversation that passed between them was scant more than murmured noises. One of the actresses, who must have had ears like a hare, picked up on snippets and relayed them to the rest of us. It transpired that the late arrival was the great-uncle of Gabriel Dean, Sir Randolph Dean by name, and had effectively tracked his elusive relative down after much searching. Great-Uncle appeared unaware of any theatrical endeavours, clearly having arrived on some other business, and it was only with some reluctance that he agreed to postpone whatever matters had prompted his journey until after the performance was done and the other guests gone home.

Giffard acted as narrator to link the three scenes and explain how they fit into the overall story. We all came on and strutted our hour, and made a fair fist of it considering we had the ghastly Ralph mumbling, tripping over the sets and forgetting his lines. Four times he had to be prompted – four! When he first came on, in black face, the guests applauded indulgently. By his third entrance they could scarcely manage to hide their embarrassment. It came as no surprise to me to overhear a sotto voce conversation during the mingling afterwards, in which Dean told Giffard that he had been a "little hard" on dear Jake and that maybe they should get the boy back. Of course Giffard was diplomat enough not to mention that Jake had never been let go in the first place. Ralph also seemed to overhear the conversation, for dark glances shot between uncle and nephew, along with a choice remark from the former that I blush to repeat here.

During my brief stints on stage, and during the mingling after, it became blatant that the normally bombastic Dean was as nervous as a schoolboy with undone homework. His much put-upon wife was pale as a sheet, constantly glancing at the bloodhound jowls of her in-law.

After an hour or so of light refreshments the assorted guests and hangers-on began to disperse. During this time raised voices could be heard from within the house, and on several occasions I saw a tense Magnolia glance red-eyed at the African idols, muttering about how unnatural they were.

As it became obvious that the event was drawing to an early close, I passed up on consuming my own bodyweight in buffet food and made myself useful. Once I'd assisted filling up the first cart with props, and seen some of the sillier members of the cast off back to town (Giffard had wisely laid on a tab for them at a watering hole near the theatre to ensure that none of them got drunk and disgraced themselves at the garden party), I decided to pause for another refreshing tipple – I shall confess that I had purloined a bottle of very pleasing white from the guests' table (which was better-appointed than the paltry affair put out for cast and crew) earlier in the day and secreted it in the cool cavity at the back of Man Friday. Both wood carvings were hollowed out at the back, presumably to make them a little lighter to carry, and made ideal wine coolers.

As I emerged refreshed I caught the eye of the crippled child who smiled sweetly at me, calling out the name of my character. Always one to entertain, I snatched up the only drum left unpacked and capered about barking, "Me great warrior Aboan", and doing what I imagined might pass for a tribal dance on the dark continent. The child, whose name was Betsy, laughed up a gale and was soon joined by her mother who seemed equally amused at my comic turn and deeply relieved to have something to take her mind off whatever was happening indoors.

Duty done, I asked Mrs Dean if I could avail myself of a mirror to remove the blackface before joining my fellows at the tavern. She directed me to a spare bedroom, and I passed the aged relative on the way. He sat roughly where Woman Saturday had once stood, glowering from the shadows and seeming a damned sight more frightening than the wooden monstrosity. He ignored my polite greeting and growled about dark creatures bringing shame upon them all, muttering more to himself than to me, I thought.

Once in the bedroom I sat about restoring myself to civilisation, when I heard that cheeky devil Gabriel stealing my act! Glancing out the window I saw him wearing one of the African headdresses, banging the drum and crashing about with all the elegance of a carthorse attempting ballet. He was doing his best to imitate my nonsense chanting and singing, making obeisance before Man Friday and even kissing the ugly brute, whilst the poor child was doing her dutiful best to laugh but clearly was less impressed by her father than by a professional such as I. Mrs Dean was nowhere to be seen, and I returned to the mirror.

I had just finished removing the last of my make-up and tidying up my attire when the scream rang out from the garden. Sticking my head out the window I spotted old Gabriel leaking his vital essences all over the makeshift stage, his wig on the stained grass like a drowned sewer rat. The wife was caterwauling and flapping about as servants and old Giffard came running.

Taking the stairs several at a time, I made my entrance upon the scene to discover Dean still wearing the silly headdress and sprawled on his back with a sizeable hole in his throat. Little Betsy was ashen-faced and pointed at Man Friday, croaking inarticulately. Magnolia Dean raised a terrible hue and cry, flailing about and decrying the evils of the heathen statues and their demonic influence. The servants, perhaps used to such melodramas, manhandled her towards a chair and set about plying her with cloths dipped in water still cold from the ice house. All the while she moaned incoherently about the curse of the African devils and their lust for innocent blood. Which seemed ironic, given that Gabriel had long since parted company with innocence.

Thankfully one of the servants had the wit to carry Betsy away from the scene of her father's demise – for even to someone with no medical training such as me, it was blatantly obvious that there was no point in sending for a physician. At least not for Dean, though maybe his widow might have benefitted from a draught of poppy juice. Indeed, someone must have thought the same for a medical gentleman did appear some half hour later and was eventually able to sedate the florid matriarch.

In the meantime a manservant (who was more hindrance than help) and I hefted up the bloated corpse and circumnavigated the floating island of histrionics and got the Dean onto a couch in the study. Well, that is to say we almost got him to the couch except I dropped him first! It was, I assure you, quite accidental and the result of the man's own appalling taste in interior décor. I tripped over the head of a lion-skin rug and lost my grip.

Blushing, I stood to find myself caught in the reptile gaze of Sir Randolph, whose only comment was to snarl that blasphemy in life led to farce in death. Glowering at the corpse he turned and hobbled out.

The scrawny old butler flapped about tending to his master and generally moaning. Though a very new actor myself, I had enough natural skill to recognise a bad actor when I heard one. It took little prompting to engage the scarecrow in conversation and, for lack of anything better to talk about, I commented upon his accent which struck me as decidedly Ipswich. He was not, he explained to me, an old family retainer though he had served the Deans since their first arrival in Suffolk. Indeed, there were no old retainers at all, the Deans having arrived by themselves. About the only thing they had ever done to endear themselves to the natives was to bring some much-needed employment to the area and take on an entirely local staff. Of course the shifty-eyed dodderer didn't put it in quite such coarse terms, but hemmed and hawed around the issue. It amounted to the same thing at the end of the day though!

Moments after we had arranged the body and draped a sheet over it, Ralph appeared looking surly and glared at the body. I made a scathing comment about his having arrived too late to help, but he just stared at me gormlessly and seemed as immune to sarcasm as he did to stagecraft advice.

It was an immense relief when the doctor and Giffard arrived some minutes later and the medic gave a cursory glance at the stiffening body before attending to the prostrate widow. The great actor and I slipped away for a pipe and a stroll in the surprisingly beautiful gardens. Who would have imagined that such ugly people could have such taste? I recalled the half-empty bottle of wine hidden behind Man Friday, and suggested that it might aid in steadying my nerves. Alas the bottle had tipped over and leaked its contents into the garden.

Dear old Giffard made a valiant attempt to produce moral outrage on behalf of the late Mister Dean before his genuine fears over the financing of the play took the fore. It was as we prognosticated the future that I caught a glimpse of a distant figure slipping out of the gates through which we had not long earlier rode. At the time I had assumed it be some servant, and may have paid no heed but for the curiously light gait for so wide a figure as she skipped away from Castle House.

Some while later the doctor emerged, wiping his hands with a bloodstained kerchief. Even at that tender age I had a degree of curiosity that my late mama would have considered vulgar. In response to my indelicate questions the flustered physician described the wound as a circular one that had penetrated the throat from beneath and torn upwards ripping open windpipe and artery alike. I suggested an Italian stiletto, but he pooh-poohed this as too narrow a diameter and suggested something more like the thickness of a walking stick. There was no such weapon anywhere near the body when I saw it, and I said as much.

We stood awhile in the sunshine trying to contemplate how Dean might have come by such a wound accidentally or through some act of self-destruction. Though I do not think any of us could seriously imagine so contentious and self-regarding a man harming his own survival. Most especially not before the eyes of his adored daughter. The alternative explanation hung unspoken between us, and it was I that finally voiced it. The doctor snorted a half-laugh and remarked that a third of the town had reason to despise Gabriel Dean. Too many lived in his filthy slums and many others (I had the impression he included himself in this) were tradesmen or professionals owed money that they were never likely to see. As with too many people, Dean's wealth was perhaps sustained through an unwillingness to share it.

Whenever Dean had appeared at the theatre it was in the company of a knuckle-dragging thug who had the look of the prison yard about him. The henchman had not been at the garden party – I supposed that Dean felt safe in his own home – but clearly the man must have had enemies to feel the need of such constant protection whenever journeying into town. Had some ill-treated tenant or unpaid tradesman snuck into the party and avenged himself?

I wondered at the time which doubtless ill-featured relative was likely to inherit the wealth, though naturally I did not ask either Giffard or the medical man (neither of whom were liable to know anyway). One assumed the grieving widow, but of course others may have had sizeable enough legacies to make it worth the risk of doing away with the man. Aside from the unexpected arrival, I did not think that any of the audience was actually related to our hosts – though there could have been some connection. Though most of them had been ushered away home by the time that Dean was struck down.

The doctor commented that the play may have proved rather too much for the unfortunate child. Further questioning elicited that, having tended to the distrait Betsy, the physician had heard the child, whose vocabulary was rather limited, croaking fearfully about a monster biting her daddy – which he had presumed was some scary figure featuring in our production. Giffard explained that there was no such beast.

A bang drew our attention to where Ralph, who was helping the stage manager tidy the last of the properties away, had dropped the African drum. I sauntered over and picked the instrument up and took the lion-skin rug off the overloaded youth. We arranged the articles on the cart, leaving enough space for Woman

Saturday and her husband. Old Brooks added an armful of spears and, as he went off for the next load, I paused to examine the weapons. Two of them were real spears from the African collection, with vicious barbed heads. I beckoned the doctor over, just before he returned to his practice, and indicated the murderous devices. However, he dismissed them as incapable of making the sort of wound that killed Dean – reiterating that it was a round wound and not the sort of jagged horizontal split that such items would make. The three stage props, made in imitation of the real thing, had spearheads forged of tin that were simply too soft to do any real damage. They might have caused a nasty scratch, dear boy, but that was about it!

Ralph called for some help in manoeuvring the two idols on to the back of the cart, and I trotted off to oblige. A deal more sweating and grunting managed the job, and I noticed that Woman Saturday was not only dusty but grimy. Wiping my hands afterwards it dawned on me that the stains were not so much grease as greasepaint. Brooks and I rode our respective carts back towards the theatre, and I deliberately allowed him to get ahead of me so that I could park in a side street and spend a few minutes tracking the black smudges to their source. The statue had small holes drilled through its eyes, almost like it were a vast and unwieldy mask, and I found traces of blackface near these eyes on the inside surface – as if someone had been staring out at the audience from the inside curve of the giant goddess.

Whilst the horse rested I fully examined both Friday and Saturday, paying particular attention to the various small angular holes carved into the wood, but could find no other traces of theatrical make-up. However, it did strike me that some of those gaps were just large enough to shove or throw something the diameter of a walking stick through. Could it be that someone might have hidden behind one of the idols, waiting for Dean to approach near enough during his cavorting to strike the deadly blow? I wondered if that was what Betsy had meant, knowing no other way to describe the carved totem but as a monster.

Once the cart was returned and unloaded (a task I happily left to the stage manager and his crew) I made a quick change of attire and decided to avail myself of the tab set up by Giffard at the bar.

I found the happy throng agog with the murder – for Giffard had made it quite clear to them that no other explanation would suffice. "God's teeth!" saucy Jake roared, unable to help himself from striking a pose as if playing Hamlet on Drury Lane. He went on to decry his ill luck at having missed the spectacle and said some very unkind things about the newly departed. I asked him what he had been doing whilst we had been singing for our suppers at Castle House, and he tipped me a lecherous wink and said he'd been looking up an old friend. Lovely Lily made an unrepeatable aside as to which part of the old friend he'd been looking up, but I draw a veil over that knowing what a sensitive creature you are.

It was as they were all guffawing and backslapping that I noticed a smear of black upon Jake's cheek. He'd had no cause to don costume or pancake since the altercation with Dean a week or more earlier, and I did but wonder. Of course, there may have been some innocuous explanation. He could have rubbed up against one of the other cast members, but to the best of my knowledge none of the other fellows were of Jake's persuasion; though sometimes you can never tell for sure.

Lily drank somewhat heavily and seemed on rather brittle form, which led me to wonder if she was either genuinely grieved for Dean and eager not to show it (something my young mind could scarcely credit), or if she was nervous. Whether those nerves were born of the expected discomfort of having one's lover and indulgent patron bumped off, or because she knew more than was good for her I found difficult to judge.

The drink flowed and eventually Jake announced, a little blearily, that he had an appointment – something celebratory with Mother Griffin – and slipped off.

A few minutes later Lily asked if I would accompany her out of the Great White Horse and escort her back to the lodgings. "Stupid fat hog!", she snarled, too drunk to be discreet, and proceeded to pour her scorn on our deceased patron and his clumsy fondling which, she belatedly assured me, were utterly unwelcome and vigorously fought off. My delusions that she had been the unwilling victim of those porcine advances soon dissolved in the face of such hollow protestations. Suddenly my summer romance was ashes. With heavy heart I steered her back to the lodgings to sleep it off until our opening night. En route she continued to complain about Gabriel, the incompetence of the other thespians, the arrogance of the stage manager who had accosted her with a lecture upon her elocution (he being a former schoolmaster), and the general vulgarity of the Ipswich populace. The last I felt somewhat unwise, given that we were moving amongst them at the time and her voice carried.

She clearly expected me to stay and comfort her, though she was all but passed out by the time I tipped her into bed. Just before she succumbed to Morpheus I queried her as to who on earth Mother Griffin was, at which she broke out in one of those grating, staccato laughs that had seemed so charming and vivacious only the day before. It transpired that this Griffin woman ran a popular molly house down by the docks, to which Jake was a frequent visitor.

A stagehand I passed in the street was able to direct me to the molly house and didn't so much as bat an eyelid at my somewhat scarlet-faced request. No doubt you'll find it hard to believe, after all these long years upon the stage, that I was once such a blushing flower in my youth, but I was! A sheltered upbringing, you see.

I spent a half-hour inhaling the reek of the Ipswich mud before plucking up the courage to knock at the bawdy house and wonder at the curious sigil carved into the doorpost (later it was explained to me that, just as the gentlemen of the road have their secret codes and signs, so do the gentlemen's gentlemen). A gruesome thug answered the door, bearing more than a passing resemblance to the ogre that served as bodyguard and enforcer to Gabriel Dean, and demanded nearly a day's wage to let me pass up the creaking staircase. I tried to explain that my attendance was not, well, a professional one, but he merely stonewalled me and held out a shovel-palm for the cash.

I entered into a parlour presided over by an enormous ageing termagant in an almost purple wig – Mother Griffin herself. She positively trilled at having what she assumed was a new customer, and clapped her hands to summon her boys (several of whom were a long way past deserving that appellation, and a couple for whom it was far too appropriate for my comfort).

A painted popinjay minced up to me, offering a drink along with services of an unrepeatable nature. His passionless and too-often parroted overtures reminded me of the worst in restoration theatre, and only resolved my wish for greater naturalism. Blessedly Jake spotted me and disentangled himself from a strapping young farmhand to come to my rescue. I decided that, with a man as drunk as Mr Barrow seemed to be, the direct approach might be the most effective. Had he been up to Castle House earlier that day, I asked. It took a moment for him to focus and he declared that he had been at Mother Griffin's since…since…and then the slightly dozy, but clearly well-meaning, farmhand provided the time as two o'clock. There, supposedly, he had stayed until departing for the free drinks at the Great White Horse. If that were true then he could not have killed Dean at, give or take, four o'clock.

However, I pushed the matter further, noting the guilty look on my drunken friend's face, and he finally confessed that he had paid a brief visit to Castle House earlier in the day – disguised in blackface in order to seem just one native amongst all the others. He tried to make light of it, insisting that he had only stayed long enough to watch Ralph making an arse of himself in his poached part. He had departed over the garden wall (the same way he had entered) just as the staged excerpts were ending, and headed to the molly house for a wash, change of costume, and probably a quick roll with the naïve lunk.

Jake expressed a wish to go back to the digs and sleep it off ready for an early start for the final rehearsal tomorrow before our opening night on Monday. Exiting towards the more salubrious atmosphere of the Carr Street coffee house in order to sober us both up a little, we fell to discussing my theories of the craft. During the course of our philosophical musings Jake let slip that Lily had been in receipt of some rather expensive gifts from an admirer. Of course I had already learnt who this was, and wondered what had so soured the relationship (how nauseous it was to admit that, whilst I had been wooing her with romantic blandishments, she had been swapping her favours for trinkets from that creature). Or maybe my lovely Lily really was one of those creatures that can fawn upon the hand that secretly she wishes to bite off? Yet to move from secretly loathing a person to ramming a weapon through their fat throat requires, surely, more than one sweaty cosseting too many.

If Dean had cast her over for some younger piece, maybe sheer spite might have led her to lash out. Though I found it hard to credit Lily doing so in such a manner – throwing anything that wasn't nailed down, certainly, maybe even braining her paramour with an empty bottle (she certainly wouldn't waste a full one) were far more in keeping with her character than having a man's throat out in full view of his simple-minded child.

This latter factor also seemed to mitigate against the unsightly wife demanding vengeance for the betrayal (probably the last in a long line of them, I shouldn't wonder). That Magnolia might have plenty of cause to wish riddance of her husband I could well believe, that she should perform the deed before her daughter's eyes I could not.

As I left Jake at the lodgings, in the room below mine, a note was pressed on me by the desiccated landlady. Thankfully it was not a plea for a perverse tryst, but a regal command from our actor-manager to attend upon him in his office at the theatre. Before departing I enquired, as casually as I could, if the late Gabriel Dean had a son and heir. The toothless harridan cackled, and suggested that he might have a hundred of them around town but none on the right side of the sheets. She went on to intimate that Ipswich was awash with impoverished women who had been obliged to find other ways of paying rent to Mister Dean. Not to mention their irate husbands, fathers and brothers for whom the necessity of keeping a roof over their heads resulted in their becoming impotent panderers to their own flesh. Innumerable suspects there, and it was always possible that one had made egress over the wall, just as Jake Barrow had, done the deed and slipped away again unnoticed. Possible, but somewhat improbable with all the people coming and going.

The landlady, a sharp creature if ever there were one, quickly cottoned to the issue of inheritance. Naturally talk of Dean's death was all round town and she probably knew almost as much about it by that stage as I did. Though she had no inside knowledge of the legal details of any will, it was widely assumed in Ipswich that the bulk of the fortune (and ownership of all those properties) would go to the lack-witted nephew Ralph. Maybe a few small bequests here and there, but certainly most of those ill-used tenants were now breathing a sigh of relief that a far less cunning (and, from the women's viewpoint, less repulsive if worst came to worst) landlord would be collecting their rents.

Some even had the impression, or false hope in her opinion, that Ralph might keep the properties in better repair.

I raised the spectre of the superannuated Sir Randolph, but the landlady had no light to shed. As far as she, or the rest of Ipswich, had been aware both Mr and Mrs Dean were without respective families. Certainly in the seventeen or so years they had dwelt in the town no relations had visited them, nor had they departed on visitations to sundry in-laws. Who exactly the old man was, where he fitted into the picture or why his relatives seemed so nervous of him remained a mystery to me.

I was almost out the door when the thought struck me, and I enquired if she knew what had happened to Ralph's parents. She did not, for the boy had already been orphaned when they arrived in Ipswich.

The theatre was empty, and I crossed the stage en route to the office when Giffard intercepted me coming in the opposite direction. I am only a little above five feet tall, whilst the good Giffard towered over six foot. He steered me like a father, his hand upon my shoulder, into an unoccupied props room where we perched on the edge of a makeshift bed (the stage manager currently having nowhere else to live).

That deep, fruity voice began to lay out his concerns about this ghastly crime and the likelihood that someone from the theatre was involved. It would be extremely bad for future funding if the charge of homicidal mania were added to all the other slurs made against us thespians. In that crowded, pungent storeroom he explained to me how the proud name of the theatre, in the hands of whichever relation of his it was, depended upon maintaining the good will of the burghers of Ipswich. A slaughtered slumlord was scarcely likely to do the play any benefit, nor launch my career upon the path I was then but dreaming of. As to what my dear brother George would have said to hear that I had forsaken respectable trade to get embroiled in a sordid crime – it didn't bear thinking about!

I suggested my theories that it could have been motivated from within the family – maybe Ralph driven by greed for inheritance – or by some ill-used tenant who had clambered over the wall and struck the blow. This latter theory struck me as especially weak, but Giffard seized upon it with undue enthusiasm.

Even as I suggested my ideas, I marked upon a broken prop in the corner of the storeroom – one of the cheap imitation spears – which brought to mind the doctor's comment that the weapon had been the diameter of a walking cane...and of course the ancient great-uncle had such an aide. There was something deeply unsettling about his arrival at the garden party and the way the Deans had reacted to him, something that begged further investigation. Yet the proposition of so arthritic and wizened a creature plunging his stick into Gabriel's throat seemed too preposterous for words. Could he have persuaded one of his servants to do the deed for him? It was unlikely, though not impossible, and still left the question of motive.

"He despises them!" Giffard interjected, and it dawned on me that (not for the last time) I'd been thinking out loud. The dear old boy went to explain that he had overheard some of the ranting in the house whilst the guests were dragging out their departures. The snippets that our manager had picked up on included Sir Randolph fulminating about a malevolent, unnatural pair looming over the proceedings and that God's misbegotten curse was upon them. The old man clearly feared the two African idols as much as Magnolia did, and Giffard conjectured that maybe he worried that the great-nephew was involved in some satanic cult worshipping those deities. I recalled Sir Randolph's comment about blasphemy, and set this strange possibility to the back of my mind for later contemplation.

The authorities had spoken to Giffard, although only briefly. Whilst theatricals were little trusted, the idea that a touring company with no real connection to the town could have felled one of the leading citizens seemed ludicrous to the man in charge of the case. Lily, whose other charms had momentarily distracted the august investigator, told me later that the arm of the law was splitting its attention between the servants and nephew Ralph as most likely to have had a motive and opportunity.

The dress rehearsal was a strangely gay affair, despite our financial uncertainties. High spirits made for a rather lairy run through. Lily's left breast managed twice to fall out of her costume – entirely by 'accident' you understand – whilst I got bellowed at by Giffard for dropping two drums and nearly impaling an understudy with a sword. Jake, not one to be outdone, managed to flash us the pride of Glasgow and even tried climbing up Man Friday, who began to rock ominously. I tried to get my head down for a few hours' kip in the dressing room, but the stage manager's stentorian snoring next door kept me awake. Turning over the events of the last few days in my mind I let phrases and images drift. The corpse, the looming statues, the beating of drums in tune with Brooks' snores, malformed Betsy pointing and croaking about monsters, and then that phrase in Giffard's orotund voice – misbegotten curse.

A rather cruel and unpleasant interpretation of those words suddenly came to me in the emptiness of the dressing room. I didn't like it, but then I don't think I would have liked Sir Randolph, who struck me on our briefest of acquaintances as decidedly cruel and unpleasant himself.

I mulled some more and one thought connected to another in a reticulate manner, as if spun by a particularly venomous spider. On one of the shelves I found a dog-eared script of *'Tis Pity She's a Whore* and reminded myself of a key point in the plot. It gave an ugly alternate light to some of what happened at the garden party, but I wasn't sure if it really brought the name of the killer into any greater focus. A wiser head than mine might be called for.

I found Giffard nursing a bottle of sherry in the stalls, and presented my ideas to him. He found it quite distasteful, but had to admit a certain logic to the train of thought. However, I was duly persuaded by Giffard to keep silent until after the first-night performance, and turn my face aside from natural justice at least for a short while.

I was later to learn that an unfortunate housemaid, no longer able to conceal her condition from the butler, was arrested on suspicion of having avenged herself on Mister Dean for getting her that way. She broke away from the constables, who I dare say were feeling churlish enough for arresting some ill-used chit of a girl, only to be fished out of the docks a few hours on. I swear to you that I knew none of this at the time, and it was only brought to my attention by Giffard when I propounded my own solution to the crime late that very night.

I see you are thinking that I placed my own urge to fame ahead of the natural demands of justice. Well, rest assured that it was not so. I have heard tell that ships, being worlds enclosed, run by their own rules of right and wrong. So it is with those who tread our boards. Giffard agreed as we sat in the stalls that I should look deeper into the matter, and I in turn consented to abide by his judgement on the facts.

The evening arrived, the audience filled the seats, and I stood quivering in the wings. Beneath the blackface I was white as a ghost. Waiting for my entrance, my mind was briefly distracted by the rack of African spears waiting by the props table. I eyed my own rather grubby weapon with its smears of greasepaint, and exchanged it for the only clean spear in the rack, smoothing out the rather battered-looking tin spearhead. I recalled Giffard's words from the dress rehearsal that I should pay more attention to my use of props and less to obsessing over character and motivation. I certainly didn't wish to trip over the flats or drop my spear mid-performance. However, it was the penny that dropped rather than any of the props. Giffard was absolutely correct, had I paid more attention to practical matters then issues may have been the sooner resolved.

I almost missed my cue but for the stage manager pushing me on, and the rest my dear is legend. The audience lionised my naturalistic style, and I noted that dear Jake began to emulate me by the second act. That was when I saw it, that look of mute rage upon lordly Oroonoko's face when the wicked plantation owner whipped the high-born slave. I stood in the wings once more, searching in vain amongst the stained spears. Giffard appeared and I appraised him as rapidly as possible before going back on. Jake appeared at our elbows, ready for his next entrance, and must have heard just enough of the conversation to realise we were discussing the murder. He advanced one of my earlier ideas that one of Dean's many ill-used women (or more likely one of their menfolk) might have climbed the wall and both entered and left the party unseen. Giffard was keen on this suggestion, but mention of the walls suddenly recalled to me my sight of them on first riding through the gates of Castle House. The walls, lined at they were with vicious spikes, were better suited to a fortress (or a prison) and I said as much. How could anyone get over such a wall, I asked – and Jake at least had the good grace to blush as he recalled the lie he had told me at the molly house. Mind you, I said, a person could slip in disguised had they jumped on the back of one of the props wagons. His burr going up an octave or three, Jake asked how someone could that unnoticed. Of course, they couldn't I responded – it would have to be done with the complicity of other cast members. That rascal giggled nervously and dived on stage a few moments too early. Images of that nimble-footed fat lady slipping out the garden gate, sometime *after* the murder, came to mind. That foolish farm boy at the male brothel no doubt had been persuaded to give a false time to anyone asking about Mister Barrow's whereabouts.

I could but wonder what other silly games my fellow thespian might be playing.

When the play was done I found a note from our august leader waiting for me in the dressing room. He had invited a 'select band' to attend upon him in his cramped office whilst the rest frolicked in the green room in traditional first-night manner.

In the proprietor's office I found the handsome Jake, a little disgruntled to be missing out on the free-flowing drink at the party, being placated by Giffard and his relative who owned the theatre. We were shortly joined by the lovely Lily, already so far gone that she was virtually carried in by the stage manager who bore an expression of long suffering. In response to my question he told me that the gormless Ralph was amusing the rest of the cast with his elephant impressions, and that the Widow Dean was hovering uncertainly in the box – torn between the social pressure to maintain a front of grief and go home, and her clear preference for being amongst the joyful living. He offered to fetch them, but I stayed his hand. As per our agreement Giffard was to sit in judgement on my evidence, and it was sufficient that we knew where the Deans were.

A copy of the playbill was pinned to the office wall and I drew attention to my name there at the base. So far as the people of Ipswich knew, my name was Lyddal. Indeed, Ralph was used to addressing me by that very cognomen. Blank faces stared back at me, so I proceeded to elaborate the point – when a stranger presents himself in a certain way it is natural to simply accept this on face value. That, it was my feeling, was what had essentially happened nigh on twenty years previously when Gabriel, Magnolia and their toddler ward arrived in Ipswich. People took them largely at face value, accepting them for who they claimed to be. Jake, lightning quick, asked me if I were claiming that Gabriel Dean was a false name – was the dead toad in fact some miscreant on the run?

He was close, and puffed like a peacock when I said so. At my prompting Giffard repeated his anecdote about discarding the original intention to play *'Tis Pity* in favour of the impulsive suggestion of *The Royal Slave.* It may be that there was some trivial reason for Dean's dislike of Webster's play but I repeated what seemed to me the salient comparisons between the days of Gabriel Dean's arrival in and departure from the town. A wealthy couple arrive new to town without any servants (surely a considerable oddity in itself) and for near two decades give every indication of having no in-laws on either side. When a relative does arrive, out of the blue, he is greeted with anxiety...one might almost say nervous horror. He reacts with hostile conversation – I repeated those phrases about malevolent looming figures and a misbegotten curse. Dear Giffard echoed his earlier notion of some sinister cult devoted to the African totems. I countered this by pointing out that Sir Randolph could have had no conception that those two idols were anything other than stage props – he would certainly have no reason to assume they were anything to do with his long lost relations. No, my theory was that the malevolences to which he referred were none other than Gabriel and Magnolia themselves, and the misbegotten curse a scathingly unkind reference to that poor child Betsy.

Blushing a trifle, I recalled my mirthful impression of poor Magnolia at our first encounter and paused a while to see if they followed my allusions. Jake, who had grown up in the Glaswegian slums and no doubt seen a thing or two, furrowed his brow and fudged for delicate words. My poor dear mother would have been mortified to think that such a notion could ever have formed in my mind, but as tactfully as possible I outlined the possible reason why Magnolia and Gabriel might bear such a tragic resemblance to each other (and why *'Tis Pity* might have touched upon a raw nerve), and why they might chose to flee to a town where they were unknown and seemingly sever all contact with their relatives. My account seemed to sober even

Lily up, who looked as if she might be violently ill at the prospect of where the warty hands that had caressed her flesh might have been previously. Brooks bore an expression of utter disdain, looking far more the schoolmaster he was at heart than the stage manager he had become.

Ever practical, Giffard then asked if Sir Randolph had slaughtered his great-nephew in order to prevent a family scandal coming to light. Admittedly I had considered this, but not only did the man's general frailty count against such likelihood but also the issue of the weapon. Whatever device had been rammed into Gabriel's throat through one of the gaps in the Woman Saturday carving it was not one that had either been found at the scene or whose absence from the house had been marked. Then it was a weapon that the killer had brought with him, and try as I might I could think of no contraption which either Sir Randolph or one of the performers (and here Giffard groaned aloud) might innocently bring with them that could fit the bill as a spontaneously seized dealer of death. Therefore this suggested, surely, that the sharpened shaft was something brought for the express purpose of killing Dean when the opportunity presented itself. All agreed to this. All also agreed that nobody had been seen parading about with a viciously pointed stick, which suggested again that the item had been concealed in some manner.

Picking up the homemade spear that I had brought with me, I unscrewed the tin spearhead, revealing nothing more than the blunt end of a pitchfork handle. Disappointed groans ensued, till I pointed out that it would be an easy thing to sharpen one of these staves – which matched the diameter of the wound – and replace the imitation spearhead until such time as it was needed. The actual murder weapon had been destroyed, and this unstained handle created in replacement of the bloodstained prop. All the props that had been taken to the garden party had been handled by greasepaint-bedecked theatricals, and all the others on the spear rack bore the signs of frequent and grubby handling. This one alone was of clean wood.

Who better to turn a harmless stage toy into a lethal weapon than the invisible keeper of the props store? Giffard recalled seeing just such a broken stick on the day we had sat in the storeroom-cum-bedroom discussing events.

I elaborated further to this small audience how I had discussed my theory of acting with Jake – that one should draw from reality in bringing characters to life. The darling boy had clearly heeded my ideas, fresh though I was to the profession. I explained how I recognised that look of futile outrage on Oroonoko's face from the same place where Jake had borrowed it. It was on the face of Brooks that day when the bloated slumlord had smashed his nose in retaliation for laughing at his split breeches. It dawned on me then that the stage manager's humiliation had only been further added to when the spiteful Dean had later evicted him from his humble home, forcing him to sleep at the theatre.

Brooks broke down quickly enough and admitted the deed. Giffard and the theatre proprietor decided between them that it would be punishment enough to subvert a little of the money from the dead man's theatrical funding to send Brooks on a one-way trip to the colonies. I was about to object to this, when Giffard explained about the unfortunate maid, recently pulled from her watery grave, and whom the authorities were content to lay the blame for Dean's demise upon. When our erstwhile angel had already caused so much misery in his life, what was to be gained from ruining yet another life? I could but agree.

How Brooks fared I cannot say, for the rave reviews that my debut earned kept my mind fully occupied, restoring warmth to my lovelorn heart. Matters of murder were soon overtaken by the call of Thespis.

As the dear Bard said, the play's the thing!

Seventh Story Notes

David Garrick was a real person, perhaps *the* major actor of his day who transformed the theatrical world by introducing a whole new style of realistic acting to counter the mannered style of Regency theatre. Though Hereford born he made his debut as a professional actor at the Tankard Street Theatre in Ipswich in the summer of 1741. This theatre, Ipswich's first known such establishment, had only opened in 1736 – a few years after the first local newspaper was printed. His first theatrical experience was playing the slave Aboan with Henry Giffard's troupe in *Oroonoko*, or *The Royal Slave*, a potboiler by Thomas Southerne. He had already written a play which Giffard's troupe had staged. He used the stage name *Lyddal* for the reason given in the story, very shortly after using his real name when he achieved enough success not to embarrass his vintner family. The rest of the characters in the story are fictional.

Molly houses were a common sight in many larger towns and cities, largely tolerated though sporadically cracked down on when the political wind blew in the wrong direction. Homosexuality was still very much illegal in those days, and some sex acts were punishable by death up until 1863.

Some three decades after the events of this tale Garrick himself was to be vilified for an alleged (though rather unlikely) relationship with the Irish playwright Isaac Bickerstaffe. The later was obliged to flee the country after a scandal with a guardsman, and died in poverty and obscurity. Ipswich may well have had one or more molly houses, being a thriving port, though I have found no definitive evidence for one.

Ipswich expanded over the 18th century, though remaining an essentially rural area it began to develop the sorts of squalid and unsanitary living conditions endemic to much larger urban areas.

This century also produced a number of colourful and notable characters, such as Margaret Catchpole who was eventually deported to Australia, where she became one of its leading citizens.

Chapter Eight

A Doctor Calls

Old Winter had just finished hanging a sprig of fresh holly from the rafter when a sharp rap at the door startled him and nearly resulted in him falling off the chair. Muttering and tut-tutting he clambered down and opened the door to admit a bustling, rather overdressed woman desperately trying to look fifteen years younger than nature intended.

"Please, Doctor, you must help me!" she declared before bursting into tears. It was not an uncommon occurrence for Old Winter's kitchen to be occupied by weeping women, and occasionally by weeping men. She divested herself of her heavy cloak, brushing the snow off, and collapsed into the chair on which he had just been standing. She deposited an aromatic and still-warm apple pie on the battered table. It took him some moments to place the name of the woman, she not being one of his regular customers.

"Ah, Mrs Shaw – would you be requiring a salve for that bruise?"

Her hand flew unconsciously to the week-old blemish on her left cheek that was still visible beneath the pancake of cosmetics. "No! I, no, I fell over and bumped against the table." The cunning man had lost track of the number of women, and occasionally men, who had such constant accidents round the house. "My health is good, unless you consider a broken heart to be an illness."

"Oh is it a love philtre that you require? I'm not sure that even my magic is sufficient to stop Harold straying. Very kind of you, ma'am." He transferred the pie to a pantry shelf. "I shall return the dish to you in due course."

"Harry hasn't run off, I tell you! He hasn't!" she shrieked

vehemently, before sinking wearily into a chair which creaked alarmingly. "Harry has been gone nearly a week now. Whatever horrible gossip you might have heard about him just isn't…isn't…oh what's the use? Look, Doctor Winter, I know my Harry puts it around something rotten, but you've got to understand that he never goes off with any of them. In fact he's never even stayed out overnight with one of those trollops; he always comes back by the early hours. Except this time – this time he hasn't come back at all. Something horrible has happened to him, I know it has! You can read the future, Doctor, look into the crystal ball or whatever it is you do and tell me where he is."

Old Winter placed a cup of weak tea in front of his unexpected visitor and poured himself a saucer. He laid out some lardy cake, moving with deliberate slowness to allow time to think on the situation and what he knew of the Shaws. Harry was a senior keeper at the Priory Asylum, though he made far more money on the side from his extra-curricular activities. In fact everyone knew, the law included – though it could find no evidence to stick or witnesses willing or capable of speaking, that Harry Shaw ran extortion rackets, was part of the Hadleigh Gang's smuggling racket, and was a general thug-for-hire to anyone who could afford him. His brutishness was widely known to extend to his own family, who were oft seen bearing the badges of the latest drunken rage.

"I haven't got a crystal ball, Mrs Shaw, but I can use ceroscopy if you wish, or we can check the tea leaves after you've finished your cup. First off though, tell me about when you last saw your husband."

"It was Saturday, Doctor, we just finished lunch and he said he was going out on business and wouldn't be back until late. He told me not to stay up for him."

"Is that normal? Saburac tells me you are holding back."

"Oh!" Elsie Shaw recognised the name of the old wizard's familiar spirit, well known to just about everyone in the poorer reaches of Ipswich. "He was acting strangely. I don't know how to put this but, he was too nice, too pleasant. Normally he's as bad-tempered and taciturn as a badger, but for Saturday lunch he was nice as pie. We talked and chatted, and he said he had a special surprise for me that he would be fetching after seeing to his business. He even went off whistling, which I've not heard him do before."

"Where was this meeting, and who with?"

"He didn't say, but then he never did. Always said that what I didn't know I couldn't be made to tell. I'm not even sure what direction he went off in, because I was washing the plates up. I've asked everyone I could think of, but none of them know either. Or they aren't saying. Which is why I'm here asking you."

"Port of last call, eh? Well, it always is with me. Tell me who you've asked, so I don't go and trouble them a second time."

"Neither of my sons has seen him since that lunch, nor has Harry's mother. He hasn't turned up for work at the asylum or sent any message to them. I had to make up a story for the doctor what runs the place, just to try and keep the job open. Told them his brother's been taken grievous ill – just as well none of them know his brother's been dead twenty years or more. Thankfully Harry left just enough money in the house to keep things ticking over, but that ain't going to last long. I spoke to Ernie, one of his friends at the asylum. He'll be livid if he finds out, he doesn't like me talking to Ernie or any of them." Old Winter well knew why. That snivelling rat Ernie Timpson was well known locally as Harry Shaw's right-hand man when it came to thieving, smuggling and extortion. "I even went and spoke to my Bobby, but he hasn't seen him either."

"That would be Bobby...Carter?" It took a few moments for the cunning man to recollect his guest's maiden name and place her brother, a painfully shy man with a crippled leg who tended the gardens at the asylum on Castle Hill. "I heard from Mrs Scroggins, who helps clean the wards up there, that Bobby has suffered some sort of injury."

"That wasn't my Harry! No, they've just started to make up their differences and talk again, Bobby was even going to be coming to dinner last Sunday, if he hadn't been set upon by one of those lunatics at the asylum on Saturday afternoon. Swung for him with a shovel and broke his arm and cracked a couple of ribs. Poor mite's laid up in their hospital wing. Free treatment of course, but then as it was one of their crazies that done it they can hardly do otherwise, can they? I'm up to take some fruit to him later today, though heaven knows how I'm going to find the time what with sorting the boys out, making their dinner and getting Grandma over to the church."

"If you like, ma'am, I could take those pears over to the asylum for you, have a word with Bobby whilst I'm there. I'm right in thinking that Ernie Timpson sometimes drinks at the Archangel near there? Hmm, well it's always best to kill two birds with one stone."

"You'll work your magic for me then, Doctor?" she looked at him with an almost childlike earnestness.

"I shall certainly look into the problem, Mrs Shaw, and apply my powers if more ordinary methods fail to turn up Mr Shaw. However, I must ask you one thing first – are you absolutely certain that you want Harry found?"

The raucous cawing of the ill-omened bird drew the elderly magician's attention. Old Winter looked at the scarecrow with utter disgust. Not only was it not one of his own creations, but it was a perversely-shaped and poorly executed effort with a snow-covered battered broad-brimmed hat jammed onto an ugly sacking head. An ill-proportioned, lumpy mawkin with peculiarly long arms better suited to a fairground freak show than a vegetable patch. The crow and, by the look of the encrusted stains on the unusual, but rather ratty old smock, a dozen of its kin had expressed their contempt for the straw effigy that clearly failed to do its job. Though, oddly, Old Winter found the empty eyes and raking stick fingers strangely disturbing.

The garden it loomed over was rather better maintained, though still not quite to the cunning man's own standard. The sprouts and cabbages looked forlorn in the frozen soil, and well overdue harvesting. The look of disdain was apparent to the day keeper, who felt unaccountably back-footed by this peculiar, scrawny old man with gimlet eyes staring out at him from behind round-rimmed glasses perched on a Roman nose.

"That old scarecrow was made by the inmates on the superintendent's orders. It's good for the mad ones to have something useful to do with their hands like, that's what he says anyway. Some of them like to help out doing the gardening too, though being high-born gentlemen they don't really know bugger all about it. Just do as Mr Carter says, at least most of the time anyway. These last few days with him laid up in the hospital wing they've just been doing whatever comes into their heads…and there ain't no accounting for that. So, Mr Winter, do you want to take the job on for a week, maybe two at the most?"

"Yes, I think I can make something of this mess, certainly that vegetable plot is in bad need of some care. I'll repair this horrid old mawkin tomorrow; it looks as if it's long past needing it."

"That was only put in a month ago! Still, what you do with the garden is up to you. I see you looking at the scarecrow's smock!" He blushed somewhat. "It is indeed my old tunic. The superintendent makes us wear them, partly to keep us clean – some of the residents are prone to hurl their food, and worse, about. He also says that having uniform helps visitors to distinguish between the staff and the inmates. As you're only likely to be here a short time, the superintendent may not bother ordering one for you. I doubt Carter's one will fit you, he being so much shorter. Does supervising the patients worry you? It puts off most who might otherwise work here."

"Not at all, Mr Fry, I have dealt with many disturbed and

unhappy people during my long life. Not many from this station of society, admittedly, but I doubt the madnesses of the rich are so much different from those of the poor."

"Good afternoon, sir!" the keeper jumped to as a tall frock-coated figure emerged from around a side door of the asylum and strode across the large intervening lawn, his old-fashioned voluminous frockcoat flapping like the wings of some enormous crow. "This here is Mr Bayldon Winter, who has agreed to take on tending the gardens until poor Mr Carter is back on his feet. He has some experience of working with the sick-minded."

"Good afternoon to you, Mr Winter, I am Dr Michaelmas the superintendent of this establishment." The large man reached out an enormous paw and shook the new gardener's hand. He had dark curling hair and piercing eyes set in a heavy countenance. "Have we met before? You seem familiar to me,"

"Briefly, several years ago now. I helped to bring a man in to your asylum after he had escaped and become confused. His name was...oh, now what was it? Quite affrighted by the thought of vampires he was. Richmond, that was his name, Sir Cardew Richmond."

"Ah, dear old Cardew. He always was prone to wander off during his forgetful periods. Sad to say he died two years ago, from a seizure. Then you are familiar with the kind of gentlemen we get here, good, good!"

He made to amble off, but Old Winter stalled him with a question.

"Before I take up my duties here, Dr Michaelmas, I should like to know precisely what happened to Carter – was he attacked by one of your inmates?"

"Well, indeed I can understand your concern to know such a thing." He dusted the snow off the rather rustic wooden bench and perched awkwardly on the edge, causing the seat to groan alarmingly. "Fry here can take you to see him so you can reassure yourself that his injuries are not deadly ones. He has a broken arm and two cracked ribs, which I tended to myself. He was set upon Saturday afternoon past by young Mr Burke, one of our regular residents. He has spent several stays with us here during his deranged episodes, though he has never shown any potential for violence before – please be assured that we do not knowingly expose our gardeners to danger! Mr Burke is prone to some rather curious fancies. This last time his family brought him in for a rest cure after he vandalised a statue at the Corn Exchange. He believed the figure was actually alive and had endeavoured to attack him. The town burghers are far from amused I can tell you, and were it not for the wealth of his family buying a new statue then he would be labouring in prison as we speak. Very sad case. Oh! Pardon me, Mr Summer…Winter, rather, but I have terrible headache again. I do not know what it is about this place, but I seem to suffer nothing but headaches whilst at work!"

The great bear of a physician rubbed his aching temples wearily, and wandered off into the gardens. Taking this as a seal of approval, the portly day keeper escorted his newest recruit to the hospital ward.

Old Winter stared down at the gaunt, pale man sleeping in the hospital bed and wondered if he really needed to wake him. There were two other patients on the ward, one with a heavily bandaged head and the other sporadically hacking up his lungs and spitting phlegm into a basin.

"Give 'im a shake, that'll wake 'im up!" The grey-haired magician was startled by the sudden appearance at his elbow of the rat-faced orderly who had, moments before, been sweeping the floor in the far corner.

"Ernie Timpson! You gave me a start."

"Do I know you, mister?" A furtive, mistrustful expression spread across the sharp features. Winter noticed the knuckles whitening on the broom.

"Your widowed sister has visited me on a number of occasions for physic and consultations about the future. I have seen you in passing, though you never stopped and spoke – you still live with her, I take it?"

The disconcerted little man nodded, and relaxed his grip on the broom. "You're the mawkin-maker. Fancy seeing you in a place like this – don't tell me this wet weekend is some relation of yours? I'll wake 'im up for yer, if yer like."

"No, I'll wait a little longer. He clearly needs his rest, and no, he is not a relation of mine. Who was it that attacked him?"

"That nutter Burke – Burke by name and berk by nature!" He sniggered at his own dazzling wit, as he confirmed the superintendent's account. "He was meant to be digging up potatoes, or whatever vegetables they need for the kitchen. Billy-boy here can't manage it himself, being a cripple. Though he still takes a wage for being head gardener, which is a bleeding cheek if you ask me."

"Of course," Old Winter murmured, his attention drawn to the patient's scarred foot that stuck out from under the bed clothes. It was the result of being trapped in a house fire in childhood, which had consumed the neighbouring house – and, indeed, the neighbours along with it. Winter himself had provided treatments and saved the child from succumbing to infectious miasmas. "Dr Edwards must be an unusual man to employ a gardener who cannot use a shovel."

"You're telling me! Sucker for a sob story, he is, and Big Harry knows how to spin them. That's the way with a lot of these educated sorts, haven't the sense to leave someone in the gutter where they belong. Part of Billy-boy's duties is to teach the crazies how to do a bit of gardening themselves. Did Fatty Fry tell you that? And you still want the job? Christ, you must be desperate for the money! Never seen what the point of that is, I mean if any of these fine gentlemen get sane again and go home it's not like they'll ever get their hands calloused picking up a trowel or a rake." The temporary gardener asked him what he'd meant about big Harry. "Billy-boy here is Harry's brother-in-law. There was a bit of trouble between them, and let's just say that this pillow-biter came off the worse. Nearly died, in fact, and Harry's missus nagged him so much eventually he got him this job just to shut her up. Billy-boy was ill for so long he lost his last job, you see. Harry can be silver-tongued when the he likes, though you'd never know it to look at the bloody great bruiser."

"Can't say as I've ever seen that side of Mr Shaw. Is he not at work today?" Old Winter conjured the very image of naivety.

"No…no, he's not been in for a few days now. His brother has died, so he's gone off to sort out the family business." The man was clearly anxious, and the older man suspected that he was as close to genuinely caring about another person's wellbeing as he was capable of being.

"Tell me, what was it that triggered Mr Burke off to attack Mr Carter here? Just so that I can avoid sparking him off to attack me."

"He shit in the garden! I bet they didn't tell you about that when you applied for the job. Oh, Burke I mean – not Carter! I can't imagine someone as refined as Billy-boy even having a bum hole let alone using it. No, Burke crapped all over the vegetable patch and the day keeper caught him and Billy-boy trying to clean it up. Burke made up one of his mad stories about what had happened and flew into a rage when Fatty Fry didn't believe him."

"Well, that would explain the peculiar smell in the vegetable patch, if it gets used in that manner. So why did he assault Mr Carter, instead of Mr Fry? Or did he attack both?"

"He blamed Billy-boy for not backing up his account, and laid into him with a shovel or rake or something. I dare say he would have set about Fry too, except Fatty knocked him flat on his arse before he had a chance. He's spent the last week locked up in the padded room screaming and ranting."

"Do the patients frequently use the vegetable garden as a

latrine?" The elderly man's voice rose querulously. Whilst he was curious to learn what had become of Harry Shaw, there were limits.

"No, not often," the scrawny man conceded, clearly getting bored and starting to edge away. "Some occasionally piss themselves, but rarely do they let rip over the cabbages. Don't think Burke has done it before, normally fairly well-behaved. Mind you, I'm indoor staff – don't often get called out to deal with anything in the grounds, unless one of the patients needs hauling away." The door to the ward banged open as another orderly entered, and Winter's unwitting informant wandered off trying to look vaguely industrious with the broom.

"How much of that did you hear?" the cunning man whispered in the apparently sleeping patient's ear, startling him sufficiently that the emaciated man's eyes sprung open with surprise.

"Just the last little bit." He had the decency to blush. "I'm awfully sorry, but why are you here? I don't think the superintendent appwoves of your sort of medicine."

"Oh, I'm not here to treat your injuries!" Bayldon Winter chuckled. "Partly I'm here to cover your gardening duties until such time as you are well enough to return to work, and partly I am here bearing gifts from your sister. So tell me, did Mr Burke batter you just because you wouldn't agree with his story? I shall make a point of avoiding him, if so."

"Well, he is a vewy sensitive man and does get easily upset," he responded with a pronounced speech impediment. "Perhaps Mr Burke is best avoided until he has calmed down. Please thank my sister for the fwuit. It's awfully kind of you to keep my job going in this way."

"Your sister is still bereft of a husband, if you have any advice to offer her…?"

"I haven't seen him since Fwiday last, the day before I was attacked. Even then it was only in passing when he came to wound up the lunatics to take them back indoors when it began to snow a little. The superintendent is quite particular about the gentlemen not catching colds. Illnesses spwead like wildfire thwough the asylum." He distractedly rubbed his high forehead, the hairline already receding despite his youth.

"Did you speak, or are things still…difficult between you?"

"Oh, well only the bwiefest of conversations about the patients. You have obviously heard about the incident, when he nearly dwowned me in the Gipping. Well that was some years ago now, and I admit to having been exceedingly angwy and bitter. However, I have wecently come to wenew my faith in the Lord and, with the help of a vewy dear fwiend, come to embwace forgiveness. My bwother-in-law is not, admittedly, the easiest of people to get along with, but I am doing my best to be a good Chwistian."

Winter thought briefly about enquiring after the dear friend, but decided that information could be more tactfully acquired by another route. He poured the patient a drink, and spent some minutes chatting about the garden and what needed doing. He could but assume that Harry Shaw really must be silver-tongued to have got his in-law a job as a gardener – the man's priorities suggested he knew next to nothing about the craft. Winter nodded vaguely at the direction to focus his efforts on the flower beds on the east side of the asylum, a nonsensical idea that would leave the cabbages and sprouts to rot. Presumably the superintendent was far more interested in just using the gardens as some means of occupying the patients than in it being a productive source of food, healing herbs or even just flowers. Sadly the week or two he was likely to be employed for was not going to be sufficient to turn this sorry state of neglect around.

"I can see that you are tiring, Mr Carter, so I shall leave you to rest. Before I go, though, have you no idea as to where Harry might have gone? Your sister is dreadfully worried, and will soon be very short of money. The pittance you earn here simply won't be enough to help her out."

"Some weeks ago I overheard…" He looked nervously about the ward and spoke in low, confidential tones. "Well, I overheard a conversation between Hawwy and Ernie Timpson whilst they were tending to the patients in the Gween Ward. I was outside the window doing some weeding – not eavesdwopping, you understand, it's just that the wards are so large and echoing that almost all sound carries. Timpson was warning Hawwy about some wival group. I expect you've heard about Hawwy's involvement in the Hadleigh Gang? It's an open secwet wound these parts of Ipswich. The Cleaver Family—"

"The Cleavers? They aren't smugglers, they're burglars and pickpockets – why would they start muscling in on the Hadleigh racket? They don't have the brains to run an operation on that scale."

The little man in the bed shrugged his shoulders, wincing at the pain in his ribs, and indicated that the shenanigans of the criminal underworld were a mystery to him.

The fat ginger tom sat athwart the terrier which in turn snuggled on Old Winter's lap. The rocking chair creaked gently and the wood crackled in the hearth, keeping the January chill at bay. The newly laid southernwood gave off a gently lemony aroma as the rockers crushed it.

"Well, my dears, it seems one of my notions has come to nothing. Whatever happened to Big Harry, he didn't do a bunk after laying into his brother-in-law for a second time. So where is the vicious bugger? Run afoul of the Cleavers maybe…but then why haven't I heard of a fight on the grapevine? Those sorts of incidents go all round town in a matter of hours." He thought for a while about how he could delve into the Cleavers' shady dealings. He had several run-ins with those thieving buggers, and they both feared and resented him. Certainly they wouldn't speak to him willingly, or honestly if they were somehow forced into conversation. "I think a visit to the Shaw house is called for, see if those boys or old Granny knows more than Mrs Shaw realises they do."

He drained his saucer of tea, and gazed gently at the dancing flames and the peculiar patterns they made. He always found it most helpful to watch the fire and the messages it brought from Saburac, his guiding spirit. Tongues of gold, red and blue writhed around the birch and apple logs, lulling Bayldon's eyes to grow heavy and filling his mind with images of a hulking figure; of piercing eyes glowering at him in a manner at once raging and pleading; of something vast, amorphous and ancient, utterly consumed with hatred.

Old Winter pulled himself out of his trance feeling quite nauseous; the cat had disappeared off and the dog sat huddled against the dresser with his hackles up. Whatever else was going on, he felt quite certain that Harry Shaw was no more. The only person who could testify to seeing him after he left home on Saturday gone was a local prostitute who was sure she'd seen Harry ambling towards the Archangel in the early afternoon. Oddly enough she'd sworn he was whistling a jaunty tune as he went. Had he died that afternoon during his supposed business meeting or later? There was also the question of what could have happened to the lumbering oaf's body.

Jake Shaw was a younger edition of his father, in looks at least. He stood six-and-a-half feet tall, with the same hefty shoulders, shovel hands and lantern jaw. Despite being a mere 15 years old he showed every sign of bulking out into the swaggering ogre that had sired him. His left eye was puffy with a yellowing bruise, seemingly the only resemblance he bore to his mother. He held the empty pie dish and looked from it to the elderly visitor, as if he had scant idea what to do with either.

"A saucer of tea would be nice, young man! There's a very sharp wind blowing in from the docks," the querulous gentleman declared.

"Oh, yeah, right. Yeah. You best come in then. Mum ain't back yet."

"Do you know how to boil a kettle?"

"Yeah, I 'spose." He slouched into the kitchen and began awkwardly blundering around, until his visitor wearily intervened and helped rekindle the neglected hearth fire before putting the iron kettle on the iron spit arm.

"Is your grandmother well?"

"Oh, yeah, she's asleep. Nods off a lot these days. If she hears you clattering about, she'll probably come down to see what's going on." Old Winter wasn't entirely sure if this was a warning to avoid rousing the aged and notoriously cantankerous relative, or a wish on the part of the youth to offload his peculiar visitor on someone else as soon as possible.

"I haven't seen her in quite some time. I take it that there's still no word from your father, Jake?" A curious expression fleeted across the young giant's face. "Ah, what a shame…this whole experience must be very distressing for your mother. Hopefully he'll return before the rent is due at the end of the month."

"I bring money in!" Jake suddenly became animated in defence of…quite what, the magician was unsure. "I earn a bit helping out on the market as a porter. Just fetching and carrying heavy loads like, I'm not quick enough with numbers to be selling anything. Not like Toby does. Dad says I'm as thick as shit, but at least I can put my back to hard labour."

"Does Toby also work on the market?"

"On Mr Griddle's grocers stall, though he's off at the moment. Had an accident." A sullen look once again took over the boy's heavyset features. "Dad wants to us to work at the asylum as soon as places become available. Seems to think something should open up soon, and the money's a bit better than on the market."

"Yet you don't fancy working at the asylum alongside your

father and uncle, why is that?" The lad's only response was an inarticulate shrug. Winter let several long minutes creep past in silence as he observed the youth before him. "Mad people can sometimes be quite frightening, can't they? Now, I have my bag of medicaments with me – what sort of accident has befallen Master Toby?"

A look of alarm crossed Jake's face as he attempted to downplay the accident or the necessity of any intervention. Winter, however, was quite used to dealing with boys, having had five of his own, and for all his immense size Jake was little more than a child at heart. Fixing the lad with his sternest stare he sent him off to fetch his older brother from the curtained-off section of the bedroom the two of them shared. If Jake was a replica of his father, then Toby had the bones and features of his mother. The delicately built blond youth limped awkwardly into the kitchen, propped up by his younger brother and showing all the recalcitrance of a schoolchild summonsed before the headmaster. He attempted to brush away all offers of help, and avoid being examined – but the elderly healer was as persistent as his own terrier that waited obediently by the hearth and watched the scene unfold. The skinny boy finally lifted his shirt to reveal a canvas of slowly fading welts in assorted shades of yellow, blue, and purple. Obviously created by a heavy leather belt, Winter also marked a number of encrusted bloody patches from what was certainly the buckle. Like most people the Shaws were wary of washing too often, and had not properly tended the injuries, some of which were now beginning to fester.

"I fell downstairs," Toby whimpered.

"Of course you did, boy," Winter muttered with disgust. "Jake, put some more water in that kettle. I want it warm, but not boiling. Now, Toby, I want you to hold still whilst I put this salve on your back, it will sting but you're clearly used to pain. Good lad, now this will be much easier if you just take the shirt off then I can tend the marks on your arms and chest as well."

"What are you doing here?" The shrill voice cracked like a whip, and the guest turned to see a dishevelled old woman of about seventy standing in much-patched gown several decades old. "Put your shirt on, boy! Your father will leather you a second time when I tell him you've been running off to strangers whining about a few paltry bruises."

"Be quiet you foul harridan!"

The matriarch's mouth spluttered with shock, before clamping shut when the guest raised his gnarled blackthorn walking stick and pointed it ominously at her. Her watery eyes took in the arcane symbols carved into the wood, which most residents of Ipswich knew to be far more dangerous than mere decorations.

"This boy should have been with me a week past for these injuries to be properly tended to," said Winter. "Haven't you or your daughter-in-law the wit to recognise the stench of a festering wound? For your information, woman, Toby did not come to me. I came here, to assist your family in finding where Harry has disappeared off to."

She eventually found her voice. "He hasn't disappeared, he's just off with one of his fancy pieces. If that lazy slut were a better wife to him, he wouldn't need to keep going off with these trollops."

"Keep? He has done this before then?"

"Well, no, not gone off with them as such. But he has plenty of women, most likely he finally just got sick of Elsie and ditched her. Though I would have thought he'd let me know what was going on, if nothing else."

"Any word from the Hadleigh Gang?" He addressed the question to Jake, who looked shifty and eyed his viperous grandmother nervously. "Oh it's no secret your father is in with that lot, boy. If he has run off with some tart, then your mother needs to know and I can stop wasting my time looking for him. If he is holed up in some woman's bedroom, then he'd still be in contact with his fellow smugglers. Knowing your father, he wouldn't be passing up the chance to make drinking money just for the sake of a leg-over. Nor would he hesitate to put a lad your size to good use working for that bunch of roughs. So I'll ask you again, Jake, has he been in contact with the gang?"

"No, mister." The boy shook his head, and looked more bewildered than usual. "They ain't heard nothing from him either. Geor—I mean, one of the blokes as runs the gang is right concerned. As you say, Mister Winter, my dad hasn't missed a chance to do a job with them in all the years I've been alive and probably longer."

"Shut your mouth, boy!" the old woman hissed between her few remaining teeth.

"Gran, what's the point in covering things up? Old Mister Winter here is trying to help. I don't know what happened to Dad, but you know full well he hasn't just done a bunk with some woman. If he had, he'd have turned up for that consignment that went down two nights ago. I know the boss is worried, 'cause he gave me more than the usual share for helping out. If we didn't have that money coming in then it wouldn't be much longer before the bailiffs would be turfing us all out into the streets."

"Jake's right," Toby pulled his shirt back on as the old man finished applying the last of the unguent to his bruises, "Mum's spoken to everyone she can think of, and nobody's heard a thing about him. Whatever's happened to Dad, we need to find out pretty bloody quick and then start making some plans. If he isn't coming back, for whatever reason, we've got to work out how to keep this roof over our heads and some food on the table. You can at me poison all you like, Gran, but you don't want to end up in the workhouse any more than I do. I'm going to speak to Mr Bridger about learning bookkeeping. He's always said he'd take me on at the drop of a hat, being as I'm so quick with numbers."

"Your father—"

"Ain't here, Gran, and that's that. Whatever he does or doesn't want, we've got bills piling up and only enough money left to see us through a couple more weeks. All that cash he made from smuggling and one thing and another, well he pissed that all away down the pubs."

The old woman lashed out a bony hand and smacked her grandson in the mouth. He wiped the blood away and made to rise, though the pain from his bruises dropped him again.

"That will be enough of that!" Winter imposed himself between the two, roughly barging the elder Mrs Shaw backwards. "Toby is coming home with me for a few days. I have spoken, Mrs Shaw, and if you dare interfere I will put the eye on you! Now this boy has serious injuries, if he is to get better and bring some much-needed money back into this house then he needs to come with me so I can tend to him properly. Jake, you can help walk your brother to my house and then come back here to support your poor mother."

The journey through town was slow, but presented a good opportunity to talk to the lads without any real concern of being overheard. Neither of the young men appeared to have heard any specific rumour about gang warfare, but both clearly assumed that their father was dead and at the hands of someone connected to his criminal activities. Toby thought it was probably someone from the Revenue who'd perhaps despaired of ever convicting him in open court and so just shot him, whilst Jake thought that it was more likely to be some rival from within the Hadleigh Gang who wanted to get his hands on Harry's turf.

Both boys were adamant that their father had left the house in good spirits Sunday morning, unaccountably so for normally he was hung-over and brutish. Instead of his usual Saturday night drinking binge down the Archangel, Harry had stayed at home and been as close to pleasant as either of them could remember him being in years. He'd even promised to treat them all, Uncle Robert included, to a meal at one of the slightly nicer pubs on

Sunday. Of course that hadn't happened, between him disappearing and their uncle being battered by the mental patient that very afternoon. One of the cleaners had brought word round of the incident after she'd finished duty that evening, and Jake had trundled dutifully up with his mother to visit the injured man. There had been neither sight nor word of Big Harry either on the way there or back. They had, the boy informed him with some degree of youthful disdain for the notion that anyone over the age of thirty might have a sex life, stopped off on the way back to inform Uncle Robert's 'lady friend' of his plight. Old Winter bottled up the identity of the lady for future reference. It was unlikely that she might have an involvement, particularly given that Robert Carter really had been assaulted by a lunatic and not his brother-in-law as Winter had first suspected, but one never knew where a trail might lead.

Despite his evident discomfort, Toby stared around the cottage wide-eyed and excitable like a child on holiday. Old Winter fielded what felt like a hundred different questions about every bunch of herbs, almanac, jar of curiously coloured lotion, talisman and amulet in the place. In many respects the boy made Old Winter think of what his youngest son might have become had he survived.

"You do not seem very grieved by the thought that your father might be dead," the aged cunning man observed once Jake had lumbered off back home with half a dozen eggs to help feed his family.

"I'm not," Toby replied with the bald simplicity of youth, "life will be a damned sight better for everyone if he is gone. Money will be in short supply for a while, but we'll muddle through and things will get easier once I've apprenticed as a bookkeeper. Gran will be dead by then too, so there'll be one less mouth to feed."

"That's certainly…possible," the old man responded, feeling rather disconcerted by this blasé approach.

The potting shed was a vision of almost obsessive orderliness, with numerous seeds and bulbs arrayed in jars shelved by size. A host of gardening implements, spotlessly clean, dangled from racks. It took some moments for Old Winter's eyes to adjust to the gloomy interior, whereupon he noticed first the large mound of straw dumped in the centre of the shed and the young man nested up asleep in the middle of it. As the gaunt man stood perplexed by the discovery, the sleeper awoke and stared at him for some moments before speaking in a cultured, but somehow strangely childlike voice.

"You won't tell him I'm here, will you?"

"Tell who?"

"Him, the Guardian! He can't see me from here. Please don't tell him where I am. Where's Mr Carter? You're not Mr Carter."

"No, I'm Mr Winter. I have been hired to take care of the gardens until Mr Carter gets out of the hospital. Who are you?"

"Oliver Burke, sir. I didn't mean to hurt Mr Carter, I just got angry when he wouldn't tell the truth about the monster."

"I think Mr Carter knows that you were…rather upset last Saturday. What Guardian is that, Mr Burke?" Winter cast a wary eye about to see if there were any potential weapons within the young man's reach.

"The one that watches me, watches everyone. I missed my dinner on Saturday! Mr Fry hit me and dragged me into the safe room. Five days they kept there, five days and I missed my dinner on Saturday. That's not right, making a chap go without his dinner. My father shall be most displeased when he hears. Dr Michaelmas wouldn't even let me make a snowman with all the others. I saw it walking, but nobody would believe me." The man's mind seemed to dart between a dozen different topics like a bee between flowers.

"You saw a snowman walking?"

"No, of course not! There weren't any snowmen till Sunday, no I saw the Guardian walking and then it did a very bad thing in the vegetable garden but nobody would believe me. Even Mr Carter and he knows, because he has seen the Guardian walking too. He just doesn't want to admit it in case they lock him up in here too. This is a horrible place, sir, I begged Father not to send me back here but he never listens. He doesn't understand about the things that live in the corners, the wraiths. You understand about them, don't you? I can tell you don't like it here either." Old Winter could scarcely disagree with this, and whilst he had yet to see any wraiths loitering in corners he had certainly felt a looming sense of hostility.

"Tell me, young man, have you seen anything of Mr Shaw, one of the keepers?"

"No, he isn't here anymore thankfully! He's a horrible man, always punching and slapping us. He twisted my arm quite badly once and Dr Michaelmas had to put a sling on it. He tried to drown Mr Carter once, so I heard. Everyone here hates him, even Dr Michaelmas is scared of him. Maybe the Guardian drove him away?" The old man lowered himself to kneel on the floor besides the troubled young man, and proffered half a sandwich whilst enquiring further about the source of his knowledge. "Oh I heard them arguing in the doctor's office before Christmas, when I was helping to weed the garden. That ugly brute threatened the doctor and said he knew things about him. He always liked to know things about people, bad things especially. Once he gave me sweets and asked me all sorts of questions about father, but I wouldn't say anything. Even when he started hitting me I refused to answer his questions."

"That was very brave of you, Mr Burke. Did he bully other patients?"

"Yes, lots – and quite a few of them are not as brave as me, they told him bad things about their families. He liked to know all sorts of things, but I know something he didn't! He thought that nasty Timpson man was his special friend, but I know better. Mr Timpson has another friend that he doesn't want Mr Shaw to know about!"

"What makes you think that?"

"The ugly man only comes to see Timpson on Saturdays, and Shaw doesn't work Saturdays. And they only ever meet in the vegetable garden!" He added this latter detail with a note of triumph, as if it proved the point beyond contestation. When Winter looked at him blankly, he swallowed the sandwich hungrily and continued, "Sitting out on the stone bench in the vegetable garden is about the only place round here where people can talk without being overheard. It's far enough from the main building that you can easily see anyone approaching before they are close enough to eavesdrop. It's where families go when they are visiting and want to talk to a patient in private."

"This ugly man…?"

"I don't know who he is, but he doesn't work here and hasn't got any relatives here either. He only comes to talk to Mr Timpson, and then goes away straight after. In fact I've seen him go straight from the main gate to the vegetable garden on two occasions. He has a big fat belly and a scruffy black beard. His hat has—"

"A white stain on the front peak," Old Winter finished, eliciting a surprised look from the patient. "That sounds an awful lot like Joshua Cleaver. Would you be good enough to take those two baskets up to the vegetable plot, we have to collect some sprouts for the kitchen."

Mr Burke took off like a rabbit pursued by a greyhound, fleeing in the opposite direction to the vegetable patch and disappearing from sight. Old Winter sat perplexed for some time, before lifting his creaking bones into a standing position. He took a broom and set about sweeping up the straw 'nest' and depositing it into one of the empty vegetable stores. As he was picking the straw up a particularly strong odour assailed his nostrils, emanating from a corner. Poking around he found a rolled-up strip of cloth that seemed to have fallen, or been shoved, behind a box of broken pottery shards. It appeared to be half an old neckerchief, but soaked with the pungent aroma of dwale. Winter rather gingerly placed it on the work bench, and scanned his eyes across the numerous jars and bottles. Just to be sure, he opened each in turn and sniffed, but his nose confirmed what his eyes had seen: not one of these containers held the incriminating preparation.

Miss Violet Stanford peered across the dainty tea things at her unexpected and largely unwanted visitor. The cunning man smiled tightly at her and took note of the cracked-and-glued saucer, chipped cups, and not-so invisible repairs to her dress. Miss Stanford's possessions had, it was fair to say, seen better times. As, indeed, had Miss Stanford herself, although she still strove to maintain genteel appearances.

"Mr Carter and I, are, well – and I hope you will keep this to yourself for the immediate future – engaged to be married. We had planned to announce this to his family over dinner on Sunday past, but one of those benighted lunatics attacked him the day before. I expect you know that already, Doctor Winter?"

"How long have you and Mr Carter known each other, may I ask?"

"Oh, well," she blushed and tittered in a slightly self-conscious manner, "we knew each other some seven years ago when he worked at the Ipswich School. He was a junior master then, teaching mathematics. He was a scholarship boy there himself, in previous years you know! My papa was also the chaplain there, and taught a little Latin."

"Does your father still preach there?" Old Winter wondered why a clergyman's daughter should be renting a tiny room in one of the poorest parts of Ipswich.

"No, Papa left the school some years ago." Discomfort touched her eyes, and her guest dimly recalled some minor scandal at the school, though the exact details escaped him.

"Things were rather…difficult for a number of years. Finding another living proved exceedingly difficult and we had to move several times. Mama died in the fever that swept town four years ago, then Papa simply lost his spirit and dwindled away. I have no siblings, sir, nor any other relatives. I am required to earn my way employing what little Latin I have in assisting students and even providing some small degree of help to Dr Michaelmas with his medication records and so forth."

"Then presumably you will have met Harry Shaw, in passing at least, at the Priory Asylum."

"Yes, I had encountered him in the corridors, and on a couple of occasions when Mr Carter and I were taking the air along the banks of the Gipping and elsewhere. He, well, without wishing to be indelicate, he made some frankly improper, not to say quite obscene, remarks. Even when he knew that his brother-in-law and I had an understanding, well he continued to be very inappropriate." Her fingers unconsciously strayed to some faded finger marks on her left wrist.

Winter placed the barely coloured cup of tea down, wishing he were not is such suffocatingly genteel company. There was no cake on offer. He looked at the leaves in the bottom of his cup for some time, and wondered how best to approach this rather brittle woman.

"Do you…that is, I've that you, well, that you can read the leaves. Is that so, Doctor Winter?"

"Indeed ma'am, tasseomancy is a particular skill of mine. Would you like me to read the leaves in your cup?" Without waiting for a response, he plucked the bone china from her hand, upended it into the saucer, spun it three times and then turned it upright to look at the patterns formed by the remaining tealeaves. "There is a terrible burden on your shoulders, one not of your making. Life gives you a chance to share this weight with a like soul, one who also has burdens to bear."

"People should not be held accountable for the acts of their relatives. It is most unfair of society to judge in these matters," she commented sadly.

"Indeed so. There is a man around you, a fatherly figure, very kindly towards you, but one who is greatly troubled…I feel there is some menace towards him. That threat is receding now, but it looms over you both."

"Dr Michaelmas – he has been very kind to me. He knew my late father a little, and did his best to help us when things became so very difficult."

"Is he being threatened in any way?"

"Yes, I think he is," she spoke very quietly. "I have often seen him these last few weeks with his head in his hands, asking himself in a despairing tone what he is to do. I fear that the Priory is not making ends meet – several of the artworks in the doctor's study have gone, and I know he has been trying to find cheaper suppliers for the patients' meals. Not a person that is threatening him, but the spectre of poverty – or rather bankruptcy in his case. I shall tell you in confidence, sir, that this is a menace that has loomed over me as well. There have been too many times of recent years when I have known hunger, and cold."

There were other reasons why Michaelmas might have been obliged to sell off his artworks, but Old Winter kept his own counsel. He glanced a final time into the tea bowl. "You will soon be facing a dilemma, Miss Stanford, an important choice that will change your life forever. I feel that compassion and forgiveness should be your watchwords in the months to come."

"Oh they always are!" his hostess replied primly. "I am still very much a regular churchgoer, regardless of what may have happened in the past."

The twins sat either side of a clearly intimidated Toby who was nervously assisting them in stuffing mince into a hollowed-out marrow. The boys had their father's Roman nose and aquiline features, but a burliness that must have skipped several generations for neither their father nor late mother could account for any relative of like size. They glared at Toby with a menace that only the elder Winter could tell was entirely faked.

"Hello, Dad," they chimed in unison.

"There's another marrow over there for tomorrow." Zack nodded towards the vegetable basket in the corner. "We've just been instructing your guest on the various tasks that need doing round the house."

"Do you want to keep these seeds for the garden? Perhaps the lunatics might like to plant some at the asylum." Zander pushed the bowl of marrow detritus towards his sire. "We asked around about Violet, and everyone says she's as sweet and fragrant as her name. Quite boring from what we hear, and very much in love with Robert Carter. The Cleavers are still up to their usual shenanigans, we had to give young Cyrus a bit of a pasting after he tried to pick Zack's pocket. He did tell us, with a bit of persuasion, that Ernie Timpson had asked for a meeting with his Uncle Josh, but he didn't know what it was about."

"Cyrus is the thickest of the bunch, so he probably would be kept in the dark if there was anything going on. He didn't have a clue about the missing man though, in fact didn't even know he was missing – which goes to show the dangers of inbreeding. Speaking of which, did you know Zander has got a new woman?" This elicited a thick ear from his twin, and a retaliatory strike that nearly and deliberately squashed the skinny adolescent trapped between them.

Rolling his eyes, Old Winter quickly snatched any breakables off the kitchen table and moved them to safety. Except he suddenly stopped midway in his rescue mission, pausing with the bowl of scooped-out marrow flesh raised midway to a shelf in the larder. Eventually his youngest surviving sons paused in their play-squabbling long enough to notice the strange tableau.

"Dad? Dad, are you alright?"

"Yes, Zack," he replied after a distracted pause.

"Zander, Zack's the ugly one. I keep telling you. Sure you're alright?"

"Yes, I... yes. Toby, I want you to go and ask your mother and brother to meet me up at the asylum. Within the hour, before we lose the light."

"Yes sir, and what about Gran – shall I bring her too?"

"Oh, her...no." Winter was clearly lost in greater thought, staring at the bowl he was holding. "No, leave her at home. This whole thing will be much easier to resolve without that miserable harpy stirring up even more trouble. Collect Miss Stanford on the way, if you would. Boys, I suspect I will need a little muscle if you would oblige accompanying me."

Dr Michaelmas shivered in the biting wind and eyed the crow perched on the mawkin's shoulder, seemingly indifferent to all the people gathered in the vegetable garden. The doctor kept a massive paw firmly but reassuringly on the narrow shoulder of Mr Burke, who looked as if he might bolt at any moment. Ernie Timpson looked, if anything, even more nervous and kept glancing at the twins who endeavoured to give their most granite-faced glower in response.

Old Winter raised a hand in greeting as the Shaws and Miss Stanford made their way across the lawn, and stood in a huddle behind the doctor.

"Have you found my Harry? Toby said he thought you had something important to tell us." Elsie Shaw pulled her shawl tight against the wind. Her face was a picture of anxiety, eyes darting constantly between Old Winter and Jake.

"Yes, Mrs Shaw, I have found Harry. I am afraid the news is not good though, I have to tell you that your husband is dead."

The widow gave a strangled sob and staggered against her youngest son, who held her upright.

"How he came to die is a matter of some conjecture on my part, and as for what to do about it...well, I may lay that decision at wiser feet than mine."

"Where is he? I want to see him, I want to see my Harry."

"Mrs Shaw, your husband has been dead probably since Sunday last. Without wishing to be graphic, he isn't a pretty sight. Maybe somebody else should take charge of the body?"

"No!" she shrieked, alarming her sons. "He's my husband, I should dress the body. Take me to him, I assume he's round here somewhere or you wouldn't have brought us here. Doctor Michaelmas, make him show me where Harry is!"

"Perhaps Mr Winter is correct. If your husband has been dead for over a week, the sight of it may cause you considerable distress." The look the superintendent received from the Widow Shaw was such that he rapidly back-pedalled. "Perhaps, Mr Winter, you would be kind enough to show us where poor Mr Shaw has been all this time?"

The cunning man nodded and walked a few paces to the where the sprouts and neglected cabbages grew. Mr Burke leapt to his feet, his free hand spasmodically tugging frantically at his ear whilst Dr Michaelmas kept his own paw clamped firmly around his patient's other wrist. Old Winter reached up and removed the broad-brimmed hat from the scarecrow, and then the ugly sacking face with its maniacal stitched-in smile. Elsie Shaw let out a low moan as the eyeless, green-hued face of her husband emerged into the weak January sun.

"Take him down from that frame, for the love of God cut him down!" Dr Michaelmas lost his grip on Mr Burke, whose attempted flight was cut short when he ran into the waiting arms of Zack Winter.

"I am afraid that will not be possible just yet, Doctor, not without a little digging anyway." He illustrated his point by reaching down and tugging up the baggy old trousers to reveal that the legs were actually buried up to the calves.

"But why? I don't understand why anyone would do such a horrible thing to a dead man," Miss Stanford exclaimed, as she placed a sisterly arm around Mrs Shaw's shoulders.

"They didn't, Miss, Harry quite willingly did this to himself."

"What on earth do you mean, sir?" Toby asked incredulously.

"Mr Burke, yesterday you told me you had seen the Guardian walking, but that nobody would believe you. Did you mean that you had seen this scarecrow walking about?" White as the snow that still covered much of the ground, the unfortunate lunatic nodded mutely. He seemed unable to tear his eyes away from the corpse, and made no effort to escape the bear hug that Zack Winter had him in. "That's what I thought. What young Mr Burke here saw was Harry Shaw disguised as the scarecrow, walking towards the vegetable patch. I suspect he had changed into the costume, if we can call it that, in the potting shed over there. I found this poor lad asleep in a mound of straw yesterday, though it only occurred to me today that the straw was the innards of the original mawkin. A more careful man might have stripped the effigy and left it intact within its string bindings, but Harry had very little regard for anyone or anything. He just threw the straw any old how, probably thinking his accomplice would clear it all up later when the disguise was no longer needed."

"Accomplice?" Ernie Timpson's high-pitched voice went up an octave higher.

"Well, he didn't tie his own wrists to the wooden frame, nor bury his own feet in the pit at the base of the frame. I imagine they dug that so that the scarecrow would not look freakishly tall and draw undue attention. Half the point of a disguise, after all is that nobody pays you any attention. Again it was Mr Burke here who pointed the way. The large echoing rooms of the asylum are such that conversations are easily overheard. You'll testify to that, I assume, Mr Timpson?"

"Me? I've got nothing to do with any of this."

"Families wanting privacy on their visits to patients often come out here and sit on the very bench where you now sit, Dr Michaelmas, is that no so?" The superintendent nodded bemusedly. "Likewise, when you have your secretive little meetings with Joshua Cleaver, you always meet him out here, don't you, Ernie? Always on a Saturday too."

"When Harry's off shift, and wouldn't notice. What the hell have you been up to, Ernie Timpson?" The quietly sobbing widow suddenly found her voice and her anger. "I'll put word round about you, Ernie, and you'll be planted in a hole all of your own."

Ernie blanched and buckled at the knees. Had Zander not caught him he would undoubtedly have collapsed, "You can't do that!" he shrilled in a pitch that would not have been out of place emanating from an excitable schoolgirl. "I didn't hurt him, none of you can prove anything!"

"I'll do it. In fact I won't even need to put the word out, I'll do you myself," Jake snarled and moved towards the cringing man.

"Jake Shaw!" Old Winter's voice halted the youth's progress. "You and your brother can take those trowels and unearth your father's feet. Now! And be careful about what you're doing. Make sure you don't touch those lengths of cloth wrapped around Harry's legs."

"So, Mr Shaw here disguised himself as a scarecrow in order to, what, spy on a meeting between Mr Timpson and this other chap, whatever you said his name was?"

"Yes, Superintendent, both Mr Shaw and Ernie have what we might call 'extracurricular business interests' separate from their employment with you. Harry quite rightly suspected Ernie of underhand dealings with a criminal rival. Oh, there's very little point in protesting, Timpson, you were as sick of being bullied by Harry as everyone else was. You tried to rope in the Cleavers to help you get rid of Harry, no doubt push your position in the gang up a notch or two. I don't know what you offered the Cleavers in exchange, but I'm sure their palms would have been well-greased. Except Harry, for all his brutishness, wasn't as thick as he looked. He'd twigged that something was going on, and being a man who loved to be in the know – particularly if he could use that knowledge to terrorise or bleed others dry – he devised a plan to overhear your conversation."

"We've finished, sir," Toby indicated the muddy feet, wrapped up in heavy bandages. Zack transferred his captive to the firm grip of Dr Michaelmas, and went to help Jake manoeuvre the hefty corpse off the wooden stand. The wooden pole creaked and then cracked with an alarmingly loud sound. Zander instinctively let go of Timpson in order to help catch the body as it tipped forward. Whilst everyone's attention was fixed on getting Harry Shaw lowered to the ground with some degree of dignity, Ernie Timpson legged it towards the main gate at top speed.

"Stop!" Zack roared and made to go after the fugitive, before his father restrained him.

"He won't get far in this town." Old Winter exchanged a look with young Jake, who merely nodded.

"Why did Ernie just leave my father propped up here?" Toby asked, staring down at the man who had made his seventeen years of life a constant misery. "He could have buried the body somewhere on the grounds and probably nobody would have found it."

"Easier said than done, given the size of your father. However, Ernie had nothing to do with your father's demise. He was the one being spied on, remember, not the one who helped Harry carry out the plan. Harry was left where he was because his accomplice was unable to do anything about him. The plan went wrong, though whether it was murder or mere incompetence I don't entirely know. I'm sorry, Mrs Shaw, really I am."

"What do you mean?" whispered the unfortunate woman, who now looked every year of her age and then some.

"When I realised where Harry was, I checked on him just before you all arrived here. The strips of cloth wrapped around his feet, and this neckerchief that kept the mask firmly in place, have been soaked in an ointment of dwale; what the Italians call belladonna. In a large enough dose it has a number of effects on both the mind and body. Maybe the intention was to play a nasty prank on Harry and give him horrible hallucinations and nightmares, or maybe the ointment was made deliberately strong enough to cause paralysis. A big dose of belladonna is fatal, but looking at him I don't think he died of poisoning. Maybe there was no intention to kill him, just to make him very ill and get revenge, but then again maybe our erstwhile poisoner just wasn't very good at it. With a man of Harry's size it wouldn't be easy to work out what a fatal dose was."

"What are you saying, Doctor Winter?"

"You told me that Harry and your brother were beginning to patch up their differences. I wonder if at least part of that was the realisation by your late husband that his brother-in-law was quite a creative man, a source of potentially useful ideas. I suspect that it was your Bobby who suggested the idea of the scarecrow disguise, though with the ulterior motive of using the opportunity to his own ends. He helped Harry get changed in the potting shed, maybe suggested wrapping his feet and calves up in this material just to keep them warm; helped tie him to the stand, ready to spy on Timpson and Cleaver. Let's be charitable and assume the belladonna was intended to just give Harry frightening hallucinations, vengeance for the assault all those years ago. Maybe some family justice too, for all the times he'd seen his sister and nephews covered in bruises and living in fear. Let's assume that he had every intention of coming back a couple of hours later to get Harry out of the hole he'd put himself in. Except three things skewed the plan: first, he had misjudged the dose and given his brother-in-law enough dwale to paralyse him rather than just cause fearful visions; second, poor Mr Burke there attacked Bobby and knocked him senseless and stuck in the hospital ward even now; and finally, it began to snow heavily that evening and continued to do so for most of last week."

"Oh, Robert..." Miss Stanford murmured.

"I don't know quite how long Harry lasted, but he froze to death, too drugged to escape from the position he was trapped in. Do you concur with the cause of death, Dr Michaelmas?"

The medical man examined the corpse and indicated agreement.

"What will happen to Uncle Robert, will they hang him?" Toby asked quietly, drawing a chorus of despairing wails from the two women.

"Tell me, Dr Michaelmas, as an educated man would you say this is a case of murder or a prank gone horribly wrong?"

"I, well, I..." The great bear of a man was clearly uncomfortable to be placed in the position of judge. "Let me see...if Mr Carter had been intending to murder Mr Shaw, then he would have had a plan to dispose of the corpse afterwards. It is difficult to see how so slightly built a man with a severe limp could drag such a heavy body away and bury it in a shallow grave. Mr Carter is a devout Christian, a good man. Therefore one can but assume that his use of the dwale ointment was just intended to teach a thuggish criminal a rather stern lesson, rather than to take a life. A misguided, perhaps spiteful act at worst, but not murder, no. We will tell the authorities that Mr Shaw froze to death after being caught outside. Would it cause you any further distress, Mrs Shaw, were we to allow the constable to assume that you late husband had fallen asleep outdoors after drinking too much? Good Lord, but my head is pounding! If I might leave you gentlemen to bring the body indoors, but please try to avoid letting the patients see. Many find death quite distressful."

Old Winter watched his sons sort out a makeshift stretcher and carry Harry Shaw away, followed by his widow and Jake in cortege. Miss Stanford stood and stared at him, pale-faced with her mouth opening and shutting like a guppy. After some moments of failing to find the words she turned and walked away towards the gravel path. She paused there, seemingly split between entering the asylum and going home. The cunning man did not observe long enough to see her decision, but turned to collect the trowels and poisoned wrappings.

"Sir?" Toby hovered, a thin wraith amidst the turnips. "Are you quite sure that it was a prank that went wrong? Is Uncle Robert a killer?"

Winter waited some time before replying, his eyes taking in the wheelbarrow propped against the side of the distant potting shed. "Robert cares for you very much, I think he sees himself in you. A bright young man thwarted by the ignorant rage of others. As Dr Michaelmas said, if he had planned to poison off your father and dispose of the body after dark then he would have prepared for that eventuality. He would have to be really rather foolish, or perhaps worked up into an irrational state of anxiety, to have imagined that he could have manhandled such a considerable dead weight alone. I don't imagine that the superintendent will feel able to continue employing your uncle under the circumstances, though your brother will have a couple of openings to choose between. Perhaps once you're a bookkeeper you'll be able to find Mr Carter a position better-suited to his skills and temperament, in an office?"

"Yes, I should like to be able to do that. Sir, might I come and visit you again in the future? I should like to learn more about herbs."

Winter smiled, nodded and walked off to finish tidying up the potting shed.

Eighth Story Notes

The Ipswich historian G.R. Clarke recorded a tale of "Doctor" Winter's interaction with a farmer at Purdis Heath in 1744, where he broke a curse laid by the witch Grace Petts, purportedly the last of the Ipswich witches! The unfortunate Mrs Petts died in an incident of what sounds like spontaneous human combustion as a result of her spell backfiring. The same story is quoted in F. Barham Zincke's 'History of Wherstead', published in 1887, and again in Murray's 'Handbook for Essex and Suffolk'. Though this latter account does not name the cunning man involved.

Zincke goes on to mention a story about Winter living at Aldborough (possibly a variant spelling of Aldeburgh) and being spotted in the company of six black imps which resembled a cross between bats and rats!

The Reverend Hollingsworth, in his 1844 'History of Stowmarket' places Old Winter (no longer given the appellation of Doctor) back in Ipswich where he was hired by a farmer to discover the thief of some bales of wool. The two keep vigil and spot a local labourer stealing more wool, whom Winter enchants so that he is forced to carry his ill-gotten gains round and round a meadow until he is fit to collapse.

A very similar tale is also told of Winter forcing a thief to carry stolen firewood round and round until he keels over. Many cunning men and wise women were called upon to administer community justice amongst the poor, particularly where the crimes were of a small-scale nature.

The reliability of these anecdotal accounts is, of course, highly debatable and no longer verifiable. If we give them the benefit of the doubt that we could conclude that Master Winter was referred to as Doctor when a young man (it not being uncommon back then to give that appellation to anyone who seemed unusually intelligent) and more commonly known by the nickname Old in his dotage. Perhaps especially so if there were by then several generations of Winters needing to be distinguished one from another. Equally it is as likely that being a cunning man was, like any other trade, the kind of skill passed down with a family such that there might have been several generations of Cunning Winters in Ipswich and the surrounding area.

Clarke states that the last cunning man of Ipswich was William Abinger, who died in approximately 1824 and was interred in an expensive tomb in St Clement's churchyard. Whether he was indeed the last, remains a matter of speculation. Cunning men and wise women plied their trade around Britain, and many other parts of the world, for a good many centuries. To a large extent they stood in the role of physicians to those too poor to afford the services of trained medical men, but also offered divination, love philtres, located lost property and the crooks who occasionally absconded with it and (one of the areas seemingly most in demand) the breaking of malevolent spells and curses. The majority of societies around the world have, throughout recorded history, drawn clear delineation between those who practice a legitimate form of magic and those whose activities draw them into the criminal realms – often through maiming and damaging people, crops or cattle through their mystical auspices.

These workers of benevolent magic seem to have been more popular in rural areas than in the growing urban centres, though event the biggest cities had (and continue to have) their resident palmists, tealeaf readers and the like.

By the 18th century pretty much all the working-class magicians and wise folk operated within a Christian context. In these days of bible-black evangelists with their interminable lists of forbidden activities, it may seem strange to think of Christians once having a largely tolerated magical tradition operating on the peripheries of the Church – though believed in by a very large number of mainstream churchgoers.

Those readers of a certain age will recognise the name Saburac, Old Winter's familiar spirit, as the name of Catweazle's supposed castle in the 1970s TV series brought to life by that excellent and prolific British character actor Geoffrey Bayldon.

Different writers work in different ways; I find it easiest to write about characters if I have a visual image of them in my head. To me Old Winter is the spitting image of another one of Mr Bayldon's wonderful characters, the otherwise unnamed Crowman in the Worzel Gummidge TV series. That character was clearly a contemporary Cunning Man, laced round with some decidedly pagan magical imagery. This story obviously owes more than a passing debt to Worzel and his magical creator.

Chapter Nine

The Black Dog

"The scandal closed down the Priory Asylum, a mere twenty years after it opened. Apparently this is where they found the superintendent, ripped apart by the hound." Thaddeus, taking on his customary role of historian-cum-tour guide, directed his small audience's gaze towards a discoloured spot on the carpet. No amount of scrubbing by the cleaners had succeeded in fully removing the stain.

"Why are the skirting boards such a peculiar shape?" Mrs Pendleton asked, peering myopically at the concave junctions of floor and walls. Her husband smiled indulgently and cleared his throat in the manner which signified a forthcoming lecture, a noise which his lean and nervous wife had come to dread over the years.

"These are a common feature of medical establishments, both those that treat diseases of the mind and those of the body. Without wishing to be vulgar, it is quite common in places of that sort for spillages to be quite common. These concave skirting boards enable the cleaning staff to more readily mop up without anything becoming grimed into conventional corners."

Mrs Pendleton grimaced at the prospect of the probable spillages that the inhabitants of Ipswich's former mental asylum for the distressed gentlefolk of Suffolk had made.

"I hear chanting in...in Latin!" Mrs Carlton announced in stentorian tones, staring into the middle distance. Naturally none of the accompanying group could hear anything unusual. Mrs Pendleton failed to contain a gasp of thrilled awe, earning yet another disdainful glance from her husband.

"It is, I believe, fairly well-known that the first superintendent, Dr Michaelmas who was there before Mr Mitchell took on the job, named this building following the discovery of some archaeological remains from a priory that stood on this site up until the Dissolution of the Monasteries."

Mrs Carlton harrumphed and walked laboriously towards the dusty chair near the bottom of the staircase. Her stentorian breathing and rattling pendants created a discordant music that Abernathy found strangely unsettling. Though perhaps it was more Lady Whittingham's barely contained combination of grief and hope that weighed heavily upon him. She deposited herself in the chair, which groaned alarmingly, and hooked her antler-headed walking stick over the bannister. One of the three tines pointed in the direction they must soon take, towards the hospital ward where parts of six young men were found preserved by a killer who had never yet been caught. The grey-haired mystic closed her eyes, slowed her breathing and seemed to enter a meditative state.

Sensing the tension between the professor and the clairvoyant whom he so palpably despised, young Abernathy rather breathlessly recounted the torrid story of the fate that befell the members of the original priory when word reached Henry VIII about an alleged plot to assassinate him. Whether or not the prior had indeed coordinated such a plot was unknown, for he had died during a brutal torture session, cursing the king's name with his final breath. Possibly a degree of poetic licence, Abernathy interpolated, but everyone agreed that forgiveness would not be at the forefront of their minds had they met with the unfortunate prior's fate.

"That was the year before the Dissolution of the Monasteries, and some historians have suggested that the incident fuelled the king's decision to disband the Orders. If Wolsey had still been alive well, maybe the situation would have been resolved differently. You've heard the other local story about how Wolsey revealed who murdered all those people in the Apothecaries' Guild? No? Well, I'll tell you that one over dinner tonight.

Anyway, one of the other legends from that era is about the phantom dog." Thaddeus picked up the tale as Abernathy looked on with relief at being spared the ordeal of entertaining strangers. "It tells that the prior kept a large black guard dog, which burst into the interrogation cell at the priory and attacked one of the torturers. The dog was killed, but the torturer died of the wounds anyway. There are accounts from the 15th century of its ghost skulking around the ruins of the destroyed priory. Some stories suggest that the prior's dog only appears to attack the enemies of the Catholic faith, whilst other accounts perceive it as a general omen of doom for whoever sees it. As with all these legends, each storyteller adds their own colour to the tapestry such that it becomes almost impossible to discern what the very first version was like."

"But surely the superintendent of the asylum cannot have been killed by a phantom dog?" Mrs Pendleton asked earnestly, eliciting a barking laugh from her silver-haired husband. Abernathy noted that the emaciated woman's hand shook just a little, causing the candle to cast dancing patterns on the walls.

"Of course not, Mavis! Clearly the poor man was attacked by his own animal, maybe he ill-treated it or possibly the creature simply went insane. It's not unknown for a devoted family pet to suddenly turn on its owners without any obvious outward cause." He took the candlestick from his wife, pulling a moue of annoyance at the sight of the wax splatters dripping down her unfashionably clunky carpetbag and on to the dusty floor.

"Actually, Professor, Mr Mitchell did not possess a dog. Indeed, I believe he suffered a terrible aversion to dog hair that rendered him almost unable to breathe in its presence." Abernathy's interjection raised a subtle smile from the supposedly entranced Mrs Carlton. "The newspapers at the time made quite an issue of that fact – because of his allergy there were no canines allowed to patrol the asylum grounds."

"Then clearly someone must have brought a dog onto the

premises, whether to deliberately terrorise the man or out of simple ignorance," Erasmus Pendleton snapped, a flush of annoyance suffusing his plump patrician features. He stalked away from them, chins wobbling, under the pretext of looking more closely at a couple of amateurish paintings that had been left on the walls when the asylum had closed down.

"Given that we are not here to commune with the spirit of the late Mr Mitchell, surely this is all somewhat moot?" Lady Whittingham sounded brittle, her grief oppressive to all in the group. She swung round, her considerable bosom invading Abernathy's personal space, clearly holding him accountable for the direction the conversation was taking. "My son was not killed by a dog, phantasmal or otherwise."

"Quite right, my Lady," the portly clairvoyant took charge, her numerous amber and jet beads clacking as she stood. Leaning heavily on her cane she waddled towards the stairs. "We should go to the room where the remains of your son were found. The vibrations are strong in this place, a manifest evil that grows stronger as we approach the centre of the web."

"Erasmus!" Lady Whittingham snapped at her cousin's contemptuous snort in response to the bustling psychic's declaration. "You promised that you would be here only as an observer and not disrupt Mrs Carlton's work. Whether you believe in the spirit or not, please for my sake allow her to at least try and find poor Timothy's body."

"Amelia, my dear, for your sake I will stay my tongue – but you must surely see that this woman's supposed powers are, at the most charitable interpretation, no more than self-delusion. Though given that she is charging a pretty penny for this charade, I am afraid I cannot be so charitable. Timothy's death, like the deaths of those other young lads, is tragic – but this charlatan cannot bring the culprit to justice. If you trust to the police authorities…"

"Authorities?" the heartbroken mother erupted. "My boy has

been dead for almost a year, so please stop singing the praises of forensic science to me. They haven't been able to find the rest of his body, or bring the killer to justice. If Mrs Carlton can do what science has failed to do, then she is worth ten times what she is charging. Now, please let her proceed without further disruption."

The party moved off towards what had once been the Chaucer Ward in rather an awkward silence, the doughty clairvoyant leading them like a tugboat ahead of a flotilla of more elegant vessels. Abernathy and Thaddeus exchanged a weary glance – this was not turning out to be their easiest investigation.

"Good God!" Thaddeus exclaimed, clapping a hand to his mouth at the grotesque altar in the centre of the otherwise empty Chaucer Ward. Lady Whittingham gave a terrible scream and collapsed insensible to the floor. Even the doughty Mrs Carlton staggered as if punched, and would have sunk to the floor had not the wall against which she slumped kept her almost upright.

Incredulity and rage battle across Professor Pendleton's face as he approached the ring of candles and what he at first took to be severed human hands. As he got closer, the wave of nausea subsided a little as he realised that the hands were actually leather gloves and the splatters of blood seemed decidedly too bright a shade of red to be real. His wife was comforting his cousin, who sobbed uncontrollably at this ghoulish recreation of the unhallowed shrine of barbarity that an unfortunate pair of inquisitive schoolgirls had discovered in this very spot exactly one year ago. Six left hands, severed from already dead wrists (according to the pathologist) and laid in a circle with a candle by each and a bowl of congealing, fly-blown blood set in the centre. Presiding over the whole affair was a curious dog-like statue carved from black basalt and accented with gold. Then, as now, words had been written in chalk around the outer edge – but words in some strange alphabet that made no sense to any but the depraved mind that had written them.

Exactly as Lady Whittingham had said, the police had laboured upon this case for a full year to scant avail. Three of the hands had been identified (young Timothy Whittingham by a signet ring and a peculiar scar on his palm that he had possessed since boyhood), but the rest were unknown – though various possibilities had been mooted as to young men whose whereabouts remained unknown. How they had died, why anyone should saw off their hands, preserve them in formaldehyde for heaven knows how long to then display them in such a perverse manner, and where the remainder of the bodies were hidden remained as mysterious as the identity of the lunatic committing the outrages.

"The symbols are different," a shaky voice murmured at his ear, as Abernathy pointed at the chalk scribbles. Pendleton occasionally employed his scientific skills in the service of the East Suffolk Constabulary, and was quite aware that the photographs of the crime scene had never been released to the public. In fact, he was quite conscious that many of the more sensational details had not been reported by the newspapers – so how the slim young man at his shoulder knew what the original symbols were was a curiosity to be noted down and investigated later.

The professor swung round with every intention of denouncing Mrs Carlton as the responsible party, but was silenced by the look of the deluded creature. If she had set up this theatrical travesty, then she was a remarkably good actress for she seemed as appalled and shocked as anyone. Her ghastly colouration suggested that a seizure was imminent.

The two young investigators, Thaddeus and Abernathy, took an arm each and gently assisted the hefty mystic out of the room and downstairs, almost tripping over her fallen walking cane on the way out. Whilst Mavis tended to his distraught cousin and helped her out on to the landing, Erasmus turned his intellect back towards the grotesque stage set, for such he had already started to think of it as.

Five pale leather gloves were each padded out with cotton wool and placed besides the kind of cheap wooden candlestick that could be found by the crate-load on market stalls around Ipswich. The candles, likewise, were unremarkable and cheap. The bowl in the centre, which appeared on closer inspection to be filled with red ink, was a brass Benares affair. It seemed a little costlier than the other items but, short of emptying the ink on the floor, he could see no unique marks upon it that might identify the owner or the retailer. Just as he was about to stand up, he noticed two tiny purple beads close to the base of the bowl. Tearing a sheet of paper from his pocketbook, he folded it into a makeshift pouch for one of the beads, leaving the other for the police.

He made a mental note to speak to his friend Dr Schofield, the alienist at St Clement's Hospital, about the possible motivations behind the bizarre recreation. If anyone understood the workings of disturbed minds, then it was the doctor.

The clairvoyant's walking stick was still in the corner, where it has fallen when she collapsed. He scooped it up and made his way out onto the landing, in search of the rest of his party, stopping dead at the sight of the strange figure emerging from one of the other old wards.

Thaddeus measured the whey-faced psychic's slowing pulse and wondered what on earth could be taking Abernathy so long just to find some cold water. The distant crash and bestial howl not only startled the investigator, but caused Mrs Carlton's heart to race.

"It's back!" she muttered as much to herself, trying to sit up but falling back into the chair with an exhausted look. Thaddeus made his excuses and darted out into the hallway to see a large Benares brass table top rolling down a side corridor and cluttering to a halt.

Abernathy emerged from a doorway holding a bowl of water. They exchanged bewildered looks before the timid voice of Mavis Pendleton startled them from behind as she asked what they were both thinking.

"I don't know," Thaddeus murmured, following the route taken by the rolling brass disc. The corridor turned a corner, where shattered glass crunched under Thaddeus' boots. "What do you think…?"

The question was cut off by the shrill scream from the far end of the corridor. They all rushed into what appeared to be some kind of solarium, Lady Whittingham crouched in a corner sobbing and pointing at the twisted body of her cousin. The professor lay face down in a pool of blood, limbs twisted at an awkward angle. Shattered lengths of wood poked out from underneath him.

The man's wife joined in the caterwauling and rushed towards the body, though Thaddeus caught her and held her back. Abernathy dropped the bowl of water he'd been so carefully transporting and approached the fallen man.

Glancing upwards he saw the gap in the balustrade around the balcony where the professor had clearly crashed through. It was a descent of some twenty-five or so feet, dangerous but not automatically lethal. A gurgle startled Abernathy out of his observations and he quickly rolled Pendleton over. Blood bubbled up out of several vicious wounds in the man's throat and chest. His eyes dilated and momentarily focused in on the young man leaning over him, lips moved but served only to cough up more blood. Rasping for breath, the dying man's lips moved again and Abernathy leaned in as close as possible to hear the words, despite his profound distaste for blood.

The creak of a floorboard drew all their attentions back up to the balcony, where the light of their collective candles barely touched. A tall figure with an indefinable air of dishevelment about it watched them for a few seconds before turning tail and running pell-mell down the corridor and disappearing entirely from sight and hearing.

"Don't you dare!" Abernathy thundered at Thaddeus, halting him in his pursuit of the watcher. "Wait ten minutes then go and fetch the police."

Mrs Puffin laid the tea tray out as Thaddeus and Abernathy discussed the case. Abernathy became quite animated describing the corpse as he'd found it, throat torn and chest ripped into. A deal of harrumphing failed to have the desired effect, forcing Thaddeus to eventually resort to an icy retort. Seeing the shocked face of their elderly landlady, Abernathy blushed and stammered into chastened silence.

"Oh don't you worry about me dear!" declared the diminutive figure, wiping her hands on her apron with relish. "My old Uncle Bert was an undertaker, and I helped him with the laying out when he was shorthanded. When I was young, like. Seen a thing or two I have."

"Well, if you don't mind. My chum in the hospital mortuary tells me that the pathologist has taken plaster casts of the wounds, and they have the very look of teeth about them. Not human teeth, Mrs P! Sorry, didn't mean to alarm you, no, rather the long, pointed teeth such as those of a large predatory animal. He won't commit himself as to which kind of animal, apparently the size of them is too large to be easily classified as a dog. Apparently they form a very strange pattern, though, not at all like a regular bite mark." Abernathy judiciously avoided the disapproving glare of his friend.

"Fancy having a dog at a séance!" the landlady muttered to herself as she placed a dish of steaming muffins before her tenants. "When I went to see that Mrs Palladino she didn't have dogs, I can tell you!"

Thaddeus explained the absence of any mundane canine

culprit, and Mrs Carlton's theory that the prior's phantom dog had manifested and struck Pendleton down in a judgement for his scepticism. The grandmotherly woman nodded in her vague way at the story, and bustled over to the fireplace to add some more coals.

"We heard the foul thing howling." Thaddeus shivered at the memory. "Abernathy, you still haven't told me what Professor Pendleton whispered to you as he was dying!"

"It was difficult to make out, what with the bite to his throat the poor man could barely speak, but I think he said 'hound'. I told the police that, when they asked. The inspector didn't seem to think much of it."

Thaddeus tapped out his pipe and made his low opinion of Inspector Grey known. Whilst Mrs Puffin was drawing the curtains Thaddeus produced the paper wrap he had found in the late professor's pocket, and passed the purple bead to Abernathy for his opinion.

"From a necklace, perhaps? I don't recall what kind of jewellery the ladies were wearing."

"Oh no dear, pardon me for interrupting, but being gentlemen you probably wouldn't know one sort of bead from another. Especially with neither of you having much to do with young ladies. No, that little bead isn't from a necklace, it's an embroidery bead from a lady's garment. Lovely amethyst colour that is. Sort of thing that Tate woman wears..." Seeing the uncertain looks on her lodgers' faces, the diminutive matron prompted them. "Surely you remember her? I recall you mentioning her from that awful soiree from back in, now that was...May or June time, I think. Lady Whittingham invited that man with the strange foreign name to give a talk and a demonstration, and then Professor Pendleton spoilt it all."

"Oh that!" Thaddeus exclaimed. "I don't remember anyone called Tate, but that was a dreadful evening. Pendleton made such a scene, exposing Dr Tiresias as a fabulist. Whilst the fellow was undoubtedly dishonest and taking advantage of a grieving mother, by the time the professor had finished his tirade I felt almost sorry for the creature. As I recall Tiresias, or whatever his real name was, didn't even have a real doctorate."

"Purple!" Abernathy declared, nearly dropping his pipe. "I remember the medium Tiresias was using was dressed in purple. Was that her? She was a local woman I recall, whilst Tiresias had come down from London. Well, well – all I really remember about her was that, by the time Tiresias stormed out in high dudgeon, she was nowhere to be found. Doubtless slipped out whilst all the attention was focused on the shenanigans going on between the two chaps. I knew you read tea leaves, Mrs P, but I didn't realise you had your finger on the pulse of paranormal life in these parts!"

"Oh yes, dear, it's always been quite a passion of mine. That's why I was quite happy to have you both take rooms here, with all your researches and experiments. Bit daft some of the things you two get up to – no offence like, Mr Abernathy – but it's awful fascinating to hear you talk nonetheless. I never dreamt to have Investigators for the Psychical Society living under my roof!"

Asked for a description of the ambitious Tate, who remained a foggy image in both Thaddeus and Abernathy's memories, Mrs Puffin drew a mental sketch of an earnest woman with an other-worldly air about her, broad in the hip with a not unattractive face and long dark hair. The landlady estimated her to be somewhere in her late 30s, and described her as being invariably dressed in shades of lavender and purple.

"Very gushy and blithers on endless about how the spirits love us all," she added with distaste. "Gives the impression that she means well, but she makes my skin crawl. There's something vaguely unpleasant about her, can't quite explain why but she strikes me as a bit unhinged, too in love with her own fantasy of being some kind of spiritual visionary."

Thaddeus poured a second round of teas whilst Abernathy picked at his porridge. He hadn't slept well, disturbed by images of the dying man. The image of an enormous black hound slavering and drooling had startled him awake more than once.

"The chalk writing was interesting – what say you, Abernathy; was this new set different from those in the old murder case because the person writing them had no idea what the first set looked like and just made up random squiggles for effect, or were they different because the killer wished to give out a new message?"

"Message, mmm, interesting that isn't it, old boy? I mean to say, does the lunatic intend to send a message but is so far gone in madness that he simply doesn't realise that nobody understands what his scrawling means? Or is it not a message intended for mortal eye? The whole *mise-en-scène* has the look of a spell or some magical ritual; if this misguided creature is offering the severed hands up to Satan, or whatever his fevered imagination perceives to be on the Other Side, then these symbols could be meant to be understood only by the spirits rather than by mortal minds."

"Different symbols, different spell you mean?" Abernathy grunted his assent, and relit his morning pipe. "Look here Thaddy, don't mean to sound silly or anything, but that chap we saw up on the balcony of the solarium. Well, do you think it was him? You know, the maniac that slaughtered all those poor lads? If it was, well, I wondered if he was there because he'd got wind of the séance or if, well, he was preparing to start again."

Thaddeus pointed out that Inspector Grey had led a thorough search of the whole asylum and found nothing new whatsoever – certainly no butchered young man, nor even the severed hand of one.

"Maybe that's because he didn't get the chance to carry out his intentions. Two of those chaps who had their hands chopped off were about the same age as us. Maybe, well…" he tailed off, staring nervously at his companion, who came over and clapped a comforting hand to his shoulder.

"That could just have been some old tramp sleeping rough in the asylum, Abbers old chap! Let's not overly complicate matters with all these ifs and buts and possiblys – you know my favourite adage old boy, Ockham's razor, look for the simplest explanation. In fact, we don't even really know it's a man; I could scarcely see the figure up there in the shadows. There's a fair old chance it was this Tate woman, spying on the competition. Don't forget those purple dress-beads."

After some quiet contemplation whilst aromatic pipe smoke filled the chamber Thaddeus announced that he intended to make an appointment to consult with Miss Tate, the up-and-coming clairvoyant. Abernathy opted to pay a sickbed visit to her professional rival.

The apple-cheeked clairvoyant was very much as Mrs Puffin had described her. Dressed in a somewhat unbecoming shade of mauve, she laid down the last of three cards and stared in the glass ball placed in the centre of the table. The room was unpleasantly chilly, with a cloying combination of lavender and the rather wilted-looking lilies that filled vases and gave the place the air of a funeral parlour. Indeed, Thaddeus could not help having an unkind thought as to the origins of the discoloured blooms when he noticed what might have been a black-edged card protruding from one of the arrangements.

"There is a terrible, suffocating grief about you, Mr Thaddeus. The dead surround you, wanting to be embraced by you…but you hold back. Are you a sceptical person, sir, because I feel this is setting up barriers to those loved ones who want so desperately to help you." She wittered on in such a vein for some minutes, till her client began to phase out and contemplate a forthcoming meeting with his bank manager. That is, until his attention was sharply pulled back. "Your uncle is here and says hands are important. Hands in a ring and a great black dog – does that mean anything to you, Mr Thaddeus?"

He nodded meekly as she continued to commune with Uncle Henry. After further intimations regarding the menace posed by the dog, Miss Tate warned him of treachery by a grey-haired woman before collapsing back into a state of somewhat theatrical exhaustion.

"I hope I haven't worn you out for your next consultation?" he asked solicitously, and received the slightly peeved assurance that she had no other clients booked for that day. "I actually saw you some months ago, Miss Tate, at a soiree held at Lady Whittingham's house."

The wan look darkened as the medium bridled, rather bitterly distancing herself from Tiresias (he noted she steadfastly refused to grant him the appellation of Doctor). Her proclaimed gratitude towards Professor Pendleton for exposing Tiresias' fraud struck Thaddeus as rather overly laboured. His revelation of the academic's death was received with shock, which again struck her client as somewhat overdone. The news had just missed the morning newspapers, but would undoubtedly be all over the town like wildfire by now. He had heard two old women talking about it on the walk over to the medium's parlour that very morning. Feeling that he had more than overstayed his welcome, Thaddeus made his excuses.

On the way out of the cluttered parlour Thaddeus nearly tripped headlong over the head of a tiger-skin rug, and only just managed to steady himself before colliding with a glass cabinet filled with curiosities.

Miss Tate bit back an acid remark and gave him her sweetest smile, along with a warning to protect himself against the hostile forces arrayed against him. She opened an ornate box bearing an Egyptian scarab design and presented him with a small ankh, effusing as to its mystical properties and refusing all offers of payment for it.

A dozen streets over Abernathy found Mrs Carlton draped inelegantly across a chaise longue, gazing disconsolately out at the River Gipping. Over tea, bought in by her granddaughter, her frosty manner began to mellow and she spoke at length about the atmosphere of malice and pending doom which events the previous day had prevented her from detailing.

"It emanated from that devilish idol, presiding over the foul circle of hands. I could not manage to sleep last night for bad dreams, so I got up in the early hours and an idea came to me." She looked at him uncertainly for some minutes, weighing him up. "That policeman came round this morning and confirmed what your friend said, that those hands were actually just padded-out gloves, he thinks it was all just a vicious trick but…well, what occurred to me in the small hours was this – suppose it's more like a blueprint?"

Abernathy stroked his moustache nervously, as he invariably did when he hadn't a clue what someone else was talking about. Quick at reading body language, Mrs Carlton clarified.

"One of my sons is a draughtsman, and he draws up plans for things before they are put in place. I only know what I read in the newspapers about that terrible discovery at the old asylum last year, but nobody knew what was going on till them little girls found all the hands. Who's to say that the maniac didn't start out with a ring of gloves, just like there was yesterday and gradually replaced each glove with a real hand? Maybe what we saw wasn't put there to shock us, but is much worse – the first stage of the whole thing beginning all over again?"

"Good God!" Abernathy felt queasy. "Whoever committed those crimes was insane, and isn't likely to stop. That's what my chum at the police pathologist's office said at the time. The only reason no more people have died is because the exposure of the altar disrupted what was happening. Disrupted, but not stopped."

"If it has stopped. Don't scoff, sir, and I'm not saying as I've had a vision or anything of that sort, just speculating. What I mean is, lads disappear all the time. Oh, not in your level of society, Mr Abernathy, but amongst the poor where the authorities cannot be bothered to look too hard. My cleaning woman's nephew went off to work three months back and hasn't been seen since. He could have run off, or fallen in the Orwell and been washed away or anything else I know; all I'm saying is that young men haven't stopped disappearing, so just because body parts haven't been turning up doesn't prove it's over."

"I understand you have had some contact with the spirit of the late Timothy Whittingham?"

"Only a little so far," Mrs Carlton demurred. "I cannot go into details clearly, but so far it has primarily been reassurances to his poor, dear mother that he is happy in the heavenly realms. When his mother's grief over the absence of his body had not abated, my guide began to give images concerning the whereabouts of the makeshift grave. Confused images, I must admit, but then I think the whole terrible incident was exceedingly confusing for Timothy. I have not said so overtly to Lady Whittingham, but it is my belief that the poor man was quite drunk when this lunatic set upon him. He was scarcely aware of what was happening."

"That was the last time anyone saw him alive," Abernathy observed, "leaving the Great White Horse Inn. I was meant to have joined him that night, but had a terrible headache after having a row with…a friend. He was, as you say, rather sloshed and apparently intending to meet with some chaps at one of the other hostelries. Except he never arrived."

After their cups had been refilled and more cake served, he asked his host how many times she had been to Lady Whittingham's house. The reply was but once, and then to visit Timothy's bedroom – by now a veritable shrine. Abernathy had been there once himself, in the week following young Whittingham's disappearance. Lady Amelia had summonsed everyone she could think of who might know or be able to guess where her son had gone. For nine agonising months they had searched in vain before the hands were found. Like pregnancy in reverse, Mrs P had described it as.

Abernathy had snuck a look in Tim's bedroom whilst on the pretext of answering a call of nature. He could smell his friend's favoured brand of tobacco in the folds of the curtains, but there had been no visions, no ghosts, no paranormal impressions, nothing. Abernathy had never had any pretensions towards mystical abilities, just an endless fascination with them in other people. However, he had hoped that if ever he were to acquire such skills then that would have been the time. Some hint, some notion, some sense as to what fate had befallen his dear friend – but nothing, except for the yawning dread.

The slavish devotion of some people to communing with the dead on a practically weekly basis had always struck him as bizarre. However, sitting on Tim's bed for those few minutes had brought home to him how painful the need for some kind of certainty in the face of nothingness was.

A large slab of fruit cake was placed before Abernathy and Thaddeus, and two bowl-sized cups filled with builder's tea. As the rain drummed on the window panes, they huddled closer to the hearth and discussed their respective discoveries of the morning.

"After I left Mrs Carlton sprawled on her couch, I went to see Lady Whittingham up at the hall. She seems to have aged ten years or more. I've never seen anyone in such a state of shock. She barely seemed to register that her cousin was dead, and just kept asking after Mrs Carlton and when she'd be up to another table-rapping session to contact Timothy. The butler said she had spent the whole night sat in a chair before the fire, not responding to a thing anyone said to her. They have sent for a doctor, though what good he'll be able to do I cannot imagine."

"Did you notice anything about the mantelpiece, dear?"

Abernathy stared open-mouthed at Mrs Puffin for some moments. "Yes! It was the only thing in the room that was mismatched. The lack of harmony kept annoying me. How did you know?"

"Elsie the housemaid is my niece. I paid a visit to her this morning, after I'd finished tidying up. She noticed yesterday when she was dusting, and told the butler. He would have asked Lady Whittingham about it on her return from the asylum, but of course what with everything that had happened it went out of his head. Then, this very morning even before I'd arrived, they found it left outside the kitchen door of all places!"

"What on earth are you both talking about?" Thaddeus asked, feeling quite left out by their exchange.

"The dog, dear. Remember you said that sitting beside the bowl of blood, or red ink rather, was a black statue of some dog-like creature. Well, according to Elsie, Lord Whittingham brought back a load of statues and whatnot from Egypt. Ancient things from the temples and pyramids. Well, she noticed one of them was missing from the mantelpiece when she was dusting. A black jackal apparently, that was the god of the dead back in those days."

"Anubis."

"That's the name, dear! Anyway, her ladyship being out the house at the time they searched high and low but couldn't find it – and assumed she'd taken it with her to show someone maybe. Well, this morning there it was as I said, sat outside the kitchen door like a dog what's had a night on the town."

"Good Lord!"

"I know, Thaddeus, quite extraordinary isn't it? I mean, are we to think that Lady W took it out the house with her and that somebody else brought it back?"

"Why on earth would a grieving woman create such an insult to her dead son? Not to mention, old boy, we both left the hall with her and travelled in her carriage. Where could she have possibly concealed a statue of those dimensions on her person? That silly little reticule could not have held such a thing. Nor was she out of sight from the moment we entered the asylum to the time we went to the Chaucer Ward."

"Actually," Abernathy replied after some thought. "None of us were. Whoever set that up and lit the candles, it wasn't any of our group. As I recall the candles were not burnt all that far down. Presumably it was whoever we saw on the balcony. What reason had he…or she…to kill the professor?"

"Do maniacs need a reason?" grumbled Thaddeus.

"Well, dear, I suppose not. Though if the person on the balcony was Miss Tate, she was all but accused of fraudulence by your Mr Pendleton. Besides which, he might have seen her retrieving that Egyptian statue and recognised her." Abernathy admitted the possibility, but could conceive little reason for her to set up the hideous altar in the first place. "Professional rivalry, maybe. Mrs Carlton does nearly all the gentry these days, and since that scene between the professor and that Tiresias character I don't think Miss Tate has had much credibility amongst the better paying customer. It might be a wicked thing to imply against someone when we don't know for a fact that it was even her, but maybe the whole thing was set up with the hope of giving Mrs Carlton such a shock she'd keel over dead on the spot. She's not a healthy woman, which is why she hobbles about on that stick."

"The shock would have been far more dangerous to Lady Whittingham. Does she have any enemies…or greedy relatives?"

"Good point, Thaddeus, I don't actually know how the will is disposed but with no husband or child left maybe there's a reasonable chance that the money would go to her cousin and his wife."

"Oh dear, I had almost forgotten about poor Mrs Pendleton, she's such a negligible person. She must be utterly devastated and neither of us even thought to go and visit her today. Has she a daughter or some other relative to comfort her?" Abernathy looked blankly at his friend's question. He couldn't recall ever hearing the professor mention his family, and had barely exchanged five words with the now widowed Mavis during their exploration of the asylum.

"But poor Lady Whittingham didn't die of shock, did she? Though if she killed her husband, maybe it wasn't for any money, his or the Whittingham estate. There was a man a bit like the professor, lived two streets over. He was a lay preacher at the Baptist church on the corner, always full of blood and thunder and certain of himself. In love with the sound of his own voice, and always right – and everyone else always wrong, of course. Treated his wife like a doormat; timid scrawny little thing she was. Hardly there at all, really."

"And did she kill him, Mrs P?"

"No dear, but she did brain him with a skillet one day. He was berating her about something or other, and she just lost her mind, picked up the skillet and knocked him out cold with it. Might have polished him off, if the scullery maid hadn't hauled her off. Poor creature is still up at St Clement's Hospital so far as I know, and I don't think her husband has ever visited her to this day."

Thaddeus and Abernathy strolled around Christchurch Park, huddled under one umbrella with their arms linked. They discussed the case at length, considering both the natural and supernatural elements. Thaddeus was particularly intrigued by the strange fusion of Egyptian mythology and Tudor folklore. He had spoken to Inspector Grey earlier in the day, and been informed that no statue, Egyptian or otherwise, had been found with the original altar. The more gruesome details of the first crime had never been fully disclosed to the newspapers, so whoever had staged the circle of gloves had either been the same lunatic or someone who knew enough about the crime to recreate it. In either case there seemed no obvious reason to innovate the additional statuary, let alone return it, though as Mrs Puffin had implied that could have been done by someone else entirely – clearly someone who recognised where it had come from and wanted to save its owner from any possible accusation.

"That means Mrs Pendleton, surely?" asked Abernathy. "It wasn't you or I, Lady Whittingham would hardly leave the statue outside the kitchen door when she could have put it back on the mantelpiece directly, and from the look of Mrs Carlton I just can't see her hobbling up the back stairs at lightning speed to retrieve the statue. However, after you went for the police I took the ladies into the visitors' room and went off in search of something warm to wrap around Mrs Carlton, she looked half dead. When I came back Mavis Pendleton was standing out on the veranda, staring into space. It took me quite a while to find some moth-eaten old blankets left in a storage cupboard, I doubt either Mrs Carlton or Lady Whittingham would have noticed if she'd disappeared off for five minutes."

"And she did have that horrible old carpetbag, quite big enough to hide that statue it. So it was either her, or the mysterious observer. I think the only thing for it, Abbers old chap, is to visit the grieving widow and see what we can divine for ourselves."

"Must we, Thaddy, you know I can't abide emotional scenes? I never know what to say to weeping women. Oh very well then, but you're going to have to provide any comforting platitudes that are needed."

Truth be told, Abernathy's anxieties were groundless for they found Mrs Pendleton stoically composed. She received them in the morning room amidst a number of tea chests, explaining that she had decided to honour her husband's memory by donating his collection of scientific books, papers and equipment to the town museum. Mr Woolnough, the curator, would be arriving the following day to collect. Neither of her two guests felt able to suggest that she seemed to be emptying her house of her husband's memory with almost indecent haste.

The conventional offers of help were made and demurred with the conventional level of appreciation. After some floundering Thaddeus eventually got to the point and asked if she had any notion as to who might have murdered the professor.

"Oh, whatever lunatic was loitering on the balcony, doubtless the same twisted creature that murdered poor Timothy and those other lads. Erasmus was of the opinion that those crimes had been performed by some former inmate of the Priory Asylum, no doubt interred in that very ward where the hands were found. If the records had not been so carelessly lost, the miscreant would be easier to track down. Assuming they were indeed lost."

"What do you mean?" Abernathy asked, somewhat taken aback by the timid woman's sudden burst of volubility.

"Well, the Priory Asylum catered for the wealthiest families in East Anglia. Once they were no longer being treated, can you imagine any such families being comfortable with the possibility that their darkest secrets might end up being scrutinised by prying eyes? Most especially those families whose relatives had a propensity towards violence. Few people would willing admit to having a cousin who thinks he is Julius Caesar; absolutely nobody would want it known that they have an uncle who enjoys maiming or killing innocents."

The logic of her point could not be denied, and suddenly introduced a very different image into Thaddeus' mind than the dishevelled imbecile he had been envisioning. The killer who had repulsed Ipswich might be living a genteel life in one of the town's grandest homes sheltered by anxious relatives, rather than sleeping in ditches and raving at demons that he alone could see.

"Mrs Pendleton, do you recall the statue of Anubis?"

"No!" The force of her response, and the fact that she knew who Anubis was, seemed to resolve that particular mystery. That she was able to think so practically within minutes of her widowhood was also noteworthy. Before any more could be asked upon the matter, a servant announced the arrival of Lady Whittingham. She looked somewhat surprised to see the gentlemen present.

The two women spoke briefly and awkwardly about the forthcoming funeral. Mrs Pendleton said that she had written to the Freethought Association for advice, as she had simply never attended a funeral that did not involve clergy of some sort and was at a loss as to how to proceed.

"We never really spoke about death," she said, with such an air of resignation that Abernathy gained the distinct impression that they probably never really spoke about much of anything. Most likely Erasmus lectured and Mavis nodded a lot. "I know what he objected to, but not really what he would have wanted instead."

They each made a few vague suggestions about music, flowers and so forth. Suddenly Lady Amelia blurted out something that made Thaddeus cringe.

"If a person doesn't believe in an afterlife do you think that means they just vanish when they're dead? Mrs Carlton says Heaven is whatever you expect it to be."

"Well, maybe that would be for the best. Erasmus hated to be proved wrong about anything. He did say to me several times that he wanted to be cremated, should he precede me. I am told there is a crematorium in Woking, though that seems an awfully long way to go."

"The Church has always taught that the body must be intact ready for the resurrection at Judgement Day."

"I cannot imagine that Erasmus would have been overly concerned about that." A trace of a smile crossed her thin lips. "It is Timothy that you are thinking of though, Amelia. I have no idea if God exists or not, but if He does then surely such a Creator could not be so callous as to reject a young man who has committed no more sin than to fall victim to a crazed mind?"

"And if there is no God?" Lady Whittingham looked paler than ever in her funereal weeds.

"Then the tragedies and triumphs of our lives will be forgotten as surely as those of the lives of the countless ancients whose names nobody remembers anymore. My husband says...said that it is only the human capacity to love each other that makes a difference. Though I do not think he ever loved much of anyone, least of all me."

"I adored Timothy!" Lady Whittingham continued as if her cousin-in-law had not just opened her heart in so bizarrely public a fashion. "Yet my love wasn't enough to protect him, or bring him justice, or even provide him a decent funeral. Love! It seems of so little use to me sometimes. Of as little use as Erasmus' lauded intellect in putting things to rights. Nothing can make things right, not if death really is the end of everything."

There was a painful silence whilst Mavis stared at Lady Amelia, who in turn stared into the hearth that so singularly failed to provide either warmth or cheer to the denuded morning room. Thaddeus and Abernathy exchanged helpless glances, each wishing the other could think of something to say to break the atmosphere. It was Abernathy who finally went against the grain of his normally unclubbable nature.

"Did either of you ladies get a clear look at the person on the balcony?"

Both of them looked perplexed for some moments, as if their minds were so far distant that the horror of a few days previous was now difficult to recall. It was Mrs Pendleton who answered first.

"I could barely see whoever it was, though I am sure it was a woman. Some short time later I felt an overwhelming need to be alone, and wandered the corridors. Foolish, I know, when a killer might be at large but for some reason I felt as if there were no risk posed to me. As I passed what turned out to be a small store room I saw that the dust upon the floor had been disturbed by the door being opened, so I looked inside. The room was empty, but there was a strong aroma of lavender. It is not a fragrance which either I or Lady Whittingham use, and I only recall Mrs Carlton smelling of carbolic soap."

"Odd, because I had the very distinct impression that it was a man on the balcony," Lady Whittingham spoke more vigorously than she had previously. She leaned forward to pick up her tea cup, but her hand shook so badly she nearly dropped it. "I said as much to that inspector person when he called upon me yesterday. He seemed a large man from what little I saw of him, and bearded I think. My son's murderer has never been caught, and the police have made it clear to me that they are of the opinion that we were unfortunate enough that our visit to the asylum coincided with the return of the villain to the scene of his previous crime."

Thaddeus cleared his throat, feeling unaccountably nervous in the face of Lady Whittingham's conviction. "It is possible that it was not a coincidence. What I mean is, the creature might live within sight of the asylum and have seen lights moving about. It could have drawn him there."

"Like a moth to a flame." The autocratic woman looked suddenly queasy. "I had not considered that. You must impress this idea upon the inspector, Mr Thaddeus! He did not strike me as a particularly insightful or resourceful man."

"Or," Abernathy chimed in, "he may have heard of our planned visit. It was not, after all, a secret. Someone may have mentioned it in passing, and he decided to make that terrible reminder of his previous deeds."

Mrs Puffin had just finished igniting the fire when she heard her lodgers arriving downstairs, complaining vigorously about the inclement weather. She smiled to herself and noted the clock – a full quarter of an hour later than planned. Knowing Mr Abernathy's obsession with punctuality that could only signify that their investigations had taken an unusual turn to keep them longer than planned.

By the time Abernathy and Thaddeus had mounted to their shared drawing room, Mrs Puffin had warmed the coffee pot over the spirit lamp and toasted the first round of crumpets. Thaddeus declared fatuously that he would surely marry Mrs P were she only not walking out with the greengrocer.

"Undoubtedly Mrs Pendleton removed the Egyptian statue from the scene of the crime and deposited it on Lady Whittingham's doorstep, yet I just cannot see how she might have smuggled in a dog, set it on her husband and then got the vicious thing out again without a soul noticing…assuming, of course, that the professor was not in truth done to death by a spectral hound instead of a living one." Abernathy swallowed a mouthful of buttered crumpet, washed down with sweet coffee. "Is it possible that we could be looking at two people working in cahoots? If so, dear boy, it does rather blow the notion of this being a spontaneous crime of passion." He tapped his pipe into the ashtray.

"Doesn't always follow, dear." Mrs Puffin cleared away the remains of the jam pot, unconsciously plucking up a stray strawberry. She noticed the bemused looks of her lodgers and blushed a little. "What I mean is, it could be like me and the Cleaver boy."

"Who?"

"Oh of course, sorry dear – that was before your time here. Danny Cleaver was a lad of about ten or so who lived three streets over. Several times I caught him stealing pies I'd left to cool on the window sill."

"Little scamp!" Abernathy chuckled.

"Not really, dear, you see he was a vicious little bugger. Excuse my language, but he was. On more than one occasion he stole money, smashed my windows if I went after him. He threatened me with a knife once."

"Well, I hope you told the lad's father, that sort of behaviour is quite beyond the pale!"

Mrs Puffin shook her head ruefully as she piled the last of the crockery on to the tea tray. "Not much point, Mr Thaddeus, it was usually the father as had sent the kids out thieving. Whole family were villains, you see; burglary, opium running, extortion – whole clan in and out of prison on a regular basis. More out than in, though, because, you see, if anyone gave evidence against them or so much as spoke to the police, then one of the Cleaver boys would be round to stave their heads in. Even Danny, young as he was, was a wrong 'un. Old Mary Tenniel, who was gone ninety, caught the little monster going through her silver drawer one day and he put her in hospital for over a month. When she got out the house had been robbed blind, and she'd never had that much to start with. I was with her when she keeled over. Dead by the afternoon, poor old thing."

"That's rather shocking, Mrs Puffin, but I'm not entirely sure what it has to do with the current situation."

"Oh just that one day I was looking out what's now your bedroom window, Mr Abernathy, when I saw Danny sitting on that roof over the way eating whatever he'd managed to steal that morning. The young Greenwood girl crept up behind him and shoved him off the roof as I watched. Broke his leg and a couple of ribs. She never knew I'd seen her do it, and I never told on her. I knew what she'd done was a crime, but those Cleavers deserved what they got. Same way it might be with your situation up at the old asylum. If a second person had a grudge against this professor, then they might have added to the crime off their own back – not always a need for careful planning and people conspiring with each other. Sometimes we just see someone else doing what we've always wanted to, and lend a hand, if you see what I mean. Even if it's only to help conceal their identity. Would you like some more coffee, dears, the pot is all but empty?"

They confirmed they would and, whilst the landlady disappeared down to her kitchen, mused in silence for some time on what she had suggested. Thaddeus finally pointed out to his companion that there was only one real conclusion that could be drawn from what Mrs P had suggested. Abernathy refuted it, and was about to suggest his alternative theory when they heard their elderly landlady mounting the stairs with her tray.

"There we go, nice and hot. I've been thinking about what you said, Mr Abernathy, about what you'd heard from your friend who works for the police doctor. Do you really think the professor was killed by a dog? It seems most unlikely to me."

"But, Mrs P, how else could we explain the fang marks?"

"Well, you did say, dear, that the teeth marks weren't in a regular patter like a normal bite mark. Well, what with what Mr Thaddeus here always saying about that razor thing – Oddems, is it?"

"Ockham's Razor, Mrs P!"

"That's the one, dear, surely the simplest answer is that the wounds ain't like a regular bite because it ain't a bite at all."

"But," Abernathy mused, "how else could a dog sink its fangs into a chap without using its mouth?"

"They're not fangs though, are they, dear?" Seeing the quizzical look pass over both her lodgers' faces, she continued, "Your doctor friend, or whatever he is, said the wounds were like animal teeth – but like doesn't mean that they definitely are, does it? Seems to me that everyone's got a bit carried away with this idea of a bleeding great big dog appearing out of thin air and disappearing as quick. If you were to stop thinking about ghost dogs, you might think of other things instead. Now I might be wrong on this, but when I saw Mrs Carlton in town this morning she was hobbling about on a silver-handled walking stick. Far too fancy for her it was, and no doubt bought for her by poor Lady Whittingham or one of her other rich clients. Anyway, my point being that her old walking cane had an antler handle. Couple of sharp prongs on that. I'm no doctor, but it seems to me if you gave someone a few good hard whacks with that it might leave holes a bit like the fangs of some big animal. Especially if it hit them in a fleshy part, like the throat."

"Mrs Carlton was downstairs with us until after the professor's body was discovered. I don't see how she—"

"She was, that's true," Thaddeus responded to his friend's musing, "but her stick was upstairs. Do you remember, old chap, how we nearly tripped over the damned thing trying to haul the Carlton creature out of that ghastly room when she took her funny turn? Somebody else could have snatched it up and polished Pendleton off."

"A crime of impulse then, not carefully organised like that staged altar of severed hands. Gloves, rather. I keep thinking the person who set up that altar must either be the same as Pendleton's killer, or at least in league with him. Though I suppose that really is little more than an assumption. Every single one of us looked utterly shocked upon seeing it, and I don't think we have any budding Beerbohm Tree's in our little circle."

"Mrs Pendleton said she smelled lavender in the disturbed storage room, and when I visited Miss Tate she seemed to have nearly bathed in the stuff."

"There you go then, dear, it's not proof but suppose she staged that nasty scene to scare the life out of Mrs Carlton. Either she stole the Egyptian dog statue herself, or maybe got one of the servants to do it for her. She could have relatives or friends working at the hall easily enough. Maybe a bit of spite against Lady Whittingham herself, for having hosted that embarrassing soiree, or just because she wanted to play up to the stories about the ghostly dog. Doesn't really matter what was going through her head, let's just say she staged it for the sake of argument."

"And unbeknownst to her, one of the party was planning to murder the professor?"

"Oh no, I don't think it was planned at all, do you, dear? No, if I was going to do someone in, I'd plan it a lot better than that. I mean, if he hadn't fallen backwards through the rotten old bannisters would he have died at all? Been badly wounded, certainly, but probably not died. Maybe his attacker was lashing out blindly in rage, not really intending to do anything as certain as murder – just flailing wildly. No, it strikes me that in a sense that silly Tate woman sort of sparked the crime."

The lodgers looked at her, and asked as one what she meant, bringing a smile to the old woman's jovial face.

"Me and Mr Puffin never had children. Don't know whose fault it was, he blamed me and I blamed him, but there we are. Things are the way they are. I think if we'd had a kiddie and my boy were done in as horribly as all those poor lads must have been, well… I'd go off my head. All the more so if I had such a vile shock as seeing that ring of gloves. Nobody in that poor woman's position would be in their right mind that evening."

"But Lady Whittingham is, well, a lady!" Even Thaddeus felt a tad fatuous saying it. "Solidly built, I'll grant you, but a lady all the same."

"She's a mother who has lost her boy and only has one slim thread that might help get him back – dead, I know, but having his body, giving it a decent burial is what she wants more than anything in the world. I'd say her sanity probably depends on it. A voice from beyond the grave is better than utter silence. I know Mrs Carlton couldn't contact the other side of a post-office counter, but would a woman unhinged by grief see it that way? The only time I met that professor was when he came here briefly the other week to meet with you gentlemen, but I could hear his voice carrying all through the house, going on and on about how he knew better than everyone else, telling you how ridiculous paranormal investigation was. He obviously had a low opinion of mediumship and weren't at all shy about saying so."

"She nearly dropped her tea cup," Abernathy observed. "I thought it was nerves, but if she had set about Pendleton with a walking stick hard enough to cause those wounds...well, whoever did it would probably have strained a muscle, tore a ligament or done some sort of injury to themselves in the process."

"It's not proof though, Abbers. None of this is, just conjecture...and can you imagine Inspector Grey or anyone else being willing to prosecute a person of Lady Whittingham's standing on nothing more than guesswork? Especially when she's managed to convince them she saw a bearded mystery man, even when she was huddled in the corner and couldn't possibly have seen who was standing on the balcony."

"I know that but, well, I mean we can't just stand by whilst someone gets away with murder. Even if the poor woman was half off her head with grief, she can't just go around killing people because they are insensitive know-alls. No matter how sanctimonious Professor Pendleton was, he didn't deserve to die. We must do something, old chap."

Mrs Puffin took her tea tray back to the kitchen, leaving her residents to silently contemplate what, if anything, they would do about their theory.

Ninth Story Notes

The Priory Asylum is, of course, completely fictional. Early records show the existence of two private mental asylums in Ipswich during the Victorian period. Grove Retreat stood opposite what is now Alexandra Park, whilst the Belle Vue Retreat was found along the Woodbridge Road. The first local institution run by the Borough for the mentally disturbed was St Clement's Hospital, built in 1870. This was built partly in response to the Lunatic Asylums Act of 1858.

The quality of treatment in such institutions was variable, but gradually improved in response to the research and guidance of the Medico-Psychological Association as it restyled itself in 1865, having previously had the cumbersome title of the Association of Medical Officers of Asylums and Hospitals for the Insane. Indeed, whilst a number of the privately run retreats had been little more than money-making endeavours and places for the well-heeled to conceal their more embarrassing relatives, under the Asylums Act humanitarianism came to the fore with the wish to help improve people's lives rather than simply lock them up.

Incidentally the Chaucer Ward, site of the grotesque collection of body parts, is named after the famous author of the Canterbury Tales who is alleged as having possibly been born in the town.

This story is set in 1896, not long after the opening of Christchurch Park, Ipswich's first public park. It might be argued that the provision of such recreational areas for rich and poor alike reflect the growing level of concern for public health – particularly mental health, and what these days would be classed as environmental psychology.

Spiritualism and all things paranormal became immensely popular in the Victorian age, initially popularised by the Fox

Sisters in America. Ipswich's first known spiritualist church (the Cedars) did not open until the 1920s, though doubtless the town had its fair share of mediums, table rappers, and other communicators with the spirit realms well before that period.

Along with a passion for contacting the dead came a love for all things Egyptian. The discovery of the Rosetta Stone in 1799 led to translations of Ancient Egyptian texts, and the urge to collect antiquities. Lady Bedford and her husband Admiral Frederick (who eventually became Governor of Western Australia) were two such collectors of ancient artworks, many of which they donated to the Ipswich Museum where they can still be seen today.

Mr Woolnough, briefly alluded to in this story, really was one of the early curators of the Ipswich Museum. In those days it was mostly a natural-history collection, before extending to a wide variety of other historical artefacts.

Suffolk has a rich tradition of spectral dog sightings and stories, and the beast in this tale is in no small part inspired by Black Shuck. This enormous hound is the focus of several legendary accounts, perhaps the most famous of which is the account of how he burst into a Blythburgh church in 1577 accompanied by a great peal of thunder, caused several deaths, toppled the steeple, and left claw marks upon the door which are still visible to this day.

Shuck and his canine compatriots crop up in accounts all over East Anglia. Sometimes these dogs cause deaths, sometimes they act as omens of forthcoming tragedy, sometimes they just scare the wits out of people and disappear without any greater grief occurring.

The theatrically inclined reader may recognise the name of Mrs Puffin as a clairvoyant character from the play *Goodnight Mrs Puffin* by Arthur Lovegrove. The part was one of the stage successes for the lovely Irene Handl in the 1960s, on whom my character of Mrs Puffin is based – the character's first name, Ada, is derived from one of Miss Handl's TV successes, *For the Love of Ada*.

Chapter Ten

No Way to Treat a Goddess

The serene face of the large marble statue gazed up from the small pool of congealed blood, partly hidden by the bead curtain at one end of a short, narrow corridor. The body of the woman it had been used to murder lay in the small therapy room at the other end of that corridor. Inspector Vincent Carfax wondered if this oriental deity was as sick of violence as he was. She looked as if she might be. Twenty-five years on the force had exposed him to virtually every conceivable act of brutality, venality and perversity. Woolf had less than half his experience, but working for the Met in London must have given her far more awareness of the extremes of human behaviour than any sane person would choose to have.

"What did you say she was called again?" he asked his tall, fiery-haired colleague standing to the other side of the corpse.

"Kwan Yin, goddess of mercy and compassion." She watched her new boss's eyebrow rise in query. "I bought a smaller version when I was on holiday in Malaysia last year. She's very popular with Buddhists and Taoists alike."

It was difficult to get much of a sense of the late Andrea Medicaster, when the left-hand side of her face was smashed to a pulp. She lay partly concealed by the massage couch that occupied the centre of the room. The pathology report would give them far more details, but it seemed fairly obvious that the killer had landed rather more than just one blow. He or she must have been in a rare fury to heft such a weighty statue time and time again. The remaining soft, pallid skin, lank black hair, puffy hamster-cheeks and pouting lips seemed uninspiring. Underpinning the stench of blood and excrement was an overwhelming combination of floral aromas from the many broken bottles of essential oils that had been swept off the shelves by the door during the struggle and shattered against the marble-topped preparation table on the opposite side of the room. Some of the bottles had evidently been trodden on, with oils and fragments of glass stomped into the lino along the narrow corridor.

Sergeant Eleanor Woolf observed the long, cadaverous form of the black-haired inspector as he leant over the mangled body. It was easy to see why colleagues nicknamed him Dracula.

"According to the other proprietor, this statue stood on that small table beside the therapy-room door."

"Seems like a weapon of opportunity. Think this was an impulse murder, sir?" she asked.

"Certainly doesn't seem very well planned. The killer must have been spattered with blood. There's some smeared on the inside of the door at the shop-end of the corridor, just above where the statue was dropped." A short passage linked the salesroom to the therapy room, with a miniscule kitchenette to one side of the passage, and a toilet and storeroom to the other. It was an old building with no fire door or rear exit. The SOCO team had already photographed the splatters arced across the mural-decorated walls. Woolf cast a jaded eye at the various wall designs of witches and wizards, badly executed and presumably intended to give the place a spiritual look. However, she found the prancing, robed figures more twee than ethereal.

"It could have spattered on a cheek, or hand. Then if the killer were leaning against the wall and peering through the bead curtain, it might easily have rubbed off."

"Yes, maybe listening to hear whatever was going on in the shop itself, or to see if there were any customers as potential witnesses? If it was a facial spatter, then that would make our suspect roughly about, what...your height?" He appraised the sergeant, who stood about 5′ 11″.

"No money stolen, apparently. Or anything else, though who

on earth would kill to acquire joss sticks or tarot cards I can't imagine! I wonder what she said or did to provoke this?" Eleanor mused, glancing again at the various mystical figures that decorated both the therapy room and continued along the walls into the shop. The shopkeepers obviously had eclectic tastes, judging from the mixture of wizened old ladies, brick-red Native American medicine men, and pseudo-Celtic elves and druids on the wall. Then again, perhaps the art was geared towards the expectations of customers rather than any personal preferences.

"This place has certainly changed since I was last here. Mind you, that was about twenty or more years ago, when this was a video shop. We raided them and found they were selling child porn from a secret room out back. Oh, it got worse! They were using the cellar to actually make some of the films they were selling. One of them was shanked in prison, as I recall. Not sure what became of the other two. What is it about this place that it just seems to attract misfortune? Anyway, tell me what you know about this new lot," Carfax enquired as he returned his spectacles to their case.

"Me? I don't know anything about them at all, sir. In fact I didn't know this shop existed until today."

"Well, I thought you might have been a customer here given that you have an interest in the esoteric." He left the unspoken question hanging in the air, a light smile playing upon his thin lips.

"I've only been in Ipswich a month, sir. I haven't had time to meet many of the locals yet." *Except for the criminally inclined ones, and their victims,* she thought. "How do you know about my interests?"

"I've seen that ring you wear. According to my friends at the Lodge on Soane Street, it's some Viking rune thing."

"Oh! Yes, it's a protective talisman. It's a gift from my grandfather, he thought it might keep me safe..." She tailed off, slightly embarrassed.

"I'm a Mason," he smiled disarmingly, "so I can hardly criticise! You know, I've lived here for forty years now, and Ipswich still surprises me with all that goes on under the surface. Remind me to tell you about that group who thought there were in touch with aliens living in a UFO crashed out at Rendlesham, when we have a bit more time. You wouldn't believe what they were getting up to, all on the telepathic instructions of the aliens apparently!"

Neville Cozener hunched behind his counter, looking rough and reeking of alcohol and stale cigarette smoke. Carfax thought there were few things sadder than a short, paunchy middle-aged man trying to look like a quarter of his age by wearing a baseball cap and a hideous shirt. The badly bleached hair poking out just added to the vision of a mid-life crisis. Woolf thought that he had probably been quite attractive when young, but far too much self-indulgence had resulted in him going to seed.

"We met about ten years ago, and went into business together soon after. We started with a stall going round psychic fairs and that sort of thing, before we got the loan to start the Prior Pagans shop. I just can't believe this has happened. Andi only ever tried to help people, why would someone harm her?"

"Presumably the door to the therapy room would have been closed, if she was seeing a patient?" the sergeant enquired, making note of the broken capillaries and puffiness that suggested a chronic drinker.

"Client, we say client. It's more empowering than patient." Neville didn't notice the inspector rolling his eyes, as he turned to gaze at the shelves full of crystals, wood carvings, tarot packs and joss sticks. "The door would have been shut, and I usually turn the radio or CD player up at this end of the corridor once the client goes through – gives them more privacy if they want to talk, otherwise any customer coming into the shop can quite easily hear what's being said. We're very professional here, you know!"

"I wasn't implying otherwise. So you wouldn't have heard much, especially if she was taken by surprise. If the first blow knocked her out, then there wouldn't even be time to yell or call for help. Many other therapy customers in today, Mr Cozener?"

"One." Neville invested the word with all the bitterness born of trying to keep a floundering business alive. "Agnes Farrier at 2.15pm, but she wouldn't have hurt Andi. She's one of our investors, and this'll hit her hard. That bitch Rhiannon did it, without a doubt. She's eaten alive with jealousy."

"What time did this Rhiannon come into the shop?"

"She didn't. I banned her two years ago. I don't have to have anyone in here if I don't want them!" he snarled defensively.

"Then how do you suggest she killed Miss Medicaster, if she wasn't in the shop?" queried Eleanor impatiently.

"Maybe when I nipped to the loo, or went out to the stock room. Or, more likely, she might have come in when I popped round the corner to the baker's. I was still feeling hungry after lunch and went to get some buns. If she'd been loitering outside somewhere biding her time she could have dived in then."

"Smashed your partner's head in and dived back out without your noticing? Were you in the stock room or at the baker an especially long time, Mr Cozener?" One of the SOCOs had reported finding two empty and one three-quarter full vodka bottles at the back of a shelf in there. "Maybe you could write down this lady's address, so we could pay her a visit?"

"With pleasure!"

"Constable Fisher found this on the toilet floor," Carfax observed once the address was handed over, holding up a bag containing shards from a small hexagonal brown bottle.

"It's one of the vials we use for essential oils, elixirs, herbal tinctures and that sort of thing," he responded, lighting up his fourth cigarette of the interview. Carfax opened the bag for a sniff, but couldn't detect any aroma. There was no suggestion of drugging or poisoning, but it was always wise to check.

"Excuse my curiosity, but what is that?" Woolf pointed towards part of a battered brass plaque contained, along with a few other oddities, in a glass-fronted cabinet fixed to the wall behind the counter.

"Oh, that's our little museum!" For the first time a smile spread across the shopkeeper's bleary face. He opened the door and took out the broken plaque which bore the partial legend 'Prior S-', inviting them to take a closer look. "When we took this place over it had been empty for a few years, we had to carry out quite a lot of repairs and renovations – including sorting out a flood in the cellar. All sorts of interesting little pieces came to light after the floor was dug up. This plaque was part of one from the Prior School that stood here back in the Edwardian era. It was a boarding school for boys, a bit like the Ipswich School but much smaller. We think the two lead soldiers belonged to one of the lads. The school took over the building from an old mental asylum. Those blue bottles are probably from the asylum's medical store. There was a bit of scandal about the school apparently, after the headmaster committed suicide. It closed down in the 1920s after an explosion in the chemistry laboratory killed quite a few pupils and some teachers. The school governors sold the land off and developers repaired the building, converted it into upmarket apartments but they were flattened by the Germans during the war. That art deco brooch probably belonged to one of the residents. It was a bombsite until the mid-50s when they erected this row of shops and flats."

"Presumably the name of the shop comes from the school?"

"Yes, well more from the plaque really. Neither of us knew about the Prior School until after the plaque was unearthed and I did some research. Up until then we were going to call the shop Ipps-Witches. Those coins are a mixture of Late Saxon and Early Medieval."

"Did anyone else come in the shop today, anyone you haven't

mentioned?" Carfax's question elicited the information that there had only been one other visitor at about 2pm, though Reg Peddlar was just collecting a treatment for his wife. The crime itself had been phoned in at half three, and Dr Godalming's initial assessment had confirmed that death would have occurred in that rough time period.

The semi-detached on Woodbridge Road had both a flourishing herb garden, and two large concrete Egyptian dog statues as door sentinels, painted rather neatly to imitate basalt.

"Once we've done with Mrs Bay here, I'll take this Mrs Farrier and you can track down the afternoon customer…what's his name?"

"Reginald Peddlar, sir. Rather fortunate that their only other customer was a known face." Woolf mused, glancing approvingly at the herb beds.

"For us…probably not much fortune for them if they get so little passing trade. Not much footfall on Castle Hill, I guess."

They were on the verge of abandoning the house as empty, when the azure door swung unexpectedly open. The inspector made the introductions, whilst wondering if Rhiannon Bay and his new sergeant had been separated at birth. Whilst noticeably shorter, the alleged killer had the same explosion of livid red hair and bottle green eyes.

"I was working all afternoon, Inspector. Usually I'm at the main Ipswich branch, but I was asked to cover someone off sick at the Woodbridge library this week. So what is it I need an alibi for?" Her voice held the pleasant lilt of South Wales. The eyes danced with mischief, as she ferreted around in the rather chaotic kitchen cabinets for extra cups.

"There was an incident today at a shop over on Castle Hill. Prior Pagans – are you familiar with that establishment, Mrs Bay?"

"Those wankers?" she snorted contemptuously. "Don't tell

me someone finally threw a brick through their window? Though I'd hardly get a fully-fledged inspector on my doorstep if it was something that minor, would I? Spill the beans!"

"It's not a laughing matter, Mrs Bay. There has been a serious incident at the shop. A homicide, in fact." Carfax found it difficult to sound censorious in the face of such an infectious smile.

"Really!" Rhiannon whistled. "So someone actually took a hatchet to the Blonde Bombsite at long last?"

"Andrea Medicaster was dark-haired, not blonde." Eleanor's attention was drawn away from the ornate framed papyrus of a cat-headed goddess.

"Andrea? Oh! That does surprise me, I was referring to Neville. I can easily imagine someone doing him over, but Andrea's such a bland, inoffensive thing. Why would anyone kill her? "

Carfax took a sip of the strong black coffee, which tasted wonderful, and relaxed in the worn upright armchair. The homemade fruit cake was also excellent. He cast an eye over the disordered but homely décor, and noted the row of family photographs on the mantelpiece. He counted three children and a dark-haired man with the look of a matinee idol – presumably the husband.

"I have the impression that there's no love lost between you and Mr Cozener. Care to give us your version of the saga?"

"Not really, but I will if you insist." She sighed with distaste and paused some moments as if marshalling her thoughts. "It's been going on for about six or so years now, and shows no signs of ending. Well, that's when the big bust-up was, though even before that the situation was strained to say the least. I've managed to avoid the pair of them since then, so I don't know what they're up to these days, but Nev always used to have a drink problem. Never understood why Andi put up with him, but there's no accounting for taste. When he was sober he could be charming, witty, erudite...but he was a vicious drunk. Not physically violent, just vitriolic. He alienated so many people by opening that big mouth of his."

"Is that what led to the rift?" Eleanor prompted when the other woman drifted off into memory.

"Not entirely, I earn my living as a librarian but I'm also a priestess in my religion – a minister, if you prefer that term. I do a lot of the same things that a vicar would…baby naming, marriages, funerals and all of that kind of thing. However, I don't charge…it's a service to my Gods and community, I think." She paused, as if waiting for them to make some acerbic comment. "Anyway, Andi and Nev started offering rites of passage, rituals, spells and whatnot professionally. A price tag for everything! Their argument was that a lot of other religions charge, so why shouldn't they."

"Which is true," Carfax interjected, "we had to pay a hefty chunk for the vicar to do my uncle's funeral."

"A thing doesn't become moral just because others do it though, does it? I doubt you'd let a crack dealer go just because they say there's someone else on the other side of the town who also deals so why shouldn't they jump on the bandwagon. Still, you're not here for a sermon! Neville never could abide anyone he saw as competition to his shop. Said I was undercutting them, which I suppose is true in as far as it goes. He'd slag off other New Age shops behind their backs, spread vicious rumours, doing his best to drive them out of business. I was conducting a baby naming once, and he turned up as someone's guest, drunk out of his skull, and turned the air blue ranting on and on about how he could have done everything so much better. The poor parents were livid. That was the last straw. Ever since then he has been slagging me off to anyone daft enough to listen. No end of people have asked me to conduct rituals for them, and then cancelled on the basis of some scurrilous slander they've heard from those idiots. I could probably write a novel about all the accusations I've had thrown at me behind my back. Mind you, plenty of them book up again after a couple of months of getting bled white paying for all sorts of spells, courses, sacred crystals and endless other crap that they never really wanted in the first place."

"To what extent was Miss Medicaster involved in all this?" Carfax asked.

"I always had the feeling that she was under Neville's thumb, and just did whatever she was told. Co-dependency and all that. I don't know what she got out of that relationship, unless maybe she was one of those people who just got off on being bossed around. Love is blind, I guess!"

"Love...are they a couple?"

"Yes, you sound surprised."

"I am." Eleanor didn't attempt to hide how startled she felt. "I must admit I assumed Cozener was gay – his mannerisms reminded me of a gay neighbour back when I lived in London. Besides, Cozener gave the impression they were just business partners. I know some people prefer to keep their emotions under wraps and be very Stoic, but he really didn't behave like a grieving lover. More like what he claimed, a shocked business partner."

"Well, as I say it's been several years since I had any contact with them so it's possible the romance may have dried up and just become a practical arrangement. You'll have to ask him... you might even get an honest answer, if he's drunk enough."

"Aside from any possible domestic disputes, can you think of anyone else who might wish to harm Miss Medicaster?" the inspector asked, gazing longingly at the fruitcake. Rhiannon Bay was obviously a noticing kind of person, as she automatically cut them both another slice.

"Not really. She always seemed so ineffectual. Plenty of people probably want to shoot Neville. You haven't said how the murder was committed. Any chance that the wrong person bought it by accident?"

"Unlikely. Obviously we can't give out the circumstances at this point in the investigation."

"I read somewhere that most murders are domestic in nature. Presumably there's a reason why you don't think it's Neville. He has an alibi? Oh, judging from your expression he doesn't."

"You're very astute, Mrs Bay. No, he doesn't have an alibi, but that in itself is rather curious." Carfax reached down and stroked the ears of the terrier that was leaning up against his calf and looking hopeful.

"How so? Oh, I get it. You mean that anyone with an ounce of sense who had killed their other half would at least attempt to create an alibi for themselves, and presumably he hasn't. So you're thinking he is either innocent or a moron. For what it's worth, Inspector, I can assure that, as much as I can't stand the man, he isn't stupid by any degree."

The interview over, Woolf sat in the car looking at an A-Z of Ipswich whilst the inspector took a call on his mobile and had a smoke, leaning against a garden wall and admiring the local gardens.

"Do people really have such long-lasting feuds over nonsense about how much someone does or doesn't charge? Or was that just a front to avoid telling us about whatever really went on?" he asked on his return to the car.

"Oddly enough they do get a bit irate over it! Admittedly it's not as major an issue as, say, the way Catholics get het up over abortion or Anglicans go on about women bishops, but it still puts backs up. For some people rituals, religious teaching and the rest of it is just another way to pay the mortgage. For others the very idea of slapping a price tag on things like that turns religion into money-grubbing. Money and religion rarely mix well, regardless of which religion."

"So where do you come down on it all, or is that too personal a question?" he asked.

"I'm all for keeping religion free and open to everyone, rich or poor. Still, that doesn't mean I automatically think Mrs Bay is innocent just because I agree with her on one issue. She doesn't seem the homicidal type, but as you say there could be a lot more that's gone on we haven't been told about. The rumour-mongering could have reached the wrong ears – if Bay's job or marriage were being threatened by it that might be enough to cause her to lash out."

"True, we'll have to dig deeper. If I take this Farrier biddy you can take Chapman and find out what he came to the shop for. Speaking of which, that was Fisher on the phone. The woman at the bakery confirms that Cozener bought some cakes there in the afternoon, though she isn't sure at what time. However, Fisher has him on the off-licence CCTV at 2.40 buying a bottle of vodka and holding what looks like a paper bag with the bakery logo on it. Neither of the shop assistants noticed him behaving in any way oddly nor registered him being spattered with blood or anything of the sort." Carfax fished the cigarette packet out of his pocket and found the final smoke broken in half and looking woeful.

"So he gets back to the shop what, five minutes later…ten at the absolute most if he stops to pet next door's dog or some silly thing and then doesn't call 999 for the best part of 45 minutes."

"Plenty enough time to cover his tracks far more efficiently than he did, if he actually smashed Medicaster's brains in."

"Or, indeed, cover up after finding his fancy piece doing the deed – if, indeed, he found her, him or it in the act of dispatching their love rival. All of which seems a bit improbable given the literally bloody mess left in that therapy room. It's blatantly obvious that nobody made any effort to tidy up or conceal any evidence at the scene. So what was he doing?" Woolf drummed her fingers on the dashboard with all the vigour of a distracted pianist.

"Presumably he arrived back shouting 'Honey, I'm home' or

words to that effect, and got no answer. If he didn't do it, then she must have been killed whilst he was out. There doesn't seem to be any chance for any other person to have slipped straight past the till to do the deed without being registered, if you'll pardon the pun. So Medicaster's dead, answer comes there none and the bun sits on the plate drying out. Why doesn't he stick his head round the door and find out what was delaying her?"

"My uncle and aunt once went seven weeks without speaking a word to each other after she caught him checking on dirty pictures emailed to him by some tart in America," Eleanor reflected.

"Oh dear! So maybe the two were on such poor terms that a glowering silence was nothing unusual, or maybe Cozener was so busy surfing the Net and looking at naughty pictures that the time just flew past. I noticed a laptop behind the counter. Make sure we check the browsing history on that, and make sure Fisher checks the phone records in case there were any time-consuming calls. Whatever happened, eventually he looks in the therapy room and sees his dearly beloved, or not so beloved as the case may be, with her skull caved in. Right, Woolf, onwards and upwards!"

Agnes Farrier's home was a shrine to kitsch. Carfax eyed the myriad ghastly cutesy angels made from porcelain, crystal, wood, and even macramé that lined every available shelf and wall space, and repressed a shudder. The Bay home had been like an extension of the Egyptian Room at the British Museum, though without the air of homesick melancholy. The abundance of pastels in this place reflected the Arran jumper sported by the cumbersome, white-haired old woman wedged into the armchair before him.

"It's just wicked," she snuffled and snorted into a large hankie, "why would anyone do that to poor Andi?"

"How did Miss...how did Andi seem during your Reiki

session, did she mention anyone she was afraid of?" He displaced the two overfed cats that were vying for a place on his lap. He had counted at least a dozen felines since entering the house. Normally he liked cats, but the miasma of ammonia made him gag, and everything seemed covered in cat hairs or drying vomit.

"No, Andi had no enemies. Well, unless you count that awful Bay woman. Though I wouldn't have thought even she was capable of murder, though some of her friends are thuggish! Maybe she egged one of them on? Yes, that must be what happened. There is one of them that's been in prison several times for GBH and heaven knows what else. Ross something-or-other, that Welsh tart would know. Go and talk to her, but don't believe a word she says."

"I already have spoken to her, Mrs Farrier." He wished he'd taken the male suspect, and left this florid-faced termagant and her cat-filled bungalow to Woolf. "Though I shall enquire further about this Ross character. I understand that you invested some money with Andi and Nev in their shop, do you have any worries about seeing a return on that?"

"None at all, Andi is, was very optimistic about the future. Oh, I know things have been a bit slow this last year or two, but both the tarot and the angel cards showed that we were just turning a corner. We talked about starting some new courses, something to attract the college students." Noticing his quizzical look, she gushed into more detail, "Nev and Andi wanted me to help them teach an Introduction to Wicca course – lots of teenagers are very into Wicca now, and Nev thought a lot of people would want to learn about angel rituals too. Five people have signed up to that already. I thought we should also run a course to help people open their awareness to the faerie realms and—" Carfax broke into the tide of vacuity and asked about the practicalities of their business plan. "Well, yes I know Castle Hill is a stretch from the college, but Andi and Nev were looking into changing premises and moving a bit closer to town. The rents go up, of course, but the footfall improves. One of their previous investors did a feng shui reading and said that the geomancy of the shop they're in was all wrong, and that's why business took a downward turn. Nobody has had much luck in that place. All that ugly 1970s concrete, hardly surprising!"

"Who was this previous investor?"

"Kathy Peddlar. Oh, wait, that wasn't her! Sorry. I mean, she has invested in the shop and all, but she wasn't the one who did the feng shui. No, that was…let me think…oh of course, that was poor old Derek. He was an artist you know, painted some wonderful pictures of the little people." She steered him into the dining room where a large sepia-toned acrylic depicted a surprisingly good image of an ethereal woman with swan wings arising from a lake.

"Why did you say 'poor old Derek'?" Carfax asked, eliciting a rambling account of how a few years earlier Derek the Druid had keeled over with a fatal heart attack just outside the Prior Pagans shop. Asked quite how many people had invested money in the business, Agnes admitted that she had no actual idea. Her financial arrangements were, Carfax felt, all somewhat vague and she had clearly not consulted a bank manager or any kind of business advisor before parting with several thousand pounds. Clearly in her mind the whole thing was some sort of gentleman's agreement in which her friends would behave honourably. A lifetime on the force had left Carfax rather too jaded to expect honour to be anything other than a rarity where large sums of money were involved.

"You mentioned Kathy Peddlar, Mrs Farrier, would she be a relative of Reginald Peddlar?"

"Reg? Oh yes, the poor thing is his wife. I do hope she recovers – cancer, not quite sure what sort but I've heard it's extensive. We've all been sending her healing energy, you know. Andi was doing everything in her power to heal Kathy, and Nev has organised several chanting circles with his coven. He doesn't do that for just anyone, you know!"

Reg stared distractedly out of the window at the distant arch of the Orwell Bridge, absently tugging at his unkempt grizzled beard. A fat tabby nudged him without success.

"Did she say anything to you that might help us?" Sergeant Woolf thought the thin man looked exhausted. The whole house had an air of being tired, threadbare and neglected. The walls were spotted with an assortment of green-men plaques, pictures of dragons, and pentagrams of every size and permutation. They were all in dire need of a good dusting.

"No, it was just a five minute in-and-out. I picked up the treatment for Kathy, exchanged some pleasantries about the weather and that was it. She seemed her usual self, not particularly bothered by anything."

"What do you do for a living, if you don't mind my asking, Mr Peddlar?"

"I'm a carer, ironically. Most of the time these days I care for my wife, but I also work part time in a home for people with learning difficulties."

"Is your wife unwell, Mr Peddlar?"

"Yes, she has leukaemia." He conveyed a world of weariness in that simple sentence. "She's upstairs as the moment, lying down."

"Were you regular customers at the shop?"

"Not me, but Kathy has spent a small fortune there over the years." He gestured to the assortment of mystical books, figurines and wall plaques that littered the room. "Have to admit I don't really believe in anything particularly, though I was raised a Baptist. Fell out of love with that pretty quickly, I can tell you! Some of what Kathy does is quite intriguing, but in honesty the only witches that interest me are up at the race track."

"How did you feel about your wife investing money with Medicaster and Cozener?" Sergeant Woolf rearranged the cat that had decided to try its luck on her lap instead of its owner's.

"I…well, I didn't know she had. Can you tell me how much?" He winced when he heard the answer. "I don't suppose we'll ever see that back. She and Andi knew each other when they both worked at the insurance company, even back before those two started running a market stall. Always on their courses, getting Reiki and Bach flower remedies and reflexology and who knows what else. Mad into these elixirs at the moment."

"I get the impression that you're not so enthused about these things, Mr Peddlar?" She noticed the bottom of the thin man's shoes as he crossed his legs. They had been resoled once already. His cuffs were badly frayed too.

"Well, herbalism's fine, there's a science to it. My grandmother was famed for her concoctions – just for minor ailments, like. But so much of what those pair of snake-oil merchants offer seems…" he paused for so long that Eleanor thought he'd phased out completely, "…just an excuse for bleeding gullible people dry!"

Holywells Park on a wet day was still more conducive to reflection than the joyless concrete of Ipswich police station.

"My dog would love this place," Eleanor mused. "I'll bring him on Sunday. Anyway, you don't reckon on this Farrier woman?"

"She invested £5,000 in that place. From what I can gather, our corpse was the main earner, what with the courses and therapies and all that palaver. Cozener seems a bit of a dead weight, driving half the customers away with drunken tantrums and then guzzling what little profit they made. With Medicaster dead, that place will almost certainly go under."

"So bang goes the investment, and Agnes kisses goodbye to ever seeing her retirement nest egg returned to her. Mind you, perhaps she'd already guessed as much and lashed out in a fit of fury. Though it's difficult to imagine a woman of her age wielding a heavy statue with quite such passion. Presumably Cozener will end up bankrupt?"

"Drunken rages aren't conducive to long-term financial planning, Sergeant. Still, if we're right about the killer leaning against the shop door there doesn't seem to be much reason for him to spy on his own premises. Oh, your fellow redhead seems to have a cast-iron alibi working in Woodbridge all day, unless she procured someone to do the deed for her. Speaking of which, we have another little trip to Castle Hill. Seems the ex-con friend that the sweetness-and-light Agnes mentioned actually lives about five minutes away from the shop. One Ross Tennant – not, as stated, in for GBH but for a couple of drug offences (once for possession of cocaine and once for speed). His mug shot seems vaguely familiar but I can't quite place him. Oh, I picked this up at the library. Most enlightening! I'm not closed-minded by any degree, but some of the things people believe beggar credulity." He showed her a slim volume on complementary healing.

It wasn't until the imposing, heavily tattooed man spoke that Carfax was able to crystallise why the face had seemed familiar. The slightest hint of a stutter sparked a flashback to a younger version of the same man with a far more pronounced speech impediment being interviewed several years earlier as a possible suspect in the brutal beating of a local heroin dealer. They had eventually arrested somebody else, but Tennant was clearly an enforcer for Atkinson, one of the minor local drug lords who had since disappeared off the scene.

"You remember me." It was a statement, not a question. The last time they had met Ross had a shaved head, but now his thick blond hair was collar length. It softened the image somewhat. "If you're about to bang on at me about drugs, I've been clean for three years now, thanks to Narcotics Anonymous and some very good friends. Don't use and don't deal."

"Pleased to hear it." The inspector leaned over and turned off the blaring radio. The smell of engine oil was overpowering, and he gestured to the younger man to go outside. "Actually I'm here to ask you were you were yesterday between 1.30pm and 3.30pm."

"Here, fixing cars. I've only got one employee, and he's been off all week with this flu virus that's going round. A customer phoned on the land line at about 3.30ish, if that proves anything. I don't expect you to believe me, but I have been going straight for four years now."

"Narcotics Anonymous, own business...I'm impressed, what happened, Ross? Tell me the magic formula so I can recommend it to others!"

"Well, let's just say that..." The tattooed man paused awkwardly and blushed, he had never been much of a talker and words didn't come easily. "...Let's say I found religion."

"Paganism, to be specific?"

"Kemeticism, if you want to be really specific, Inspector."

"What's that?"

"Egyptian religion. I know you probably think it's all a bit mental and daft, but it works for me."

"I'm not criticising, Ross. So presumably you know Rhiannon Bay?"

"Yes...has something happened to her?"

"No, why would you think that?"

"You ask me for my whereabouts, and then you ask me about Rhiannon. What else am I supposed to think?"

"Fair point, Ross. I can't imagine for a minute that you haven't heard about the murder just round the corner yesterday."

"Because I've got a criminal record, you think I must be involved in every crime that takes place around here?"

"Not at all. However, I do think when a member of a small community gets killed and another member of that community lives and works five minutes round the corner, it must be worth asking what you know or suspect. At the moment, Ross, you're not a suspect so much as a potential witness. Now can we drop the hostility and maybe you can just tell me what you know about Andrea Medicaster's death?"

"OK. Look, I've managed to avoid both you lot and my old cronies for a good few years now and stay clean in more ways than one. This is just starting to bring back bad memories. I don't know anything much about the murder. I knew her, and had a run-in with the pair of them about two years back now. If someone told you I'm pagan, I guess they will probably have told you that too. Oh bugger it!" He sat down heavily on the low wall outside the garage and lit up a cigarette, he offered one to the policeman, but the offer was turned down. "I don't want to bore you with my life story, but, well look...I spent my childhood in and out of foster homes and care homes, and then I was on the streets for a few years. Nobody ever showed the slightest interest in me till I ran into Frank Atkinson, and yes I do know that he wouldn't have bothered with me if I weren't built like a brick shithouse. Well, I guess you know how I ended up working for him. Whatever else you might think of him, Inspector, at least he got me off the streets. A few years back there was an incident, let's call it that, with one of the suppliers up north. I got this limp and nearly bled to death. That was my signal to get out."

"What happened to Atkinson?"

"He won't be troubling you anymore, Inspector. Nor will half of his other associates, for that matter. When I was in hospital the bloke in the next bed had a regular visitor who came up to read to him. Poor sod was having an eye operation. It was all these books about paganism. I laid there listening to it. Can't stand people, but I've always loved dogs, always liked getting out by myself into the country, sitting under a tree, soaking my feet in a river. Probably sounds a bit naff to you, I guess."

"Not at all, I'm never happier than when I'm gardening or walking the dogs over in Rendlesham Forest."

"Oh, right." Ross mellowed, and the inspector noticed the

man's tense shoulders relaxing a little. "Anyway, when I got back to Ipswich I had nothing in my life. Didn't know what to do with it, so I put it away and got a job as a bouncer. Kept thinking about the books I'd listened to, and after a few months of moping about I heard this woman talking on Radio Suffolk. Rhiannon that was, and she mentioned meetings in a pub. So along I went, expecting them to take one look at me and turf me out. But no, they couldn't have been more welcoming. Spent the evening talking to Rhiannon – she's got a Master's Degree in Egyptology. A degree and talking to me like I was intelligent and understood what she was on about! I think that was about the first time that anyone ever treated me like I had a brain. Well I've never looked back. People were actually willing to help me, even when they found out about my record. Helped me with my reading and writing, helped me with all those bloody forms and things at the bank when I needed the loan to set this place up."

"What about the people at Prior Pagans?"

"Oh them! They were all right at first, though always trying to flog me stuff I didn't want. Kept trying to get me to sign up to all these expensive courses, and when I told them that Rhiannon was teaching me all I needed to know for free they went mental. Started slagging her off something chronic. Whatever else people say about me, Inspector, I'm loyal to a fault and wasn't about to listen to all their mudslinging. So I told them to eff off, and never shopped there again. That's all I did, Mr Carfax, just give them a mouthful and leave. Didn't so much as put a brick through their window! As I say I'm a reformed character."

"Presumably your friend Mrs Bay must feel quite aggrieved at the hostility that has been shown towards her?"

"She's more than just a friend. Oh, I don't mean anything like that. I mean she practically saved my life, without her I would have ended up going the same way as Fred. Never thought I would have college qualifications, a home, love and my own business. Without Rhiannon's help none of that would have happened. So no doubt you're thinking that I owe her one and the pay back was my going round and doing that Andrea over. Well I didn't, not sure I can prove it except to say that I was in the business long enough to do a proper job of it. I can assure you I'd have done that fucker Neville over as well, and there'd have been nothing whatsoever to connect it to me."

It was a rather unexpected admission, but Inspector Carfax felt it to be a genuine one. He enquired why Neville particularly should be the target of the mechanic's ire, and this time a veil of caginess descended over the previously open features.

"Can't keep his hands to himself, that's why he and Andrea had split. Guess she finally got fed up with it. Given that he's no respecter of other people's relationships, I'm guessing that you'll have no shortage of people who'd happily put a cleaver through his head."

"Thank you for your honesty, Mr Tennant. Were you wearing those work boots on the day of the murder? I'll need to take them for testing – if you're innocent, you'll get them back in due course."

All of which may well be true, the inspector thought, except it wasn't Neville Cozener that had been killed. Despite the possibility that Mrs Bay had raised, he couldn't see any likelihood of the killer having attacked the wrong person. It was bright daylight when the attack took place in a room with large windows and only someone who was practically blind could mistake Medicaster for Cozener.

Musing on that conversation as he took his leave of Tennant, another possibility floated into Carfax's mind. Sergeant Woolf had assumed, rightly or wrongly, that Cozener was gay – so maybe his hands hadn't wandered towards whoever Tennant's girlfriend was, but to Tennant himself? Though either way, would it make the slightest difference to the matter of who had smashed Andrea's head in? Unless the answer was the commonest one, and Cozener himself had done it to pave the way for some new business-cum-romantic partner to revitalise the shop and the bedroom.

Carfax sat down wearily at his desk and closed his eyes for a few moments, wondering if anyone would notice if he slipped his shoes off. The clink of a cup was rapidly followed by the aroma of decent coffee, rather than the slurry served in the canteen.

"Black and two," his sergeant announced. "Path report pretty much confirms what we already knew. Three blows in all, first one probably killed her. Quite an array of DNA in the therapy room, pretty much as you'd expect from somewhere that has an assortment of visitors and doesn't get cleaned as often as it ought to be. Oh, the brown glass vial on the toilet floor contained nothing but tap water – and no sign of any kind of drug or poison in the victim's system. Doc says that there were three blows altogether, the first to the back of the head would probably have knocked her flat – quite a serious wound that one. No sign of defensive wounds, at any rate. The angle of the next two blows to the side of the head suggests that she was on the floor already when they were delivered. Someone clearly wanted to make absolutely sure she was dead. Anyway, should we be going back to talk to anyone in particular?"

"Several. I suspect this is likely to be another dreary domestic, though whether Cozener acted entirely off his own bat or if there is another woman…or, indeed, man involved I'm not yet sure. Most of the people we've spoken to so far seem to have plenty of reason to kill him, but less so to smash Medicaster's skull in. We need to establish where the money goes – probably no inheritance from the sound of all their business chaos, but there could well be some insurance involved. Who do you fancy for our culprit?"

"Actually, I was wondering about Mr Bay – Rhiannon's husband." She unconsciously drummed a heartbeat on the desk with a pencil, a sign that Carfax had already come to register as a sign that she was ruminating. "She has an alibi at work, not that she strikes me as a murderous sort anyway, but we don't know a thing about her husband. Maybe he's the old-fashioned chivalrous sort that leaps to his wife's defence when her name is being besmirched."

"By bashing a woman's head in with a statue…doesn't sound very chivalrous to me!"

"True, but people are rarely consistent. I'd like to talk to him, as much to eliminate the possibility as anything."

"OK, we can sort that out. Any other possibilities?"

"Well, there's the Farrier woman. She strikes me as a bit unstable, and I never trust anyone as saccharine as she pretends to be. However, like you I can't see someone her age being physically strong enough to commit this sort of crime. Even if she has finally been disillusioned about her investment, she doesn't sound like the sort to vent her spleen in so bloodthirsty and futile a manner. I know you don't think the garage mechanic bloke did it, despite his dodgy past, but maybe he has a girlfriend. You said he'd talked about Cozener having wandering hands."

"Again, we're back to him as a probable target and no further towards establishing why anyone would want to kill the actual victim."

"True…and what about this Derek character that the Farrier woman mentioned as having keeled over outside Prior Pagans? I wonder if there's anything untoward in that – if there's anything suspicious about it then there might be some irate relative with a grudge."

"Good point. You get onto those two possibilities, and I'll go and speak to the noticeably not-grieving boyfriend again."

Neville Cozener slumped on the sofa in the flat above the shop. The peeling wallpaper and damp patches seemed testament to the dwindled income. Though maybe the mound of empties in the recycling box was more testament to the decision to spend what little money there was on drowning sorrows rather than tackling basic problems.

A near-empty bottle of vodka sat amidst a morass of bank statements, accounts books and red bills.

"The shop was in her name." Cozener answered the question wearily. "Andi's credit history was better than mine when it came to getting bank loans. Now it's all falling apart, I just don't know what to do anymore. I'm not sure how much longer I can even keep a roof over my head. One of your constables was round here asking about insurance policies. If you're thinking that I killed Andi to lay hands to a fortune then think again."

"When we first met, Mr Cozener, you gave me the impression that you and Miss Medicaster were just business partners. Others have told me that you were actually lovers. Is that true?"

"We were for the first few years, Inspector, but the passion died. We haven't actually been a couple for about ten or so months now, though we hadn't told anyone. Most of our customers got to know us as a pair, and we didn't want to say anything that might alienate them. People might feel awkward with a split. Neither of us could afford to move out or start again, so we agreed to continue as previous and just sleep in separate rooms. Not that it matters anymore."

"Was there anyone else, for either of you?"

"Not for me," he replied after a long pause. "She had a few dates over the last year, but nothing came of them."

That Cozener was lying was palpably obvious, though the inspector was uncertain whether the lie concerned his own love life, that of the late Andrea Medicaster, or maybe both.

"What can you tell me about Derek's death?"

"Derek Nolan? But that was ages ago, what has he got to do with anything? I suppose that ginger cow has been mudslinging again. Look, Derek had a heart attack and died before the ambulance got here – an ambulance which I phoned for, incidentally. So don't try and put the blame for that on me. Derek was always ranting and roaring about one thing and another – a magistrate sent him to anger management after he punched a doctor's receptionist. Even his wife said he was a seizure waiting to happen. There was nothing untoward about it."

Carfax and Woolf sat in the station canteen quietly reading through the old inquest notes that did indeed confirm Derek Nolan had died of a heart seizure outside Prior Pagans, despite the first aid attempted by Andrea Medicaster. Mr Nolan was childless and had no immediate relatives beyond his widow Lydia. Further investigation had revealed that she was currently sectioned up at St Clement's Hospital having thrown a heavy glass bottle filled with supposedly holy water at the Ipswich mayor, whilst yelling some sort of exorcism ritual.

She had, it transpired, believed the mayor to part of the fabled Illuminati cult and her prime persecutor in some incomprehensible worldwide conspiracy. Woolf had spent some time talking to the unfortunate woman, to scant avail. Whether it was her mental illness or the side effect of the medication, Woolf was unsure but Lydia Nolan had done little more than hint at plots, intrigues and cover-ups involving everyone from the Knights Templars to the BBC World Service to Al Qaeda. Exactly why anyone should want to persecute her was anybody's guess. On the topic of her husband she had alternated between outright accusations that Neville Cozener had killed him by means unspecified, and starry-eyed praise of Andrea Medicaster as a virtual messiah of wisdom and light.

"So, we can eliminate Lydia Nolan from our enquiries. It's possible that Derek keeled over with a heart attack following a blazing row with Neville or Andrea, but we'll never be able to prove it now. Even if we could it wouldn't make any difference, there'd be no criminal culpability. We're no closer to identifying who Ross Tennant's girlfriend might be, let alone if she might have any involvement in Andrea's death. Likewise, we've got no clear notion as to whether either Andrea or Neville had some other love interest who might have an axe to grind. We don't seem to be much further forward," Carfax reflected.

"None of the shoes that our suspects offered up had any signs of broken glass or essential oils, except for Cozener himself but then he walked into the murder room so that's only to be expected. Mind you, a killer with any sense would have given up a different pair of shoes and destroyed the incriminating pair. Bay is too short to have left the blood smear in the corridor, and Tennant too tall, unless he was hunched over. Cozener, Farrier and Peddlar are all about the right height."

"Oh, of course, the broken glass!" the inspector exclaimed, "Should have thought of that before, instead of getting caught up in all this petty politics of who-hates-who."

"Unfortunately for you, I read this little book about complementary therapies. It struck me as slightly odd that anyone would fill a little bottle with water, till I read about gem elixirs. Then I remembered what you'd gone into the shop to collect. I thought at first this was an impulse crime, and it was after a fashion – except you must have hidden long enough in the toilet, waiting until Mrs Farrier had finished her Reiki session, to have produced some kind of plan. My sergeant tells me you're a carer at one of the supported living homes. Did you have any latex gloves with you that day?"

"Yes, I came straight from work. By chance I had some gloves in my pocket, but I would have done it even if I hadn't." He looked more exhausted than ever, and slumped into another prolonged silence before eventually stirring to life again. "Kathy is dying. A matter of months, they say. She…she stopped taking the medication, thought that all that bloody Reiki and whatever other claptrap those two spun her would cure it instead. Kathy got her latest test results back this morning. The tumour's grown, and now it's too late."

"Did Miss Medicaster tell her to stop the medication? Is that why you killed her?" Carfax probed.

"No, she never said it, but they're always droning on about how toxic conventional medicine is. My wife took it all to heart. Kathy's in so much pain, Andrea said this gem elixir stuff would help. Do you know what it is?" Seeing the nonplussed look in the sergeant's eyes, his tone grew even angrier. "It's fucking tap water that bloody charlatan waved an amethyst over. £15 she charged me for that! Andrea gave me a leaflet along with the bottle. I popped into the loo before leaving, and just read it over whilst I was on the throne. I was so angry. She was vulnerable, desperate for hope and those parasites just milked her for every penny. I just sat there feeling poleaxed by the bloody audacity of it."

"So you hurled the bottle away in a fit of anger and went back and confronted Andrea."

"That daft old sow Agnes Farrier turned up whilst I was in the loo, I could hear her gabbling away nine to the dozen. So I waited for her to leave, then went in and asked her if the elixir really was just water like the leaflet said. She smiled at me, like it were all a joke! The statue was right by my hand, and…." He rubbed his grey eyes, his voice tailing off.

"Those bottles on the shelf, presumably you swept them off after killing her? I thought at first there been a struggle, but the pathologist said the first blow to the back of the head would have floored her. There wouldn't really have been a chance for any kind of fight back. You weren't just angry at her, but at her supposed tools of healing. Did you carry the statue to the end of the corridor with the intention of disposing of it?"

"I was going to sort that other parasite out too, but he wasn't in the shop when I left. In the stockroom getting pissed, no doubt, but I wasn't thinking straight enough to actually go and check. I could hardly believe what I'd just done. Suddenly all I wanted was to get out of that miserable place and check on Kathy. Now she'll die alone whilst I'm inside. They were supposed to be healing people, helping them – not just bleeding them dry."

Physician heal thyself, Carfax thought as he turned off the tape.

Tenth Story Notes

In an anthology of Suffolk murder mysteries, one can scarcely avoid mentioning the horrific real-life murders that gave Ipswich a notoriety it could have done without. Steve Wright became Suffolk's first known serial killer when he was convicted of strangling five sex workers in 2006. Speculation has linked him to other murders in different parts of the country, but nothing has yet been proven. The motive for these crimes has remained unclear, and Wright protested his innocence at the time.

As the reader may imagine, many people living in Ipswich at the time felt very nervous during that period – and not just those who plied their trade walking the streets. Subsequent to the crime a lot of effort went in to getting a lot of women off the streets. Some quit prostitution entirely, whilst others no doubt moved area or transferred to brothel work. Suffolk, like just about every other part of the country, continues to have a sex industry worked by both women and lads.

Wright's crimes also brought to the fore that fact that many of the women killed had drug issues, and that dealing and use of a wide range of narcotics is as prevalent in our county as anywhere. Smuggling has been part of Suffolk life going back many centuries, particularly around the coastal areas. The previously mentioned Hadleigh gangs were notorious for their brutality and run-ins with the customs men in the 16th and 17th centuries. Today drug smuggling has probably outstripped most other forms of illicit trade, and raids on crack dens and cannabis plants have become commonplace features of the local newspaper reports. The chocolate-box image of thatched cottages is only one part of Suffolk life.

In the story, Reg Peddlar professes himself an admirer of the Ipswich Witches – for those (hopefully numerous) readers not

MOON
BOOKS

Moon Books invites you to begin or deepen your encounter with Paganism, in all its rich, creative, flourishing forms.

local to the area, the witches are not a coven but the nickname of the local speedway team who race round Foxhall Stadium. The sports world is quite a prominent part of Ipswich life (most prominently with the football club), and a far more positive one than the aforementioned seedy world of the sex and drugs trade.

Another positive feature is the pagan subculture of Ipswich, which is curiously active for such a small town, and has been flourishing for several decades now. An assortment of covens, groves, hearths and other ritual groups have sprung up over the years, many still in existence at the time of writing.

The presence of esoteric groups in the town is nothing new, indeed there are records of a druid group meeting at the Sun Inn on St Stephen's Lane in 1795. The Ancient and Most Venerable Order of Druids met there under the auspices of 'Brother' William Phillip. This building still stands, and is now part of a shop that has changed hands numerous times. Who knows what else has gone on in the town, perhaps less well documented!

The Ipswich Pagan Council (which draws many of these smaller groups, as well as lone pagans, together to socialise, learn and interact with the wider world) has been in existence for over two decades now, and has the rare achievement of having been invited along to participate in numerous civic events by a succession of mayors. Given the political climate, this would be no small achievement for the pagan community of a metropolitan area, let alone a small rural town. Like any community, paganism has its good and bad eggs as this story hopefully illustrates.

Doubtless the dour Puritan ancestors of the town are spinning in their graves!